Great Violinists And Pianists

George T. Ferris

Contents

GREAT VIOLINISTS
AND PIANISTS

BY

George T. Ferris

NOTE

The title of this little book may be misleading to some of its readers, in its failure to include sketches of many eminent artists well worthy to be classed under such a head. There has been no attempt to cover the immense field of executive music, but only to call attention to the lives of those musical celebrities who are universally recognized as occupying the most exalted places in the arts of violin and pianoforte playing; who stand forth as landmarks in the history of music. To do more than this, except in a merely encyclopedic fashion, within the allotted space, would have been impossible. The same necessity of limits has also compelled the writer to exclude consideration of the careers of noted living performers; as it was thought best that discrimination should be in favor of those great artists whose careers have been completely rounded and finished.

An exception to the above will be noted in the case of Franz Liszt; but, aside from the fact that this greatest of piano-forte virtuosos, though living, has practically retired from the held of art, to omit him from such a volume as this would be an unpardonable omission. In connection with the personal lives of the artists sketched in this volume, the attempt has been made, in a general, though necessarily imperfect, manner, to trace the gradual development of the art of playing from its cruder beginnings to the splendid virtuosoism of the present time. The sources from which facts have been drawn are various, and, it is believed, trustworthy, including French, German, and English authorities, in some cases the personal reminiscences of the artists themselves.

THE VIOLIN AND EARLY VIOLINISTS.

The Ancestry of the Violin.--The Origin of the Cremona School of Violin-Making.--The Amatis and Stradiuarii.--Extraordinary Art Activity of Italy at this Period.--Antonius Stradiuarius and Joseph Guarnerius.--Something about the Lives of the Two Greatest Violin-Makers of the World.--Corelli, the First Great Violinist.--His Contemporaries and Associates.--Anecdotes of his Career.--Corelli's Pupil, Geminiani.--Philidor, the Composer, Violinist, and Chess-Player.--Giuseppe Tartini.--Becomes an Outcast from his Family on Account of his Love of Music.--Anecdote of the Violinist Veracini.--Tartini's Scientific Discoveries in Music.--His Account of the Origin of the "Devil's Trill."--Tartini's Pupils.

I.

The ancestry of the violin, considering this as the type of stringed instruments played with a bow, goes back to the earliest antiquity; and innumerable passages might be quoted from the Oriental and classical writers illustrating the important part taken by the forefathers of the modern violin in feast, festival, and religious ceremonial, in the fiery delights of battle, and the more dulcet enjoyments of peace. But it was not till the fifteenth century, in Italy, that the art of making instruments of the viol class began to reach toward that high perfection which it speedily attained. The long list of honored names connected with the development of art in the fifteenth, sixteenth, and seventeenth centuries is a mighty roll-call, and among these the names of the great violin-makers, beginning with Gaspard de Salo, of Brescia, who first raised a rude craft to an art, are worthy of being included. From Brescia came the masters who established the Cremona school, a name not only immortal in the history of music, but full of vital significance; for it was not till the violin was perfected, and a distinct school of violin-playing founded, that the creation of the symphony, the highest form of music, became possible.

The violin-makers of Cremona came, as we have said, from Brescia, beginning with the Ama-tis. Though it does not lie within the province of this work to discuss in any special or technical sense the history of violin-making, something concerning the greatest of the Cremona masters will be found both interesting and valuable as preliminary to the sketches of the great players which make up the substance of the volume. The Amatis, who established the violin-making art at Cremona, successively improved, each member of the class stealing a march on his predecessor, until the peerless masters of the art, Antonius Stradiuarius and Joseph Guarnerius del Jesu, advanced far beyond the rivalry of their contemporaries and successors. The pupils of the Amatis, Stradiuarius, and Guarnerius settled in Milan, Florence, and other cities, which also became centers of violin-making, but never to an extent which lessened the preeminence of the great Cremona makers. There was one significant peculiarity of all the leading artists of this violin-making epoch: each one as a pupil never contented himself with making copies of his master's work, but strove incessantly to strike out something in his work which should be an outcome of his own genius, knowledge, and investigation. It was essentially a creative age.

Let us glance briefly at the artistic activity of the times when the violin-making craft leaped so swiftly and surely to perfection. If we turn to the days of Gaspard di Salo, Morelli, Magini, and the Amatis, we find that when they were sending forth their fiddles, Raphael, Leonardo da Vinci, Titian, and Tintoretto were busily painting their great canvases. While Antonius Stradiuarius and Joseph Guarnerius were occupied with the noble instruments which have immortalized their names, Canaletto was painting his Venetian squares and canals, Giorgio was superintending the manufacture of his inimitable maiolica, and the Venetians were blowing glass of marvelous beauty and form. In the musical world, Corelli was writing his gigues and sarabandes, Geminiani composing his first instruction book for the violin, and Tartini dreaming out his "Devil's Trill"; and while Guadognini (a pupil of Antonius Stradiuarius), with the stars of lesser magnitude, were exercising their calling, Viotti, the originator of the school of modern violin-playing, was beginning to write his concertos, and Boccherini laying the foundation of chamber music.

Such was the flourishing state of Italian art during the great Cremona period, which opened up a mine of artistic wealth for succeeding generations. It is a curious fact that not only the violin but violin music was the creature of the most luxurious period of art; for, in that golden age of the creative imagination, musicians contemporary with the great violin-makers were writing music destined to be better understood and appreciated when the violins then made should have reached their maturity.

There can be no doubt that the conditions were all highly favorable to the manufacture of great instruments. There were many composers of genius and numerous orchestras scattered over Italy, Germany, and France, and there must have been a demand for bow instruments of a high order. In the sixteenth century, Palestrina and Zarlino were writing grand church music, in which violins bore an important part. In the seventeenth, lived Stradella, Lotti, Buononcini, Lulli, and Corelli. In the eighteenth, when violin-making Avas at its zenith, there were such names among the Italians as Scarlatti, Geminiani, Vivaldi, Locatelli, Boccherini, Tartini, Piccini, Viotti, and Nardini; while in France it was the epoch of Lecler and Gravinies, composers of violin music of the highest class. Under the stimulus of such a general art culture the makers of the violin must have enjoyed large patronage, and the more eminent artists have received highly remunerative prices for their labors, and, correlative to this practical success, a powerful stimulus toward perfecting the design and workmanship of their instruments. These plain artisans lived quiet and simple lives, but they bent their whole souls to the work, and belonged to the class of minds of which Carlyle speaks: "In a word, they willed one thing to which all other things were made subordinate and subservient, and therefore they accomplished it. The wedge will rend rocks, but its edge must be sharp and single; if it be double, the wedge is bruised in pieces and will rend nothing."

II.

So much said concerning the general conditions under which the craft of violin-making reached such splendid excellence, the attention of the reader is invited to the greatest masters of the Cremona school.

"The instrument on which he played
Was in Cremona's workshops made,
By a great master of the past,
Ere yet was lost the art divine;
Fashioned of maple and of pine,
That in Tyrolean forests vast
Had rooked and wrestled with the blast.

"Exquisite was it in design,
A marvel of the lutist's art,
Perfect in each minutest part;
And in its hollow chamber thus
The maker from whose hand it came
Had written his unrivaled name,
'Antonius Stradivarius.'"

The great artist whose work is thus made the subject of Longfellow's verse was born at Cremona in 1644. His renown is beyond that of all others, and his praise has been sounded by poet, artist, and musician. He has received the homage of two centuries, and his name is as little likely to be dethroned from its special place as that of Shakespeare or Homer. Though many interesting particulars are known concerning his life, all attempt has failed to obtain any connected record of the principal events of his career. Perhaps there is no need, for there is ample reason to believe that Antonius Stradiuarius lived a quiet, uncheckered, monotonous existence, absorbed in his labor of making violins, and caring for nothing in the outside world which did not touch his all-beloved art. Without haste and without rest, he labored for the perfection of the violin. To him the world was a mere workshop. The fierce Italian sun beat down and made Cremona like an oven, but it was good to dry the wood for violins. On the slopes of the hills grew grand forests of maple, pine, and willow, but he cared nothing for forest or hillside except as they grew good wood for violins. The vineyards yielded rich wine, but, after all, the main use of the grape was that it furnished the spirit wherewith to compound varnish. The sheep, ox, and horse were good for food, but still more important because from them came the hair of the bow, the violin strings, and the glue which held the pieces together. It was through this single-eyed devotion to his life-work that one great maker was enabled to gather up all the perfections of his predecessors, and stand out for all time as the flower of the Cremonese school and the master of the world. George Eliot, in her poem, "The Stradivari," probably pictures his life accurately:

"That plain white-aproned man, who stood at work,
Patient and accurate full fourscore years,
Cherished his sight and touch by temperance;
And since keen sense is love of perfectness,
Made perfect violins, the needed paths
For inspiration and high mastery."

M. Fetis, in his notice of the greatest of violin-makers, summarizes his life very briefly. He tells us the life of Antonius Stradiuarius was as tranquil as his calling was peaceful. The year 1702 alone must have caused him some disquiet, when during the war the city of Cremona was taken by Marshal Villeroy, on the Imperialist side, retaken by Prince Eugene, and finally taken a third time by the French. That must have been a parlous time for the master of that wonderful workshop whence proceeded the world's masterpieces, though we may almost fancy the absorbed master, like Archimedes when the Romans took Syracuse, so intent on his labor that he hardly heard the din and roar of battle, till some rude soldier disturbed the serene atmosphere of the room littered with shavings and strewn with the tools of a peaceful craft.

Polledro, not many years ago first violin at the Chapel Royal of Turin, who died at a very advanced age, declared that his master had known Stradiuarius, and that he was fond of talking about him. He was, he said, tall and thin, with a bald head fringed with silvery hair, covered with a cap of white wool in the winter and of cotton in the summer. He wore over his clothes an apron of white leather when he worked, and, as he was always working, his costume never varied. He had acquired what was regarded as wealth in those days, for the people of Cremona were accustomed to say "As rich as Stradiuarius." The house he occupied is still standing in the Piazza Roma, and is probably the principal place of interest in the old city to the tourists who drift thitherward. The simple-minded Cremonese have scarcely a conception to-day of the veneration with which their ancient townsman is regarded by the musical connoisseurs of the world. It was with the greatest difficulty that they were persuaded a few years ago, by the efforts of Italian and French musicians, to name one street Stradiuarius, and another Amati. Nicholas Amati, the greatest maker of his family, was the instructor of Antonius Stradiuarius, and during the early period of the latter artist the instruments could hardly be distinguished from those of Amati. But, in after-years, he struck out boldly in an original line of his own, and made violins which, without losing the exquisite sweetness of the Amati instruments, possessed far more robustness and volume of tone, reaching, indeed, a combination of excellences which have placed his name high above all others. It may be remarked of all the Cremona violins of the best period, whether Amati, Stradiuarius, Guarnerius, or Steiner, that they are marked no less by their perfect beauty and delicacy of workmanship than by their charm of tone. These zealous artisans were not content to imprison the soul of Ariel in other form than the lines and curves of ideal grace, exquisitely marked woods, and varnish as of liquid gold. This external beauty is uniformly characteristic of the Cremona violins, though shape varies in some degree with each maker. Of the Stradiuarius violins it may be said, before quitting the consideration of this maker, that they have fetched in latter years from one thousand to five thousand dollars. The sons and grandsons of Antonius were also violin-makers of high repute, though inferior to the chief of the family.

The name of Joseph Guarnerius del Jesu is only less in estimation than that of Antonius Stradiuarius, of whom it is believed by many he was a pupil or apprentice, though of this there is no proof. Both his uncle Andreas and his cousin Joseph were distinguished violin-makers, but the Guarnerius patronymic has now its chiefest glory from that member known as "del Jesu." This great artist in fiddle-making was born at Cremona in the year 1683, and died in 1745. He worked in his native place till the day of his death, but in his latter years Joseph del Jesu became dissipated, and his instruments fell off somewhat in excellence of quality and workmanship. But his ***chef d'oeuvres*** yield only to those of the great Stradiuarius in the estimation of connoisseurs. Many of the Guarnerius violins, it is said, were made in prison, where the artist was confined for debt, with inferior tools and material surreptitiously obtained for him by the jailer's daughter, who was in love with the handsome captive. These fruits of his skill were less beautiful in workmanship, though marked by wonderful sweetness and power of tone. Mr. Charles Reade, a great violin amateur as well as a novelist, says of these "prison" fiddles, referring to the comical grotesqueness of their form: "Such is the force of genius, that I believe in our secret hearts we love these impudent fiddles best, they are so full of ***chic***." Paganini's favorite was a Guarnerius del Jesu, though he had no less than seven instruments of the greatest Cremona masters. Spohr, the celebrated violinist and composer, offered to exchange his Strad, one of the finest in the world, for a Guarnerius, in the possession of Mr. Mawkes, an English musician.

Carlo Bergonzi, the pupil of Antonius Stradiuarius, was another of the great Cremona makers, and his best violins have commanded extraordinary prices. He followed the model of his master closely, and some of his instruments can hardly be distinguished in workmanship and tone from genuine Strads. Something might be said, too, of Jacob Steiner, who, though a German (born about 1620), got the inspiration for his instruments of the best period so directly from Cremona that he ought perhaps to be classified with the violin-makers of this school. His famous violins, known as the Elector Steiners, were made under peculiar circumstances. Almost heartbroken by the death of his wife, he retired to a Benedictine monastery with the purpose of taking holy orders. But the art-passion of his life was too strong, and he made in his cloister-prison twelve instruments, on which he lavished the most jealous care and attention. These were presented to the twelve Electors of Germany, and their extraordinary merit has caused them to rank high among the great violins of the world. A volume might be easily compiled of anecdotes concerning violins and violin-makers. The vicissitudes and changes of ownership through which many celebrated instruments have passed are full of romantic interest. Each instrument of the greatest makers has a pedigree, as well authenticated as those of the great masterpieces of painting, though there have been instances where a Strad or a Guarnerius has been picked up by some strange accident for a mere trifle at an auction. There have been many imitations of the genuine Cremonas palmed off, too, on the unwary at a high price, but the connoisseur rarely fails to identify the great violins almost instantly. For, aside from their magical beauty of tone, they are made with the greatest beauty of form, color, and general detail. So much has been said concerning the greatest violin-makers, in view of the fact that coincident with the growth of a great school of art-manufacture in violins there also sprang up a grand school of violin-playing; for, indeed, the one could hardly have existed without the other.

III.

The first great performer on the violin whose career had any special significance, in its connection with the modern world of musical art, was Archangelo Corelli, who was born at Fusignano, in the territory of Bologna, in the year 1653. Corelli's compositions are recognized to-day as types of musical purity and freshness, and the great number of distinguished pupils who graduated from his teaching relate him closely with all the distinguished violinists even down to the present day. In Corelli's younger days the church had a stronger claim on musicians than the theatre or concert-room. So we find him getting his earliest instruction from the Capuchin Simonelli, who devoted himself to the ecclesiastical style. The pupil, however, yielded to an irresistible instinct, and soon put himself under the care of a clever and skillful teacher, the well-known Bassani. Under this tuition the young musician made rapid advancement, for he labored incessantly in the practice of his instrument. At the age of twenty Corelli followed that natural bent which carried him to Paris, then, as now, a great art capital; and we are told, on the authority of Fetis, that the composer Lulli became so jealous of his extraordinary skill that he obtained a royal mandate ordering Corelli to quit Paris, on pain of the Bastille.

In 1680 he paid a visit to Germany, and was specially well received, and was so universally admired, that he with difficulty escaped the importunate invitations to settle at various courts as chief musician. After a three years' absence from his native land he returned and published his first sonatas. The result of his assiduous labor was that his fame as a violinist had spread all over Europe, and pupils came from distant lands to profit by his instruction. We are told of his style as a solo player that it was learned and elegant, the tone firm and even, that his playing was frequently impressed with feeling, but that during performance "his countenance was distorted, his eyes red as fire, and his eyeballs rolled as if he were in agony." For about eighteen years Corelli was domiciled at Rome, under the patronage of Cardinal Ottoboni. As leader of the orchestra at the opera, he introduced many reforms, among them that of perfect uniformity of bowing. By the violin sonatas composed during this period, it is claimed that Corelli laid the foundation for the art of violin-playing, though it is probable that he profited largely by those that went before him. It was at the house of Cardinal Ottoboni that Corelli met Handel, when the violent temper of the latter did not hesitate to show itself. Corelli was playing a sonata, when the imperious young German snatched the violin from his hand, to show the greatest virtuoso of the age how to play the music. Corelli, though very amiable in temper, knew how to make himself respected. At one of the private concerts at Cardinal Ottoboni's, he observed his host and others talking during his playing. He laid his violin down and joined the audience, saying he feared his music might interrupt the conversation.

In 1708, according to Dubourg, Corelli accepted a royal invitation from Naples, and took with him his second violin, Matteo, and a violoncellist, in case he should not be well accompanied by the Neapolitan orchestra. He had no sooner arrived than he was asked to play some of his concertos before the king. This he refused, as the whole of his orchestra was not with him, and there was no time for a rehearsal. However, he soon found that the Neapolitan musicians played the orchestral parts of his concertos as well as his own accompanists did after some practice; for, having at length consented to play the first of his concertos before the court, the accompaniment was so good that Corelli is said to have exclaimed to Matteo: "*Si suona a Napoli!*"--"They *do* play at Naples!" This performance being quite successful, he was presented to the king, who afterward requested him to perform one of his sonatas; but his Majesty found the adagio "so long and so dry that he got up and *left the room* (!), to the great mortification of the eminent virtuoso." As the king had commanded the piece, the least he could have done would have been to have waited till it was finished. "If they play at Naples, they are not very polite there," poor Corelli must have thought! Another unfortunate mishap also occurred to him there, if we are to believe the dictum of Geminiani, one of Corelli's pupils, who had preceded him at Naples. It would appear that he was appointed to lead a composition of Scarlatti's, and on arriving at an air in C minor he led off in C major, which mistake he twice repeated, till Scarlatti came on the stage and showed him the difference. This anecdote, however, is so intrinsically improbable that it must be taken with several "grains of salt." In 1712 Corelli's concertos were beautifully engraved at Amsterdam, but the composer only survived the publication a few weeks. A beautiful statue, bearing the inscription " ***Corelli princeps musicorum*** ," was erected to his memory, adjacent that honoring the memory of Raffaelle in the Pantheon. He accumulated a considerable fortune, and left a valuable collection of pictures. The solos of Corelli have been adopted as valuable studies by the most eminent modern players and teachers.

Francesco Geminiani was the most remarkable of Corelli's pupils. Born at Lucca in 1680, he finished his studies under Corelli at Rome, and spent several years with great musical *eclat* at Naples. In 1714 he went to England, in which country he spent many years. His execution was of great excellence, but his compositions only achieved temporary favor. His life is said to have been full of romance and incident. Geminiani's connection with Handel has a special musical interest. The king, who arrived in England in September, 1714, and was crowned at Westminster a month later, was irritated with Handel for having left Germany, where he held the position of chapel-master to George, when Elector of Brunswick, and still more so by his having composed a *Te Deum* on the Peace of Utrecht, which was not favorably regarded by the Protestant princes of Germany. Baron Kilmanseck, a Hanoverian, and a great admirer of Handel, undertook to bring them together again. Being informed that the king intended to picnic on the Thames, he requested the composer to write something for the occasion. Thereupon Handel wrote the twenty-five little concerted pieces known under the title of "Water Music." They were executed in a barge which followed the royal boat. The orchestra consisted of four violins, one tenor, one violoncello, one double-bass, two hautboys, two bassoons, two French horns, two flageolets, one flute, and one trumpet. The king soon recognized the author of the music, and his resentment against Handel began to soften. Shortly after this Geminiani was requested to play some sonatas of his own composition in the king's private cabinet; but, fearing that they would lose much of their effect if they were accompanied in an inferior manner, he expressed the desire that Handel should play the accompaniments. Baron Kilmanseck carried the request to the king, and supported it strongly. The result was that peace was made, and an extra pension of two hundred pounds per annum settled upon Handel. Geminiani, after thirty-five years spent in England, went to Paris for five years, where he was most heartily welcomed by the musical world, but returned across the Channel again to spend his latter years in Dublin. It was here that Matthew Dubourg, whose book on "The Violin and Violinists" is a perfect treasure-trove of anecdote, became his pupil.

Another remarkable violinist was an intimate friend of Geminiani, a name distinguished alike in the annals of chess-playing and music, Andre Danican Philidor. This musician was born near Paris in 1726, and was the grandson of the hautboy-player to the court of Louis XIII. His father and several of his relations were also eminent players in the royal orchestras of Louis XIV and Louis XV. Young Philidor was received into the Chapel Royal at Versailles in 1732, being then six years old, and when eleven he composed a motette which extorted much admiration. In the Chapel Royal there were about eighty musicians daily in attendance, violins, haut-boys, violas, double-basses, choristers, etc.; and, cards not being allowed, they had a long table inlaid with a number of chess-boards, with which they amused their leisure time. When fourteen years old Philidor was the best chess-player in the band. Four years later he played at Paris two games of chess at the same time, without seeing the boards, and afterward extended this feat to playing five games simultaneously, which, though far inferior to the wonderful feats of Morphy, Paulsen, and others in more recent years, very much astonished his own generation. Philidor was an admirable violinist, and the composer of numerous operas which delighted the French public for many years. He died in London in 1759.

There were several other pupils of Corelli who achieved rank in their art and exerted a recognizable influence on music. Locatelli displayed originality and genius in his compositions, and his studies, "Arte di Nuova Modulazione," was studied by Paganini. Another pupil, Lorenzo Somis, became noted as the teacher of Lecler, Pugnani (the professor of Viotti), and Giardini. Visconti, of Cremona, who was taught by Corelli, is said to have greatly assisted by his counsels the constructive genius of Antonius Stradiuarius in making his magnificent instruments.

IV.

The name of Giuseppe Tartini will recur to the musical reader more familiarly than those previously mentioned. He was the scion of a noble stock, and was born in Istria in 1692. Originally intended for the law, he was entered at the University of Padua at the age of eighteen for this profession, but his time was mostly given to the study of music and fencing, in both of which he soon became remarkably proficient, so that he surpassed the masters who taught him. It may be that accident determined the future career of Tartini, for, had he remained at the university, the whole bent of his life might have been different. Eros exerted his potent sway over the young student, and he entered into a secret marriage, that being the lowest price at which he could win his *bourgeois* sweetheart. Tartini became an outcast from his family, and was compelled to fly and labor for his own living. After many hardships, he found shelter in a convent at Assisi, the prior of which was a family connection, who took compassion on the friendless youth. Here Tartini set to work vigorously on his violin, and prosecuted a series of studies which resulted in the "Sonata del Diavolo" and other remarkable compositions. At last he was reconciled to his family through the intercession of his monastic friend, and took his abode in Venice that he might have the benefit of hearing the playing of Veracini, a great but eccentric musician, then at the head of the Conservatario of that city. Veracini was nicknamed "Capo Pazzo," or "mad-head," on account of his eccentricity. Dubourg tells a curious story of this musician: Being at Lucca at the time of the annual festival called "Festa della Croce," on which occasion it was customary for the leading artists of Italy to meet, Veracini put his name down for a solo. When he entered the choir, he found the principal place occupied by a musician of some rank named Laurenti. In reply to the latter's question, "Where are you going?" Veracini haughtily answered, "To the place of the first violinist." It was explained by Laurenti that he himself had been engaged to fill that post, but, if his interlocutor wished to play a solo, he could have the privilege either at high mass or at vespers. Evidently he did not recognize Veracini, who turned away in a rage, and took his position in the lowest place in the orchestra. When his turn came to play his concerto, he begged that instead of it he might play a solo where he was, accompanied on the violoncello by Lanzetti. This he did in so brilliant and unexpected a manner that the applause was loud and continued, in spite of the sacred nature of the place; and whenever he was about to make a close, he turned toward Laurenti and called out: "Cost se suona per fare il primo violino"--"This is the way to play first violin."

Veracini played upon a fine Steiner violin. The only master he ever had was his uncle Antonio, of Florence; and it was by traveling all over Europe, and by numerous performances in public, that he formed a style of playing peculiar to himself, very similar to what occurred to Pa-ganini and the celebrated De Beriot in later years. It does not appear certain that Tartini ever took lessons from Ve-racini; but hearing the latter play in public had no doubt a very great effect upon him, and caused him to devote many years to the careful study of his instrument. Some say that Veracini's performance awakened a vivid emulation in Tartini, who was already acknowledged to be a very masterly player. Up to the time, however, that Tartini first heard Veracini, he had never attempted any of the more intricate and difficult feats of violin-playing, as effected by the management of the bow. An intimate friendship sprang up between the two artists and another clever musi-cian named Marcello, and they devoted much time to the study of the principles of violin-playing, particularly to style and the varied kinds of bowing. Veracini's mind afterward gave way, and Tartini withdrew himself to Ancona, where in utter solitude he applied himself to working out the fundamental principles of the bow in the technique of the violin--principles which no succeeding violinist has im-proved or altered. Tartini, even while absorbed in music, did not neglect the study of science and mathematics, of which he was passionately fond, and in the pursuit of which he might have made a name not less than his reputation as a musician. It was at this time that Tartini made a very curious discovery, known as the ***phenom-enon of the third sound***, which created some sensation at the time, and has since given rise to numerous learned discourses, but does not appear to have led to any great practical result. Various memoirs or treatises were written by him, and that in which he develops the nature of the ***third sound*** is his "Tratto di Musica se-condo la vera scienza de l'Armonia." In this and others of his works, he appears much devoted to ***theory***, and endeavors to place all his practical facts upon a thoroughly scientific basis. The effect known as the ***third sound*** consists in the sympathetic resonance of a third note when the two upper notes of a chord are played in perfect tune. "If you do not hear the bass," Tartini would say to his pupils, "the thirds or sixths which you are playing are not perfect in intonation."

At Ancona, Tartini attained such reputation as a player and musician that he was appointed, in 1721, to the directorship of the orchestra of the church of St. Anthony at Padua. Here, according to Fetis, he spent the remaining forty-nine years of his life in peace and comfort, solely occupied with the labors connected with the art he loved.

His great fame brought him repeated offers from the principal cities of Europe, even London and Paris, hat nothing could induce him to leave his beloved Italy. Though Tartini could not have been heard out of Italy, his violin school at Padua graduated many excellent players, who were widely known throughout the musical world. Tartini's compositions reached no less than one hundred and fifty works, distinguished not only by beauty of melody and knowledge of the violin, but by soundness of musical science. Some of his sonatas are still favorites in the concert-room. Among these, the most celebrated is the "Trille del Dia-volo," or "Devil's Sonata," composed under the following circumstances, as related by Tartini himself to his pupil Lalande:

"One night in 1713," he says, "I dreamed that I had made a compact with the devil, who promised to be at my service on all occasions. Everything succeeded according to my mind; my wishes were anticipated and desires always surpassed by the assistance of my new servant. At last I thought I would offer my violin to the devil, in order to discover what kind of a musician he was, when, to my great astonishment, I heard him play a solo, so singularly beautiful and with such superior taste and precision, that it surpassed all the music I had ever heard or conceived in the whole course of my life. I was so overcome with surprise and delight that I lost my power of breathing, and the violence of this sensation awoke me. Instantly I seized my violin in the hopes of remembering some portion of what I had just heard, but in vain! The work which this dream suggested, and which I wrote at the time, is doubtless the best of all my compositions, and I still call it the 'Sonata del Diavolo'; but it sinks so much into insignificance compared with what I heard, that I would have broken my instrument and abandoned music altogether, had I possessed any other means of subsistence."

Tartini died at Padua in 1770, and so much was he revered and admired in the city where he had spent nearly fifty years of his life, that his death was regarded as a public calamity. He used to say of himself that he never made any real progress in music till he was more than thirty years old; and it is curious that he should have made a great change in the nature of his performance at the age of fifty-two. Instead of displaying his skill in difficulties of execution, he learned to prefer grace and expression. His method of playing an adagio was regarded as inimitable by his contemporaries; and he transmitted this gift to his pupil Nardini, who was afterward called the greatest adagio player in the world. Another of Tartini's great *eleves* was Pugnani, who before coming to him had been instructed by Lorenzo Somis, the pupil of Corelli. So it may be said that Pugnani united in himself the schools of Corelli and Tartini, and was thus admirably fitted to be the instructor of that grand player, who was the first in date of the violin virtuosos of modern times, Viotti.

Both as composer and performer, Pugnani was held in great esteem throughout Europe. His first meeting with Tartini was an incident of considerable interest. He made the journey from Paris to Padua expressly to see Tartini, and on reaching his destination he proceeded to the house of the great violinist.

Tartini received him kindly, and evinced some curiosity to hear him play. Pugnani took up his instrument and commenced a well-known solo, but he had not played many bars before Tartini suddenly seized his arm, saying, "Too loud, my friend, too loud!" The Piedmontese began again, but at the same passage Tartini stopped him again, exclaiming this time, "Too soft, my good friend, too soft!" Pugnani therefore laid down the violin, and begged of Tartini to give him some lessons. He was at once received among Tartini's pupils, and, though already an excellent artist, began his musical education almost entirely anew. Many anecdotes have been foisted upon Pugnani, some evidently the creation of rivals, and not worth repeating. Others, on the contrary, tend to enlighten us upon the character of the man. Thus, when playing, he was so completely absorbed in the music, that he has been known, at a public concert, to walk about the platform during the performance of a favorite cadenza, imagining himself alone in the room. Again, at the house of Madame Denis, when requested to play before Voltaire, who had little or no music in his soul, Pugnani stopped short, when the latter had the bad taste to continue his conversation, remarking in a loud, clear voice, "M. de Voltaire is very clever in making verses, but as regards music he is devilishly ignorant." Pugnani's style of play is said to have been very broad and noble, "characterized by that commanding sweep of the bow, which afterward formed so grand a feature in the performance of Viotti." He was distinguished as a composer as well as a player, and among his numerous works are some seven or eight operas, which were very successful for the time being on the Italian stage.

VIOTTI.

Viotti, the Connecting Link between the Early and Modern Violin Schools.--His Immense Superiority over his Contemporaries and Predecessors.--Other Violinists of his Time, Giornowick and Boccherini.--Viotti's Early Years--His Arrival in Paris, and the Sensation he made--His Reception by the Court.--Viotti's Personal Pride and Dignity.--His Rebuke to Princely Impertinence.--The Musical Circles of Paris.--Viotti's Last Publie Concert in Paris.--He suddenly departs for London.--Becomes Director of the King's Theatre.--Is compelled to leave the Country as a Suspected Revolutionist.--His Return to England, and Metamorphosis into a Vintner.--The French Singer, Garat, finds him out in his London Obscurity.--Anecdote of Viotti's Dinner Party.--He quits the Wine Trade for his own Profession.--Is made Director of the Paris Grand Opera.--Letter from Rossini.--Viotti's Account of the "Ranz des Vaches."--Anecdotes of the Great Violinist.--Dies in London in 1824.--Viotti's Place as a Violinist, and Style of Playing.--The Tourte Bow first invented during his Time.--An Indispensable Factor in Great Playing on the Violin.--Viotti's Pupils, and his Influence on the Musical Art.

I.

In the person of the celebrated Viotti we recognize the link connecting the modern school of violin-playing with the schools of the past. He was generally hailed as the leading violinist of his time, and his influence, not merely on violin music but music in general, was of a very palpable order. In him were united the accomplishments of the great virtuoso and the gifts of the composer. At the time that Viotti's star shot into such splendor in the musical horizon, there were not a few clever violinists, and only a genius of the finest type could have attained and perpetuated such a regal sway among his contemporaries. At the time when Viotti appeared in Paris the popular heart was completely captivated by Giornowick, whose eccentric and quarrelsome character as a man cooperated with his artistic excellence to keep him constantly in the public eye. Giornowick was a Palermitan, born in 1745, and his career was thoroughly artistic and full of romantic vicissitudes. His style was very graceful and elegant, his tone singularly pure. One of the most popular and seductive tricks in his art was the treating of well-known airs as rondos, returning ever and anon to his theme after a variety of brilliant excursions in a way that used to fascinate his hearers, thus anticipating some of his brilliant successors.

Michael Kelly heard him at Vienna. "He was a man of a certain age," he tells us, "but in the full vigor of talent. His tone was very powerful, his execution most rapid, and his taste, above all, alluring. No performer in my remembrance played such pleasing music." Dubourg relates that on one occasion, when Giornowick had announced a concert at Lyons, he found the people rather retentive of their money, so he postponed the concert to the following evening, reducing the price of the tickets to one half. A crowded company was the result. But the bird had flown! The artist had left Lyons without ceremony, together with the receipts from sales of tickets.

In London, where he was frequently heard between 1792 and 1796, he once gave a concert which was fully attended, but annoying to the player on account of the indifference of the audience and the clatter of the tea-cups; for it was then the custom to serve tea during the performance, as well as during the intervals. Giornowick turned to the orchestra and ordered them to cease playing. "These people," said he, "know nothing about music; anything is good enough for drinkers of warm water. I will give them something suited to their taste." Whereupon he played a very trivial and commonplace French air, which he disguised with all manner of meretricious flourishes, and achieved a great success. When Viotti arrived in Paris in 1779, Giornowick started on his travels after having heard this new rival once.

A distinguished virtuoso and composer, with whom Viotti had already been thrown into contact, though in a friendly rather than a competitive way, was Boccherini, who was one of the most successful early composers of trios, quartets, and quintets for string instruments. During the latter part of Boccherini's life he basked in the sunlight of Spanish royalty, and composed nine works annually for the Royal Academy of Madrid, in which town he died in 1806, aged sixty-six. A very clever saying is attributed to him. The King of Spain, Charles IV, was fond of playing with the great composer, and was very ambitious of shining as a great violinist; his cousin, the Emperor of Austria, was also fond of the violin, and played tolerably well. One day the latter asked Boccherini, in a rather straightforward manner, what difference there was between his playing and that of his cousin Charles IV. "Sire," replied Boccherini, without hesitating for a moment, "Charles IV plays like a king, and your Majesty plays like an emperor."

Giovanni Battista Viotti was born in a little Piedmontese village called Fontaneto, in the year 1755. The accounts of his early life are too confused and fragmentary to be trustworthy. It is pretty well established, however, that he studied under Pugnani at Turin, and that at the age of twenty he was made first violin at the Chapel Royal of that capital. After remaining three years, he began his career as a solo player, and, after meeting with the greatest success at Berlin and Vienna, directed his course to Paris, where he made his ***debut*** at the "Concerts Spirituels."

II.

Fetis tells us that the arrival of Viotti in Paris produced a sensation difficult to describe. No performer had yet been heard who had attained so high a degree of perfection, no artist had possessed so fine a tone, such sustained elegance, such fire, and so varied a style. The fancy which was developed in his concertos increased the delight he produced in the minds of his auditory. His compositions for the violin were as superior to those which had previously been heard as his execution surpassed that of all his predecessors and contemporaries. Giornowick's style was full of grace and suave elegance; Viotti was characterized by a remarkable beauty, breadth, and dignity. Lavish attentions were bestowed on him from the court circle. Marie Antoinette, who was an ardent lover and most judicious patron of music, sent him her commands to play at Versailles. The haughty artistic pride of Viotti was signally displayed at one of these concerts before royalty. A large number of eminent musicians had been engaged for the occasion, and the audience was a most brilliant one. Viotti had just begun a concerto of his own composition, when the arrogant Comte d'Artois made a great bustle in the room, and interrupted the music by his loud whispers and utter indifference to the comfort of any one but himself. Viotti's dark eyes flashed fire as he stared sternly at this rude scion of the blood royal. At last, unable to restrain his indignation, he deliberately placed his violin in the case, gathered up his music from the stand, and withdrew from the concert-room without ceremony, leaving the concert, her Majesty, and his Royal Highness to the reproaches of the audience. This scene is an exact parallel of one which occurred at the house of Cardinal Ottoboni, when Corelli resented in similar fashion the impertinence of some of his auditors.

Everywhere in artistic and aristocratic circles at the French capital Viotti's presence was eagerly sought. Private concerts were so much the vogue in Paris that musicians of high rank found more profit in these than in such as were given to the miscellaneous public. A delightful artistic rendezvous was the hotel of the Comte de Balck, an enthusiastic patron and friend of musicians. Here Viotti's friend, Garat, whose voice had so great a range as to cover both the tenor and barytone registers, was wont to sing; and here young Orfila, the brilliant chemist, displayed his magnificent tenor voice in such a manner as to attract the most tempting offers from managers that he should desert the laboratory for the stage. But the young Portuguese was fascinated with science, and was already far advanced in the career which made him in his day the greatest of all authorities on toxicological chemistry. The most brilliant and gifted men and women of Paris haunted these reunions, and Viotti always appeared at his best amid such surroundings. Another favorite resort of his was the house of Mme. Montegerault at Montmorency, a lady who was a brilliant pianist. Sometimes she would seat herself at her instrument and begin an improvisation, and Viotti, seizing his violin, would join in the performance, and in a series of extemporaneous passages display his great powers to the delight of all present.

He evinced the greatest distaste for solo playing at public concerts, and, aside from charity performances, only consented once to such an exhibition of his talents. A singular concert was arranged to take place on the fifth story of a house in Paris, the apartment being occupied by a friend of Viotti, who was also a member of the Government. "I will play," he said, on being urged, "but only on one condition, and that is, that the audience shall come up here to us--we have long enough descended to them; but times are changed, and now we may compel them to rise to our level"; or something to that effect. It took place in due course, and was a very brilliant concert indeed. The only ornament was a bust of Jean Jacques Rousseau. A large number of distinguished artists, both instrumental and vocal, were present, and a most aristocratic audience. A good deal of Boccherini's music was performed that evening, and though many of the titled personages had mounted to the fifth floor for the first time in their lives, so complete was the success of the concert that not one descended without regret, and all were warm in their praise of the performances of the distinguished violinist.

What the cause of Viotti's sudden departure from Paris in 1790 was, it is difficult to tell. Perhaps he had offended the court by the independence of his bearing; perhaps he had expressed his political opinions too bluntly, for he was strongly democratic in his views; perhaps he foresaw the terrible storm which was gathering and was soon to break in a wrack of ruin, chaos, and blood. Whatever the cause, our violinist vanished from Paris with hardly a word of farewell to his most intimate friends, and appeared in London at Salomon's concerts with the same success which had signalized his Parisian *debut*. Every one was delighted with the originality and power of his playing, and the exquisite taste that modified the robustness and passion which entered into the substance of his musical conceptions.

Viotti was one of the artistic celebrities of London for several years, but his eccentric and resolute nature did not fail to involve him in several difficulties with powerful personages. He became connected with the management of the King's Theatre, and led the music for two years with signal ability. But he suddenly received an order from the British Government to leave England without delay. His sharp tongue and outspoken language were never consistent with courtly subserviency. We can fancy our musician shrugging his shoulders with disdain on receiving his order of banishment, for he was too much of a cosmopolite to be disturbed by change of country. He took up his residence at Schoenfeld, Holland, in a beautiful and splendid villa, and produced there several of his most celebrated compositions, as well as a series of studies of the violin school.

III.

The edict which had sent Viotti from England was revoked in 1801, and he returned with commercial aspirations, for he entered into the wine trade. It could not be said of him, as of another well-known composer, who attempted to conduct a business in the vending of sweet sounds and the juice of the grape simultaneously, that he composed his wines and imported his music; for Viotti seems to have laid music entirely aside for the nonce, and we have no reason to suspect that his port and sherry were not of the best. Attention to business did not keep him from losing a large share of his fortune, however, in this mercantile venture, and for a while he was so completely lost in the London Babel as to have passed out of sight and mind of his old admirers. The French singer, Garat, tells an amusing story of his discovery of Viotti in London, when none of his Continental friends knew what had become of him.

In the very zenith of his powers and height of his reputation, the founder of a violin school which remains celebrated to this day, Viotti had quitted Paris suddenly, and since his departure no one had received, either directly or indirectly, any news of him. According to Garat, some vague indications led him to believe that the celebrated violinist had taken up his residence in London, but, for a long time after his (Garat's) arrival in the metropolis, all his attempts to find him were fruitless. At last, one morning he went to a large export house for wine. It had a spacious courtyard, filled with numbers of large barrels, among which it was not easy to move toward the office or counting-house. On entering the latter, the first person who met his gaze was Viotti himself. Viotti was surrounded by a legion of employees, and so absorbed in business that he did not notice Garat. At last he raised his head, and, recognizing his old friend, seized him by the hand, and led him into an adjoining room, where he gave him a hearty welcome. Garat could not believe his senses, and stood motionless with surprise.

"I see you are astonished at the metamorphosis," said Viotti; "it is certainly *drole*--unexpected; but what *could* you expect? At Paris I was looked upon as a ruined man, lost to all my friends; it was necessary to do something to get a living, and here I am, making my fortune!"

"But," interrupted Garat, "have you taken into consideration all the drawbacks and annoyances of a profession to which you were not brought up, and which must be opposed to your tastes?"

"I perceive," continued Viotti, "that you share the error which so many indulge in. Commercial enterprise is generally considered a most prosaic undertaking, but it has, nevertheless, its seductions, its prestige, its poetical side. I assure you no musician, no poet, ever had an existence more full of interesting and exciting incidents than those which cause the heart of the merchant to throb. His imagination, stimulated by success, carries him forward to new conquests; his clients increase, his fortune augments, the finest dreams of ambition are ever before him."

"But art!" again interrupted his friend; "the art of which you are one of the finest representatives--you can not have entirely abandoned it?"

"Art will lose nothing," rejoined Viotti, "and you will find that I can conciliate two things without interfering with either, though you doubtless consider them irreconcilable. We will continue this subject another time; at present I must leave you; I have some pressing business to transact this afternoon. But come and dine with me at six o'clock, and be sure you do not disappoint me."

Garat, who relates this conversation, tells us that at the appointed time he returned to the house. All the barrels and wagons that had encumbered the courtyard were cleared away, and in their place were coroneted carriages, with footmen and servants. A lackey in brilliant livery conducted the visitor to the drawing-room on the first floor. The apartments were magnificently furnished, and glittered with mirrors, candelabra, gilt ornaments, and the most quaint and costly **bric-a-brac**. Viotti received his guests at the head of the staircase, no longer the plodding man of business, but the courtly, high-bred gentleman. Garat's amazement was still further increased when he heard the names of the other guests, all distinguished men. After an admirably cooked dinner, there was still more admirable music, and Viotti proved to the satisfaction of his French friend that he was still the same great artist who had formerly delighted his listeners in Paris.

The wine business turned out so badly for our violinist that he was fain to return to his old and legitimate profession. Through the intervention of powerful friends in Paris, he was appointed director of the Grand Opera, but he became discontented in a very onerous and irritating position, and was retired at his own request with a pension. An interesting letter from the great Italian composer Rossini, who was then first trying his fortune in the French metropolis, written to Viotti in 1821, is pleasant proof of the estimate placed on his talents and influence:

"Most esteemed Sir: You will be surprised at receiving a letter from an individual who has not the honor of your personal acquaintance, but I profit by the liberality of feeling existing among artists to address these lines to you through my friend Herold, from whom I have learned with the greatest satisfaction the high, and, I fear, somewhat undeserved opinion you have of me. The oratorio of 'Moise,' composed by me three years ago, appears to our mutual friend susceptible of dramatic adaptation to French words; and I, who have the greatest reliance on Herold's taste and on his friendship for me, desire nothing more than to render the entire work as perfect as possible, by composing new airs in a more religious style than those which it at present contains, and by endeavoring to the best of my power that the result shall neither disgrace the composer of the partition, nor you, its patron and protector. If M. Viotti, with his great celebrity, will consent to be the Mecaenas of my name, he may be assured of the gratitude of his devoted servant,

"Gioacchino Rossini.

"P.S.--In a month's time I will forward you the alterations of the drama 'Moise,' in order that you may judge if they are conformable to the operatic style. Should they not be so, you will have the kindness to suggest any others better adapted to the purpose."

IV.

Viotti, though in many respects proud, resolute, and haughty in temperament, was simple-hearted and enthusiastic, and a passionate lover of nature. M. Eymar, one of his intimate friends, said of him, "Never did a man attach so much value to the simplest gifts of nature, and never did a child enjoy them more passionately." A modest flower growing in the grass of the meadow, a charming bit of landscape, a rustic *fete*, in short, all the sights and sounds of the country, filled him with delight. All nature spoke to his heart, and his finest compositions were suggested and inspired by this sympathy. He has left the world a charming musical picture of the feelings experienced in the mountains of Switzerland. It was there he heard, under peculiar circumstances, and probably for the first time, the plaintive sound of a mountain-horn, breathing forth the few notes of a kind of "Ranz des Vaches."

"The 'Ranz des Vaches' which I send you," he says in one of his letters, "is neither that with which our friend Jean Jacques has presented us, nor that of which M. De la Bord speaks in his work on music. I can not say whether it is known or not; all I know is, that I heard it in Switzerland, and, once heard, I have never forgotten it. I was sauntering along, toward the decline of day, in one of those sequestered spots.... Flowers, verdure, streamlets, all united to form a picture of perfect harmony. There, without being fatigued, I seated myself mechanically on a fragment of rock, and fell into so profound a reverie that I seemed to forget that I was upon earth. While sitting thus, sounds broke on my ear which were sometimes of a hurried, sometimes of a prolonged and sustained character, and were repeated in softened tones by the echoes around. I found they proceeded from a mountain-horn; and their effect was heightened by a plaintive female voice. Struck as if by enchantment, I started from my dreams, listened with breathless attention, and learned, or rather engraved upon my memory, the 'Ranz des Vaches' which I send you. In order to understand all its beauties, you ought to be transplanted to the scene in which I heard it, and to feel all the enthusiasm that such a moment inspired." It was a similar delightful experience which, according to Rossini's statement, first suggested to that great composer his immortal opera, "Guillaume Tell."

Among many interesting anecdotes current of Viotti, and one which admirably shows his goodness of heart and quickness of resource, is one narrated by Ferdinand Langle to Adolph Adam, the French composer. The father of the former, Marie Langle, a professor of harmony in the French Conservatoire, was an intimate friend of Viotti, and one charming summer evening the twain were strolling on the Champs Elysees. They sat down on a retired bench to enjoy the calmness of the night, and became buried in reverie. But they were brought back to prosaic matters harshly by a babel of discordant noises that grated on the sensitive ears of the two musicians. They started from their seats, and Viotti said:

"It can't be a violin, and yet there is some resemblance to one."

"Nor a clarionet," suggested Langle, "though it is something like it."

The easiest manner of solving the problem was to go and see what it was. They approached the spot whence the extraordinary tones issued, and saw a poor blind man standing near a miserable-looking candle and playing upon a violin--but the latter was an instrument made of tin-plate.

"Fancy!" exclaimed Viotti, "it is a violin, but a violin of tin-plate! Did you ever dream of such a curiosity?" and, after listening a while, he added, "I say, Langle, I must possess that instrument. Go and ask the old blind man what he will sell it for."

Langle approached and asked the question, but the old man was disinclined to part with it.

"But we will give you enough for it to enable you to purchase a better," he added; "and why is not your violin like others?"

The aged fiddler explained that, when he got old and found himself poor, not being able to work, but still able to scrape a few airs upon a violin, he had endeavored to procure one, but in vain. At last his good, kind nephew Eustache, who was apprenticed to a tinker, had made him one out of a tin-plate. "And an excellent one, too," he added; "and my poor boy Eustache brings me here in the morning when he goes to work, and fetches me away in the evening when he returns, and the receipts are not so bad sometimes--as, when he was out of work, it was I who kept the house going."

"Well," said Viotti, "I will give you twenty francs for your violin. You can buy a much better one for that price; but let me try it a little."

He took the violin in his hands, and produced some extraordinary effects from it. A considerable crowd gathered around, and listened with curiosity and astonishment to the performance. Langle seized on the opportunity, and passed around the hat, gathering a goodly amount of chink from the bystanders, which, with the twenty francs, was handed to the astonished old beggar.

"Stay a moment," said the blind man, recovering a little from his surprise; "just now I said I would sell the violin for twenty francs, but I did not know it was so good. I ought to have at least double for it."

Viotti had never received a more genuine compliment, and he did not hesitate to give the old man two pieces of gold instead of one, and then immediately retired from the spot, passing through the crowd with the tin-plate instrument under his arm. He had scarcely gone forty yards when he felt some one pulling at his sleeve; it was a workman, who politely took off his cap, and said:

"Sir, you have paid too dear for that violin; and if you are an amateur, as it was I who made it, I can supply you with as many as you like at six francs each."

This was Eustache; he had just come in time to hear the conclusion of the bargain, and, little dreaming that he was so clever a violin-maker, wished to continue a trade that had begun so successfully. However, Viotti was quite satisfied with the one sample he had bought. He never parted with that instrument; and, when the effects of Viotti were sold in London after his death, though the tin fiddle only brought a few shillings, an amateur of curiosities sought out the purchaser, and offered him a large sum if he could explain how the strange instrument came into the possession of the great violinist.

After resigning his position as director of the Grand Opera, Viotti returned to London, which had become a second home to him, and spent his remaining days there. He died on the 24th of March, 1824.

V.

Viotti established and settled for ever the fundamental principles of violin-playing. He did not attain the marvelous skill of technique, the varied subtile and dazzling effects, with which his successor, Paganini, was to amaze the world, but, from the accounts transmitted to us, his performance must have been characterized by great nobility, breadth, and beauty of tone, united with a fire and agility unknown before his time. Viotti was one of the first to use the Tourte bow, that indispensable adjunct to the perfect manipulation of the violin. The value of this advantage over his predecessors cannot be too highly estimated.

The bows used before the time of Francois Tourte, who lived in the latter years of the last century in Paris, were of imperfect shape and make. The Tourte model leaves nothing to be desired in all the qualities required to enable the player to follow out every conceivable manner of tone and movement--lightness, firmness, and elasticity. Tartini had made the stick of his bow elastic, an innovation from the time of Corelli, and had thus attained a certain flexibility and brilliancy in his bowing superior to his predecessors. But the full development of all the powers of the violin, or the practice of what we now call virtuosoism on this instrument, was only possible with the modern bow as designed by Tourte, of Paris. The thin, bent, elastic stick of the bow, with its greater length of sweep, gives the modern player incalculable advantages over those of an earlier age, enabling him to follow out the slightest gradations of tone from the fullest *forte* to the softest *piano*, to mark all kinds of strong and gentle accents, to execute staccato, legato, saltato, and arpeggio passages with the greatest ease and certainty. The French school of violin-playing did not at first avail itself of these advantages, and even Viotti and Spohr did not fully grasp the new resources of execution. It was left for Paganini to open a new era in the art. His daring and subtile genius perceived and seized the wonderful resources of the modern bow at one bound. He used freely every imaginable movement of the bow, and developed the movement of the wrist to that high perfection which enabled him to practice all kinds of bowing with celerity. Without the Tourte bow, Paganini and the modern school of virtuosos, which has followed so splendidly from his example, would have been impossible. To many of our readers an amplification of this topic may be of interest. While the left hand of the violin-player fixes the tone, and thereby does that which for the pianist is already done by the mechanism of the instrument, and while the correctness of his intonation depends on the proficiency of the left hand, it is the action of the right hand, the bowing, which, analogous to the pianist's touch, makes the sound spring into life. It is through the medium of the bow that the player embodies his ideas and feelings. It is therefore evident that herein rests one of the most important and difficult elements of the art of violin-playing, and that the excellence of a player, or even of a whole school of playing, depends to a great extent on its method of bowing. It would have been even better for the art of violin-playing as practiced to-day that the perfect instruments of Stradiuarius and Guarnerius should not have been, than that the Tourte bow should have been uninvented.

The long, effective sweep of the bow was one of the characteristics of Viotti's playing, and was alike the admiration and despair of his rivals. His compositions for the violin are classics, and Spohr was wont to say that there could be no better test of a fine player than his execution of one of the Viotti sonatas or concertos. Spohr regretted deeply that he could not finish his violin training under this great master, and was wont to speak of him in terms of the greatest admiration. Viotti had but few pupils, but among them were a number of highly gifted artists. Rode, Robrechts, Cartier, Mdlle. Gerbini, Alday, La-barre, Pixis, Mari, Mme. Paravicini, and Vacher are well-known names to all those interested in the literature of the violin. The influence of Viotti on violin music was a very deep one, not only in virtue of his compositions, but in the fact that he molded the style not only of many of the best violinists of his own day, but of those that came after him.

LUDWIG SPOHR.

Birth and Early Life of the Violinist Spohr.--He is presented with his First Violin at six.--The French *Emigre* Dufour uses his Influence with Dr. Spohr, Sr., to have the Boy devoted to a Musical Career.--Goes to Brunswick for fuller Musical Instruction.--Spohr is appointed *Kammer-musicus* at the Ducal Court.--He enters under the Tuition of and makes a Tour with the Violin Virtuoso Eck.--Incidents of the Russian Journey and his Return.--Concert Tour in Germany.--Loses his Fine Guarnerius Violin.--Is appointed Director of the Orchestra at Gotha.--He marries Dorette Schiedler, the Brilliant Harpist.--Spohr's Stratagem to be present at the Erfurt Musical Celebration given by Napoleon in Honor of the Allied Sovereigns.--Becomes Director of Opera in Vienna.--Incidents of his Life and Production of Various Works.--First Visit to England.--He is made Director of the Cassel Court Oratorios.--He is retired with a Pension.--Closing Years of his Life.--His Place as Composer and Executant.

I.

"The first singer on the violin that ever appeared!" Such was the verdict of the enthusiastic Italians when they heard one of the greatest of the world's violinists, who was also a great composer. The modern world thinks of Spohr rather as the composer of symphony, opera, and oratorio than as a wonderful executant on the violin; but it was in the latter capacity that he enjoyed the greatest reputation during the earlier part of his lifetime, which was a long one, extending from the year 1784 to 1859. The latter half of Spohr's life was mostly devoted to the higher musical ambition of creating, but not until he had established himself as one of the greatest of virtuosos, and founded a school of violin-playing which is, beyond all others, the most scientific, exhaustive, and satisfactory. All of the great contemporary violinists are disciples of the Spohr school of execution. Great as a composer, still greater as a player, and widely beloved as a man--there are only a few names in musical art held in greater esteem than his, though many have evoked a deeper enthusiasm.

Ludwig Spohr was born at Brunswick, April 5, 1784, of parents both of whom possessed no little musical talent. His father, a physician of considerable eminence, was an excellent flutist, and his mother possessed remarkable talent both as a pianist and singer. To the family concerts which he heard at home was the rapid development of the boy's talents largely due. Nature had given him a very sensitive ear and a fine clear voice, and at the age of four or five he joined his mother in duets at the evening gatherings. From the very first he manifested a taste for the instrument for which he was destined to become distinguished. He so teased his father that, at the age of six, he was presented with his first violin, and his joy on receiving his treasure was overpowering. The violin was never out of his hand, and he continually wandered about the house trying to play his favorite melodies. Spohr tells us in his "Autobiography": "I still recollect that, after my first lesson, in which I had learned to play the G-sharp chord upon all four strings, in my rapture at the harmony, I hurried to my mother, who was in the kitchen, and played the chord so incessantly that she was obliged to order me out."

Young Spohr was placed under the tuition of Dufour, a French *emigre* of the days of '91, who was an excellent player, though not a professional, then living at the town of Seesen, the home of the Spohr family; and under him the boy made very rapid progress. It was Dufour who, by his enthusiastic representations, overcame the opposition of Ludwig's parents to the boy's devoting himself to a life of music, for the notion of the senior Spohr was that the name musician was synonymous with that of a tavern fiddler, who played for dancers. In Germany, the land *par excellence* of music, there was a general contempt among the educated classes, during the latter years of the eighteenth century, for the musical profession. Spohr remained under the care of Dufour until he was twelve years old, and devoted himself to his work with great sedulity. Though he as yet knew but little of counterpoint and composition, his creative talent already began to assert itself, and he produced several duos and trios, as well as solo compositions, which evinced great promise, though crude and faulty in the extreme. He was then sent to Brunswick, that he might have the advantage of more scientific instruction, and to this end was placed under the care of Kunisch, an excellent violin teacher, and under Hartung for harmony and counterpoint. The latter was a sort of Dr. Dryasdust, learned, barren, acrid, but an efficient instructor. When young Spohr showed him one of his compositions, he growled out, "There's time enough for that; you must learn something first." It may be said of Spohr, however, that his studies in theory were for the most part self-taught, for he was a most diligent student of the great masters, and was gifted with a keenly analytic mind.

At the age of fourteen young Spohr was an effective soloist, and, as his father began to complain of the heavy expense of his musical education, the boy determined to make an effort for self-support. After revolving many schemes, he conceived the notion of applying to the duke, who was known as an ardent patron of music. He managed to place himself in the way of his Serene Highness, while the latter was walking in his garden, and boldly preferred his request for an appointment in the court orchestra. The duke was pleased to favor the application, and young Spohr was permitted to display his skill at a court concert, in which he acquitted himself so admirably as to secure the cordial patronage of the sovereign. Said the duke: "Be industrious and well behaved, and, if you make good progress, I will put you under the tuition of a great master." So Louis Spohr was installed as a ***Kammermusicus***, and his patron fulfilled his promise in 1802 by placing his ***protege*** under the charge of Francis Eck, one of the finest violinists then living. Under the tuition of this accomplished instructor, the young virtuoso made such rapid advance in the excellence of his technique, that he was soon regarded as worthy of accompanying his master on a grand concert tour through the principal cities of Germany and Russia.

II.

This concert expedition of the two violinists, as narrated in Spohr's "Autobiography," was full of interesting and romantic episodes. Both master and pupil were of amorous and susceptible temperaments, and their affairs were rarely regulated by a common sense of prudence. Spohr relates with delightful ***naivete*** the circumstances under which he fell successively in love, and the rapidity with which he recovered from these fitful spasms of the tender passion. Herr Eck, in addition to his tendency to intrigues with the fairer half of creation, was also of a quarrelsome and exacting disposition, and the general result was ceaseless squabbling with authorities and musical societies in nearly every city they visited. In spite of these drawbacks, however, the two violinists gained both in fame and purse, and were everywhere well received. If Herr Eck carried off the palm over the boyish Spohr as a mere executant, the impression everywhere gained ground that the latter was by far the superior in real depth of musical science, and many of his own violin concertos were received with the heartiest applause. The concert tour came to an end at St. Petersburg in a singular way. Eck fell in love with a daughter of a member of the imperial orchestra, but the idea of marriage did not enter into his project. As the young lady soon felt the unfortunate results of her indiscretion, her parents complained to the Empress, at whose instance Eck was given the choice of marrying the girl or taking an enforced journey to Siberia. He chose the former, and determined to remain in St. Petersburg, where he was offered the first violin of the imperial orchestra. Poor Eck found he had married a shrew, and, between matrimonial discords and ill health brought on by years of excess, he became the victim of a nervous fever, which resulted in lunacy and confinement in a mad-house.

Spohr returned to his native town in July, 1803, and his first meeting with his family was a curious one. "I arrived," he says, "at two o'clock in the morning. I landed at the Petri gate, crossed the Ocker in a boat, and hastened to my grandmother's garden, but found that the house and garden doors were locked. As my knocking didn't arouse any one, I climbed over the garden wall and laid myself down in a summer-house at the end of the garden. Wearied by the long journey, I soon fell asleep, and, notwithstanding my hard couch, would probably have slept for a long while had not my aunts in their morning walk discovered me. Much alarmed, they ran and told my grandmother that a man was asleep in the summer-house. Returning together, the three approached nearer, and, recognizing me, I was awakened amid joyous expressions, embraces, and kisses. At first, I did not recollect where I was, but soon recognized my dear relations, and rejoiced at being once again in the home and scenes of my childhood."

Spohr was most graciously received by the duke, who was satisfied with the proofs of industry and ambition shown by his *protege*. The celebrated Rode, Viotti's most brilliant pupil, was at that time in Brunswick, and Spohr, who conceived the most enthusiastic admiration of his style, set himself assiduously to the study and imitation of the effects peculiar to Rode. On Rode's departure, Spohr appeared in a concert arranged for him, in which he played a new concerto dedicated to his ducal patron, and created an enthusiasm hardly less than that made by Rode himself. He was warmly congratulated by the duke and the court, and appointed first court-violinist, with a salary more than sufficient for the musician's moderate wants. Shortly after this he undertook another concert tour in conjunction with the violoncellist, Benike, through the principal German cities, which added materially to his reputation. But no amount of world's talk or money could fully compensate him for the loss of his magnificent violin, one of the *chefs-d'ouvre* of Guarnerius del Gesu when that great maker was at his best. This instrument he had brought from Russia, and it was an imperial gift. A concert was announced for Gottingen, and Spohr, with his companion, was about to enter the town by coach, when he asked one of the soldiers at the guard-house if the trunk, which had been strapped to the back of the carriage, and which contained his precious instrument, was in its place. "There is no trunk there," was the reply.

"With one bound," says Spohr, "I was out of the carriage, and rushed out through the gate with a drawn hunting-knife. Had I, with more reflection, listened a while, I might have heard the thieves running out through a side path. But in my blind rage I had far overshot the place where I had last seen the trunk, and only discovered my overhaste when I found myself in the open field. Inconsolable for my loss, I turned back. While my fellow-traveler looked for the inn, I hastened to the post-office, and requested that an immediate search might be made in the garden houses outside the gate. With astonishment and vexation, I was informed that the jurisdiction outside the gate belonged to Weende, and that I must prefer my request there. As Weende was half a league from Gottingen, I was compelled to abandon for that evening all further steps for the recovery of my things. That these would prove fruitless on the following morning I was well assured, and I passed a sleepless night in a state of mind such as in my hitherto fortunate career had been unknown to me. Had I not lost my splendid Guarneri violin, the exponent of all the artistic success I had so far attained, I could have lightly borne the loss of clothes and money." The police recovered an empty trunk and the violin-case despoiled of its treasure, but still containing a magnificent Tourte bow, which the thieves had left behind. Spohr managed to borrow a Steiner violin, with which he gave his concert, but he did not for years cease to lament the loss of his grand Guarneri fiddle.

In 1805 Spohr was quietly settled in his avocation at Brunswick as composer and chief ***Kam-mer-musicus*** of the ducal court, when he received an offer to compete for the direction of the orchestra at Gotha, then one of the most magnificent organizations in Europe, to be at the head of which would give him an international fame. The offer was too tempting to be refused, and Spohr was easily victorious. His new duties were not onerous, consisting of a concert once a week, and in practicing and rehearsing the orchestra. The annual salary was five hundred thalers.

One of the most interesting incidents of Spohr's life now occurred. The susceptible heart, which had often been touched, was firmly enslaved by the charms of Dorette Schiedler, the daughter of the principal court singer, and herself a fine virtuoso on the harp. Dorette was a woman whose personal loveliness was an harmonious expression of her beauty of character and artistic talent, and Spohr accepted his fate with joy. This girl of eighteen was irresistible, for she was accomplished, beautiful, tender, as good as an angel, and with the finest talent for music, for she played admirably, not only on the harp, but on the piano and violin. Spohr had reason to hope that the attachment was mutual, and was eager to declare his love. One night they were playing together at a court concert, and Spohr after the performance noticed the duchess, with an arch look at him, whispering some words to Dorette which covered her cheeks with blushes. That night, as the lovers were returning home in the carriage, Spohr said to her, "Shall we thus play together for life?" Dorette burst into tears, and sank into her lover's arms. The compact was sealed by the joyous assent of the mother, and the young couple were united in the ducal chapel, in the presence of the duchess and a large assemblage of friends, on the 2d of February, 1806.

III.

In the following year Spohr and his young wife set out on a musical tour, "by which," he says, "we not only reaped a rich harvest of applause, but saved a considerable sum of money." On his return to Gotha he was met by a band of pupils, who unharnessed the horses from the coach and drew him through the streets in triumph. He now devoted himself to composition largely, and produced his first opera, "Alruna," which is said to have been very warmly received, both at Gotha and Weimar, in which latter city it was produced under the superintendence of the poet Goethe, who was intendant of the theatre. Spohr, however, allowed it to disappear, as his riper judgment condemned its faults more than it favored its excellences. Among his amusing adventures, one which he relates in his "Autobiography" as having occurred in 1808 is worth repeating. He tells us: "In the year 1808 took place the celebrated Congress of Sovereigns at Erfurt, on which occasion Napoleon entertained his friend Alexander of Russia and the various kings and princes of Germany. The lovers of sights and the curious of the whole country round poured in to see the magnificence displayed. In the company of some of my pupils, I made a pedestrian excursion to Erfurt, less to see the great ones of the earth than to see and admire the great ones of the French stage, Talma and Mars. The Emperor had sent to Paris for his tragic performers, who played every evening in the classic works of Corneille and Racine. I and my companions had hoped to have seen one such representation, but unfortunately I was informed that they took place for the sovereigns and their suites alone, and that everybody else was excluded from them." In this dilemma Spohr had recourse to stratagem. He persuaded four musicians of the orchestra to vacate their places for a handsome consideration, and he and his pupils engaged to fill the duties. But one of the substitutes must needs be a horn-player, and the four new players could only perform on violin and 'cello. So there was nothing to be done but for Spohr to master the French horn at a day's notice. At the expense of swollen and painful lips, he managed this sufficiently to play the music required with ease and precision. "Thus prepared," he writes, "I and my pupils joined the other musicians, and, as each carried his instrument under his arm, we reached our place without opposition. We found the saloon in which the theatre had been erected already brilliantly lit up and filled with the numerous suites of the sovereigns. The seats for Napoleon and his guests were right behind the orchestra. Shortly after, the most able of my pupils, to whom I had assigned the direction of the music, and under whose leadership I had placed myself as a new-fledged hornist, had tuned up the orchestra, the high personages made their appearance, and the overture began. The orchestra, with their faces turned to the stage, stood in a long row, and each was strictly forbidden to turn around and look with curiosity at the sovereigns. As I had received notice of this beforehand, I had provided myself secretly with a small looking-glass, by the help of which, as soon as the music was ended, I was enabled to obtain in succession a good view of those who directed the destinies of Europe. Nevertheless, I was soon so engrossed with the magnificent acting of the tragic artists that I abandoned my mirror to my pupils, and directed my whole attention to the stage. But at every succeeding *entr'acte* the pain of my lips increased, and at the close of the performance they had become so much swollen and blistered that in the evening I could scarcely eat any supper. Even the next day, on my return to Gotha, my lips had a very negro-like appearance, and my young wife was not a little alarmed when she saw me. But she was yet more nettled when I told her that it was from kissing to such excess the pretty Erfurt women. When I had related, however, the history of my lessons on the horn, she laughed heartily at my expense."

In October, 1809, Spohr and his wife started on an art journey to Russia, but they were recalled by the court chamberlain, who said that the duchess could not spare them from the court concerts, but would liberally indemnify them for the loss. Spohr returned and remained at home for nearly three years, during which time he composed a number of important works for orchestra and for the violin. In 1812 a visit to Vienna, during which he gave a series of concerts, so delighted the Viennese that Spohr was offered the direction of the Ander Wien theatre at a salary three times that received at Gotha, besides valuable emoluments. This, and the assurance of Count Palffy, the imperial intendant, that he meant to make the orchestra the finest in Europe, induced Spohr to accept the offer.

When it became necessary for our musician to search for a domicile in Vienna, he met with another piece of good fortune. One morning a gentleman waited on him, introducing himself as a wealthy clock manufacturer and a passionate lover of music. The stranger made an eccentric proposition. Spohr should hand over to him all that he should compose or had composed for Vienna during the term of three years, the original scores to be his sole property during that time, and Spohr not even to retain a copy. "But are they not to be performed during that time?" "Oh, yes! as often as possible; but each time on my lending them for that purpose, and when I can be present myself." The bargain was struck, and the ardent connoisseur agreed to pay thirty ducats for a string quartet, five and thirty for a quintet, forty for a sextet, etc., according to the style of composition. Two works were sold on the spot, and Spohr said he should devote the money to house-furnishing. Herr Von Tost undertook to provide the furniture complete, and the two made a tour among the most fashionable shops. When Spohr protested against purchasing articles of extreme beauty and luxury, Von Tost said, "Make yourself easy, I shall require no cash settlement. You will soon square all accounts with your manuscripts." So the Spohr domicile was magnificently furnished from kitchen to attic, more fitly, as the musician said, for a royal dignitary or a rich merchant than for a poor artist. Von Tost claimed he would gain two results: "First, I wish to be invited to all the concerts and musical circles in which you will play your compositions, and to do this I must have your scores in my possession; secondly, in possessing such treasures of art, I hope upon my business journeys to make a large acquaintance among the lovers of music, which I may turn to account in my manufacturing interests." Let us hope that this commercial enthusiast found his calculations verified by results.

Spohr soon gave two important new works to the musical world, the opera of "Faust," and the cantata, "The Liberation of Germany," neither of which, however, was immediately produced. Weber brought out "Faust" at Prague in 1816, and the cantata was first performed at Franken-hausen in 1815, at a musical festival on the anniversary of the battle of Leipsic, a battle which turned the scale of Napoleon's career. The same year (1815) also witnessed the quarrel between Spohr and Count Palffy, which resulted in the rupture of the former's engagement. Spohr determined to make a long tour through Germany, Switzerland, and Italy. Before shaking the dust of Vienna from his feet, he sold the Von Tost household at auction, and the sum realized was even larger than what had been paid for it, so vivid were the public curiosity and interest in view of the strange bargain under which the furniture had been bought. On the 18th of March, 1815, Louis Spohr, with his beloved

Dorette and young family, which had increased with truly German fecundity, bade farewell to Vienna.

Two years of concert-giving and sight-seeing swiftly passed, to the great augmentation of the German violinist's fame. On Spohr's return home he was invited to become the opera and music director of the Frankfort Theatre, and for two years more he labored arduously at this post. He produced the opera of "Zemire and Azar" (founded on the fairy fable of "Beauty and the Beast") during this period among other works, and it was very enthusiastically received by the public. This opera was afterward given in London, in English, with great success, though the opinion of the critics was that it was too scientific for the English taste.

IV.

Louis Spohr's first visit to England was in 1820, whither he went on invitation of the Philharmonic Society. He gives an amusing account of his first day in London, on the streets of which city he appeared in a most brilliantly colored shawl waistcoat, and narrowly escaped being pelted by the enraged mob, for the English people were then in mourning for the death of George III, which had recently occurred, and Spohr's gay attire was construed as a public insult. He played several of his own works at the opening Philharmonic concert, and the brilliant veteran of the violin, Viotti, to become whose pupil had once been Spohr's darling but ungratified dream, expressed the greatest admiration of the German virtuoso's magnificent playing. The "Autobiography" relates an amusing interview of Spohr with the head of the Rothschild's banking establishment, to whom he had brought a letter of introduction from the Frankfort Rothschild, as well as a letter of credit. "After Rothschild had taken both letters from me and glanced hastily over them, he said to me, in a subdued tone of voice, 'I have just read (pointing to the "Times") that you manage your business very efficiently; but I understand nothing of music. This is my music (slapping his purse); they understand that on the exchange.' Upon which with a nod of the head he terminated the audience. But just as I had reached the door he called after me, 'You can come out and dine with me at my country house.' A few days afterward Mme. Rothschild also invited me to dinner, but I did not go, though she repeated the invitation."

While in London on this visit Spohr composed his B flat Symphony, which was given by the Philharmonic Society under the direction of the composer himself, and, as he tells us in his "Autobiography," it was played better than he ever heard it afterward. His English reception, on the whole, was a very cordial one, and he secured a very high place in public estimation, both as a violinist and orchestral composer. On returning to Germany, Spohr gave a series of concerts, during which time he produced his great D minor violin concerto, making a great sensation with it. He had not yet visited Paris in a professional way, and in the winter of 1821 he turned his steps thitherward, in answer to a pressing invitation from the musicians of that great capital. On January 20th he made his ***debut*** before a French audience, and gave a programme mostly of his own compositions. Spohr asserts that the satisfaction of the audience was enthusiastically expressed, but the fact that he did not repeat the entertainment would suggest a suspicion that the impression he made was not fully to his liking. It may be he did not dare take the risk in a city so full of musical attractions of every description. Certainly he did not like the French, though his reception from the artists and literati was of the most friendly sort. He was disgusted "with the ridiculous vanity of the Parisians." He writes: "When one or other of their musicians plays anything, they say, 'Well! can you boast of that in Germany?' Or when they introduce to you one of their distinguished artists, they do not call him the first in Paris, but at once the first in the world, although no nation knows less what other countries possess than they do, in their--for their vanity's sake most fortunate--ignorance."

Spohr's appointment to the directorship of the court theatre at Cassel occurred in the winter of 1822, and he confesses his pleasure in the post, as he believed he could make its fine orchestra one of the most celebrated in Germany. He remained in this position for about thirty years, and during that time Cassel became one of the greatest musical centers of the country. His labors were assiduous, for he had the true tireless German industry, and he soon gave the world his opera of "Jessonda," which was first produced on July 28, 1823, with marked success. "Jessonda" has always kept its hold on the German stage, though it was not received with much favor elsewhere. Another opera, "Der Berg Geist" ("The Mountain Spirit"), quickly followed, the work having been written to celebrate the marriage of the Princess of

Hesse with the Duke of Saxe-Meiningen. One of his most celebrated compositions, the oratorio "Die Letzten Dinge" ("The Last Judgment"), which is more familiar to English-speaking peoples than any other work of Spohr, was first performed on Good Friday, 1826, and was recognized from the first as a production of masterly excellence. Spohr's ability as a composer of sacred music would have been more distinctly accepted, had it not been that Handel, Haydn, and, in more recent years, Mendelssohn, raised the ideal of the oratorio so high that only the very loftiest musical genius is considered fit to reign in this sphere. The director of the Cassel theatre continued indefatigable in producing works of greater or less excellence, chamber-music, symphonies, and operas. Among the latter, attention may be called to "Pietro Albano" and the "Alchemist," clever but in no sense brilliant works, though, as it became the fashion in Germany to indulge in enthusiasm over Spohr, they were warmly praised at home. The best known of his orchestral works, "Die Weihe der Tone " ("The Power of Sound"), a symphony of unquestionable greatness, was produced in 1832. We are told that Spohr had been reading a volume of poems which his deceased friend Pfeiffer had left behind him, when he alighted on "Die Weihe der Tone," and the words delighted him so much that he thought of using them as the basis of a cantata. But he changed his purpose, and finally decided to delineate the subject of the poem in orchestral composition. The finest of all Spohr's symphonies was the outcome, a work which ranks high among compositions of this class. His toil on the new oratorio of "Calvary" was sadly interrupted by the death of his beloved wife Dorette, who had borne him a large family, and had been his most sympathetic and devoted companion. Spohr was so broken down by this calamity that it was several months before he could resume his labors, and it was because Dorette during her illness had felt such a deep interest in the progress of the work that the desolate husband so soon plucked heart to begin again. When the oratorio was produced on Good Friday, 1835, Spohr records in his diary: "The thought that my wife did not live to listen to its first performance sensibly lessened the satisfaction I felt at this my most successful work." This oratorio was not given in England till 1839, at the Norwich festival, Spohr being present to conduct it. The zealous and narrow-minded clergy of the day preached bitterly against it as a desecration, and one fierce bigot hurled his diatribes against the composer, when the latter was present in the cathedral. A journal of the day describes the scene: "We now see the fanatical zealot in the pulpit, and sitting right opposite to him the great composer, with ears happily deaf to the English tongue, but with a demeanor so becoming, with a look so full of pure good-will, and with so much humility and mildness in the features, that his countenance alone spoke to the heart like a good sermon. Without intending it, we make a comparison, and can not for a moment doubt in which of the two dwelt the spirit of religion which denoted the true Christian."

Spohr had been two years a widower when he became enamored of one of the daughters of Court Councilor Pfeiffer. He tells us he had long been acquainted "with the high and varied intellectual culture of the two sisters, and so I became fully resolved to sue for the hand of the elder, Marianne, whose knowledge of music and skill in pianoforte playing I had already observed when she sometimes gave her assistance at the concerts of the St. Cecilia Society. As I had not the courage to propose to her by word of mouth, there being more than twenty years difference in our ages, I put the question to her in writing, and added, in excuse for my courtship, the assurance that I was as yet perfectly free from the infirmities of age." The proposition was accepted, and they were married without delay on January 3, 1836. The bridal couple made a long journey through the principal German cities, and were universally received with great rejoicings. Musical parties and banquets were everywhere arranged for them, at which Spohr and his young wife delighted every one by their splendid playing. The "Historical" symphony, descriptive of the music and characteristics of different periods, was finished in 1839, and made a very favorable impression both in Germany and England. Spohr had now become quite at home in England, where his music was much liked, and during different years went to the country, where oratorio music is more appreciated than anywhere else in the musical world, to conduct the Norwich festival. One of his most successful compositions of this description, "The Fall of Babylon," was written expressly for the festival of 1842. When it was given the next year in London under Spohr's own direction, the president of the Sacred Harmonic Society presented the composer at the close of the performance with a superb silver testimonial in the name of the society.

V.

Louis Spohr had now become one of the patriarchs of music, for his life spanned a longer arch in the history of the art than any contemporary except Cherubini. He was seven years old when Mozart died, and before Haydn had departed from this life Spohr had already begun to acquire a name as a violinist and composer. He lived to be the friend of Mendelssohn, Meyerbeer, Liszt, and Wagner. Everywhere he was held in veneration, even by those who did not fully sympathize with his musical works, for his career had been one of great fecundity in art. In addition to his rank as one of the few very great violin virtuosos, he had been indefatigable in the production of compositions in nearly all styles, and every country of Europe recognized his place as a musician of supereminent talent, if not of genius, one who had profoundly influenced contemporary music, even if he should not mold the art of succeeding ages. Testimonials of admiration and respect poured in on him from every quarter.

He composed the opera of "The Crusaders" in 1845, and he was invited to conduct the first performance in Berlin. He relates two pleasing incidents in his "Autobiography." He had been invited to a select dinner party given at the royal palace, and between the king and Spohr, who was seated opposite, there intervened an ornamental centerpiece of considerable height in the shape of a flower vase. This greatly interfered with the enjoyment by the king of Spohr's conversation. At last his Majesty, growing impatient, removed the impediment with his own hands, so that he had a full view of Spohr.

The other incident was a pleasing surprise from his colleagues in art. He was a guest of the Wickmann family, and they were all gathered in the illuminated garden saloon, when there entered through the gloom of the garden a number of dark figures swiftly following each other, who proved to be the members of the royal orchestra, with Meyerbeer and Taubert at their head. The senior member then presented Spohr with a beautifully executed gold laurel-wreath, while Meyerbeer made a speech full of feeling, in which he thanked him for his enthusiastic love of German art, and for all the grand and beautiful works which he had created, specially "The Crusaders." The twenty-fifth anniversary of Spohr's connection with the court theatre of Cassel occurred in 1847, and was to have been celebrated with a great festival. The death of Felix Bartholdy Mendelssohn cast a great gloom over musical Germany that year, so the festival was held not in honor of Spohr, but as a solemn memorial of the departed genius whose name is a household word among all those who love the art he so splendidly illustrated.

Spohr's next production was the fine symphony known as "The Seasons," one of the most picturesque and expressive of his orchestral works, in which he depicts with rich musical color the vicissitudes of the year and the associations clustering around them. This symphony was followed by his seventh quintet, in G minor, another string quartet, the thirty-second, and a series of pieces for the violin and piano, and in 1852 we find the indefatigable composer busy in remodeling his opera of "Faust" for production by Mr. Gye, in London. It was produced with great splendor in the English capital, and conducted by Spohr himself; but it did not prove a great success, a deep disappointment to Spohr, who fondly believed this work to be his masterpiece. "On this occasion," writes a very competent critic, *a propos* of the first performance, "there was a certain amount of heaviness about the performance which told very much against the probability of that opera ever becoming a favorite with the Royal Italian Opera subscribers. Nothing could possibly exceed the poetical grace of Eonconi in the title role, or surpass the propriety and expression of his singing. Mme. Castellan's *Cunegonda* was also exceedingly well sung, and Tamberlik outdid himself by his thorough comprehension of the music, the splendor of his voice, and the refinement of his vocalization in the character of *Ugo*.... The *Mephistopheles* of Herr Formes was a remarkable personation, being truly demoniacal in the play of his countenance, and as characteristic as any one of Retsch's drawings of Goethe's fiend-tempter. His singing being specially German was in every way well suited to the occasion." In spite of the excellence of the interpretation, Spohr's "Faust" did not take any hold on the lovers of music in England, and even in Germany, where Spohr is held in great reverence, it presents but little attraction. The closing years of Spohr's active life as a musician were devoted to that species of composition where he showed indubitable title to be considered a man of genius, works for the violin and chamber music. He himself did not recognize his decadence of energy and musical vigor; but the veteran was more than seventy years old, and his royal master resolved to put his baton in younger and fresher hands. So he was retired from service with an annual pension of fifteen hundred thalers. Spohr felt this deeply, but he had scarcely reconciled himself to the change when a more serious casualty befell him. He fell and broke his left arm, which never gained enough strength for him to hold the beloved instrument again. It had been the great joy and solace of his life to play, and, now that in his old age he was deprived of this comfort, he was ready to die. Only once more did he make a public appearance. In the spring of 1859 he journeyed to Meiningen to direct a concert on behalf of a charitable fund. An ovation was given to the aged master. A colossal bust of himself was placed on the stage, arched with festoons of palm and laurel, and the conductor's stand was almost buried in flowers. He was received with thunders of welcome, which were again and again reiterated, and at the close of the performance he could hardly escape for the eager throng who wished to press his hand. Spohr died on October 22, 1859, after a few days' illness, and in his death Germany at least recognized the loss of one of its most accomplished and versatile if not greatest composers.

VI.

Dr. Ludwig Spohr's fame as a composer has far overshadowed his reputation as a violin virtuoso, but the most capable musical critics unite in the opinion that that rare quality, which we denominate genius, was principally shown in his wonderful power as a player, and his works written for the violin. Spohr was a man of immense self-assertion, and believed in the greatness of his own musical genius as a composer in the higher domain of his art. His "Autobiography," one of the most fresh, racy, and interesting works of the kind ever written, is full of varied illustrations of what Chorley stigmatizes his "bovine self-conceit." His fecund production of symphony, oratorio, and opera, as well as of the more elaborate forms of chamber music, for a period of forty years or more, proves how deep was his conviction of his own powers. Indeed, he half confesses himself that he is only willing to be rated a little less than Beethoven. Spohr was singularly meager, for the most part, in musical ideas and freshness of melody, but he was a profound master of the orchestra; and in that variety and richness of resources which give to tone-creations the splendor of color, which is one of the great charms of instrumental music, Spohr is inferior only to Wagner among modern symphonists. Spohr's more pretentious works are a singular union of meagerness of idea with the most polished richness of manner; but, in imagination and thought, he is far the inferior of those whose knowledge of treating the orchestra and contrapuntal skill could not compare with his. There are more vigor and originality in one of Schubert's greater symphonies than in all the multitudinous works of the same class ever written by Spohr. In Spohr's compositions for the violin as a solo instrument, however, he stands unrivaled, for here his true *genre* as a man of creative genius stamps itself unmistakably.

Before the coming of Spohr violin music had been illustrated by a succession of virtuosos, French and Italian, who, though melodiously charming, planned in their works and execution to exhibit the effects and graces of the players themselves instead of the instrument. Paganini carried this tendency to its most remarkable and fascinating extreme, but Spohr founded a new style of violin playing, on which the greatest modern performers who have grown up since his prime have assiduously modeled themselves. Mozart had written solid and simple concertos in which the performer was expected to embroider and finish the composer's sketch. This required genius and skill under instant command, instead of merely phenomenal execution. Again, Beethoven's concertos were so written as to make the solo player merely one of the orchestra, chaining him in bonds only to set him free to deliver the cadenza. This species of self-effacement does not consort with the purpose of solo playing, which is display, though under that display there should be power, mastery, and resource of thought, and not the trickery of the accomplished juggler. Spohr in his violin music most felicitously accomplished this, and he is simply incomparable in his compromise between what is severe and classical, and what is suave and delightful, or passionately exciting. In these works the musician finds nerve, sparkle, *elan*, and brightness combined with technical charm and richness of thought. Spohr's unconscious and spontaneous force in this direction was the direct outcome of his remarkable power as a solo player, or, more properly, gathered its life-like play and strength from the latter fact. It may be said of Spohr that, as Mozart raised opera to a higher standard, as Beethoven uplifted the ideal of the orchestra, as Clementi laid a solid foundation for piano-playing, so Spohr's creative force as a violinist and writer for the violin has established the grandest school for this instrument, to which all the foremost contemporary artists acknowledge their obligations.

Dr. Spohr's style as a player, while remarkable for its display of technique and command of resource, always subordinated mere display to the purpose of the music. The Italians called him "the first singer on the violin," and his profound musical knowledge enabled him to produce effects in a perfectly legitimate manner, where other players had recourse to meretricious and dazzling exhibition of skill. His title to recollection in the history of music will not be so much that of a great general composer, but that of the greatest of composers for the violin, and the one who taught violinists that height of excellence as an excutant should go hand in hand with good taste and self-restraint, to produce its most permanent effects and exert its most vital influence.

NICOLO PAGANINI.

The Birth of the Greatest of Violinists.--His Mother's Dream--Extraordi-
nary Character and Genius.--Heine's Description of his Playing.--Leigh
Hunt on Paganini.--Superstitious Rumors current during his Life.--He is
believed to be a Demoniac.--His Strange Appearance.--Early Training and
Surroundings.--Anecdotes of his Youth.--Paganini's Youthful Dissipations.-
-His Passion for Gambling.--He acquires his Wonderful Guarnerius
Violin.--His Reform from the Gaming-table.--Indefatigable Practice and
Work as a Young Artist.--Paganini as a *Preux Chevalier*.--His Powerful
Attraction for Women.--Episode with a Lady of Rank.--Anecdotes of his
Early Italian Concertizing.--The Imbroglio at Ferrant.--The Frail Health
of Paganini.--Wonderful Success at Milan, where he first plays One of the
Greatest of his Compositions, "Le Streghe."--Duel with Lafont.--Incidents
and Anecdotes.--His First Visit to Germany.--Great Enthusiasm of his
Audiences.--Experiences at Vienna, Berlin, and other German Cities.--
Description of Paganini, in Paris, by Castil-Blaze and Fetis.--His English
Reception and the Impression made.--Opinions of the Critics.--Paganini
not pleased with England.--Settles in Paris for Two Years, and becomes the
Great Musical Lion.--Simplicity and Amiability of Nature.--Magnificent
Generosity to Hector Berlioz.--The Great Fortune made by Paganini.--His
Beautiful Country Seat near Parma.--An Unfortunate Speculation in Paris.-
-The Utter Failure of his Health.--His Death at Nice.--Characteristics and
Anecdotes.--Interesting Circumstances of his Last Moments.--The Peculiar
Genius of Paganini, and his Influence on Art.

I.

In the latter part of the last century an Italian woman of Genoa had a dream which she thus related to her little son: "My son, you will be a great musician. An angel radiant with beauty appeared to me during the night and promised to accomplish any wish that I might make. I asked that you should become the greatest of all violinists, and the angel granted that my desire should be fulfilled." The child who was thus addressed became that incomparable artist, Paganini, whose name now, a glorious tradition, is used as a standard by which to estimate the excellence of those who have succeeded him.

No artist ever lived who so piqued public curiosity, and invested himself with a species of weird romance, which compassed him as with a cloud. The personality of the individual so unique and extraordinary, the genius of the artist so transcendant in its way, the mystery which surrounded all the movements of the man, conspired to make him an object of such interest that the announcement of a concert by him in any European city made as much stir as some great public event. Crowds followed his strange figure in the streets wherever he went, and, had the time been the mediaeval ages, he himself a celebrated magician or sorcerer, credited with power over the spirits of earth and air, his appearance could not have aroused a thrill of attention more absorbing. Over men of genius, as well as the commonplace herd, he cast the same spell, stamping himself as a personage who could be compared with no other.

The German poet Heine thus describes his first acquaintance with this paragon of violinists:

"It was in the theatre at Hamburg that I first heard Paganini's violin. Although it was fast-day, all the commercial magnates of the town were present in the front boxes, the goddesses Juno of Wandrahm, and the goddesses Aphrodite of Dreckwall. A religious hush pervaded the whole assembly; every eye was directed toward the stage, every ear was strained for hearing. At last a dark figure, which seemed to ascend from the under world, appeared on the stage. It was Paganini in full evening dress, black coat and waistcoat cut after a most villainous pattern, such as is perhaps in accordance with the infernal etiquette of the court of Proserpine, and black trousers fitting awkwardly to his thin legs. His long arms appeared still longer as he advanced, holding in one hand his violin, and in the other the bow, hanging down so as almost to touch the ground--all the while making a series of extraordinary reverences. In the angular contortions of his body there was something so painfully wooden, and also something so like the movements of a droll animal, that a strange disposition to laughter overcame the audience; but his face, which the glaring footlights caused to assume an even more corpse-like aspect than was natural to it, had in it something so appealing, something so imbecile and meek, that a strange feeling of compassion removed all tendency to laughter. Had he learned these reverences from an automaton or a performing dog? Is this beseeching look the look of one who is sick unto death, or does there lurk behind it the mocking cunning of a miser? Is that a mortal who in the agony of death stands before the public in the art arena, and, like a dying gladiator, bids for their applause in his last convulsions? or is it some phantom arisen from the grave, a vampire with a violin, who comes to suck, if not the blood from our hearts, at least the money from our pockets? Questions such as these kept chasing each other through the brain while Paganini continued his apparently interminable series of complimentary bows; but all such questionings instantly take flight the moment the great master puts his violin to his chin and began to play.

"Then were heard melodies such as the nightingale pours forth in the gloaming when the perfume of the rose intoxicates her heart with sweet forebodings of spring! What melting, sensuously languishing notes of bliss! Tones that kissed, then poutingly fled from another, and at last embraced and became one, and died away in the ecstasy of union! Again, there were heard sounds like the song of the fallen angels, who, banished from the realms of bliss, sink with shame-red countenance to the lower world. These were sounds out of whose bottomless depth gleamed no ray of hope or comfort; when the blessed in heaven hear them, the praises of God die away upon their pallid lips, and, sighing, they veil their holy faces." Leigh Hunt, in one of his essays, thus describes the playing of this greatest of all virtuosos: "Paganini, the first time I saw and heard him, and the first moment he struck a note, seemed literally to strike it, to *give* it a blow. The house was so crammed that, being among the squeezers in the standing room at the side of the pit, I happened to catch the first glance of his face through the arms akimbo of a man who was perched up before me, which made a kind of frame for it; and there on the stage through that frame, as through a perspective glass, were the face, the bust, and the raised hand of the wonderful musician, with the instrument at his chin, just going to begin, and looking exactly as I describe him in the following lines:

> "His hand, Loading the air with dumb expectancy,
> Suspended, ere it fell, a nation's breath.
> He _smote_; and clinging to the serious chords
> With Godlike ravishment drew forth a breath,
> So deep, so strong, so fervid, thick with love--
> Blissful, yet laden as with twenty prayers--
> That Juno yearned with no diviner soul
> To the first burthen of the lips of Jove.
> The exceeding mystery of the loveliness
> Sadden'd delight; and, with his mournful look,
> Dreary and gaunt, hanging his pallid face
> Twixt his dark flowing locks, he almost seemed
> Too feeble, or to melancholy eyes
> One that has parted from his soul for pride,
> And in the sable secret lived forlorn.

"To show the depth and identicalness of the impression which he made on everybody, foreign or native, an Italian who stood near me said to himself, with a long sigh, 'O Dio!' and this had not been said long, when another person in the same tone uttered 'Oh Christ!' Musicians pressed forward from behind the scenes to get as close to him as possible, and they could not sleep at night for thinking of him."

The impression made by Paganini was something more than that of a great, even the greatest, violinist. It was as if some demoniac power lay behind the human, prisoned and dumb except through the agencies of music, but able to fill expression with faint, far-away cries of passion, anguish, love, and aspiration--echoes from the supernatural and invisible. His hearers forgot the admiration due to the wonderful virtuoso, and seemed to listen to voices from another world. The strange rumors that were current about him, Paganini seems to have been not disinclined to encourage, for, mingled with his extraordinary genius, there was an element of charlatanism. It was commonly reported that his wonderful execution on the G-string was due to a long imprisonment, inflicted on him for the assassination of a rival in love, during which he had a violin with one string only. Paganini himself writes that, "At Vienna one of the audience affirmed publicly that my performance was not surprising, for he had distinctly seen, while I was playing my variations, the devil at my elbow, directing my arm and guiding my bow. My resemblance to the devil was a proof of my origin." Even sensible people believed that Paganini had some uncanny and unlawful secret which enabled him to do what was impossible for other players. At Prague he actually printed a letter from his mother to prove that he was not the son of the devil. It was not only the perfectly novel and astonishing character of his playing, but to a large extent his ghostlike appearance, which caused such absurd rumors. The tall, skeleton-like figure, the pale, narrow, wax-colored face, the long, dark, disheveled hair, the mysterious expression of the heavy eye, made a weirdly strange *ensemble*. Heine tells us in "The Florentine Nights" that only one artist had succeeded in delineating the real physiognomy of Paganini: "A deaf and crazy painter, called Lyser, has in a sort of spiritual frenzy so admirably portrayed by a few touches of his pencil the head of Paganini that one is dismayed and moved to laughter at the faithfulness of the sketch! 'The devil guided my hand,' said the deaf painter to me, with mysterious gesticulations and a satirical yet good-natured wag of the head, such as he was wont to indulge in when in the midst of his genial tomfoolery."

II.

Nicolo Paganini was born at Genoa on the night of February 18, 1784, of parents in humbly prosperous circumstances, his father being a ship-broker, and, though illiterate in a general way, a passionate lover of music and an amateur of some skill. The father soon perceived the child's talent, and caused him to study so severely that it not only affected his constitution, but actually made him a tolerable player at the age of six years. The elder Paganini's knowledge of music was not sufficient to carry the lad far in mastering the instrument, but the extraordinary precocity shown so interested Signor Corvetto, the leader at the Genoese theatre, that he undertook to instruct the gifted child. Two years later the young Paganini was transferred to the charge of Signor Giacomo Costa, an excellent violinist, and director of church music at one of the cathedrals, under whom he made rapid progress in executive skill, while he studied harmony and counterpoint under the composer Gnecco. It was at this time, Paganini not yet being nine years of age, that he composed his first piece, a sonata now lost. In 1793 he made his first appearance in public at Genoa, and played variations on the air "La Carmagnole," then so popular, with immense effect. This *debut* was followed by several subsequent appearances, in which he created much enthusiasm. He also played a violin concerto every Sunday in church, an attraction which drew great throngs. This practice was of great use to Paganini, as it forced him continually to study fresh music. About the year 1795 it was deemed best to place the boy under the charge of an eminent professor, and Alessandro Rolla, of Parma, was pitched on. When the Paganinis arrived, they found the learned professor ill, and rather surly at the disturbance. Young Paganini, however, speedily silenced the complaints of the querulous invalid. The great player himself relates the anecdote: "His wife showed us into a room adjoining the bedroom, till she had spoken to the sick man. Finding on the table a violin and the music of Rolla's latest concerto, I took up the instrument and played the piece at sight. Astonished at what he heard, the composer asked for the name of the player, and could not believe it was only a young boy till he had seen for himself. He then told me that he had nothing to teach me, and advised me to go to Paer for study in composition." But, as Paer was at this time in Germany, Paganini studied under Ghiretti and Rolla himself while he remained in Parma, according to the monograph of Fetis.

The youthful player had already begun to search out new effects on the violin, and to create for himself characteristics of tone and treatment hitherto unknown to players. After his return to Genoa he composed his first "Etudes," which were of such unheard-of difficulty that he was sometimes obliged to practice a single passage ten hours running. His intense study resulted not only in his acquirement of an unlimited execution, but in breaking down his health. His father was a harsh and inexorable taskmaster, and up to this time Paganini (now being fourteen) had remained quiescent under this tyrant's control. But the desire of liberty was breeding projects in his breast, which opportunity soon favored. He managed to get permission to travel alone for the first time to Lucca, where he had engaged to play at the musical festival in November, 1798. He was received with so much enthusiasm that he determined not to return to the paternal roof, and at once set off to fulfill engagements at Pisa and other towns. In vain the angry and mortified father sought to reclaim the young rebel who had slipped through his fingers. Nicolo found the sweets of freedom too precious to go back again to bondage, though he continued to send his father a portion of the proceeds of his playing.

The youth, intoxicated with the license of his life, plunged into all kinds of dissipation, specially into gambling, at this time a universal vice in Italy, as indeed it was throughout Europe. Alternate fits of study and gaming, both of which he pursued with equal zeal, and the exhaustion of the life he led, operated dangerously on his enfeebled frame, and fits of illness frequently prevented his fulfillment of concert engagements. More than once he wasted in one evening the proceeds of several concerts, and was obliged to borrow money on his violin, the source of his livelihood, in order to obtain funds wherewith to pay his gambling debts. Anything more wild, debilitating, and ruinous than the life led by this boy, who had barely emerged from childhood, can hardly be imagined. On one occasion he was announced for a concert at Leghorn, but he had gambled away his money and pawned his violin, so that he was compelled to get the loan of an instrument in order to play in the evening. In this emergency he applied to M. Livron, a French gentleman, a merchant of Leghorn, and an excellent amateur performer, who possessed a Guarneri del Gesu violin, reputed among connoisseurs one of the finest instruments in the world. The generous Frenchman instantly acceded to the boy's wish, and the precious violin was put in his hands. After the concert, when Paganini returned the instrument to M. Livron, the latter, who had been to hear him, exclaimed, "Never will I profane the strings which your fingers have touched! That instrument is yours." The astonishment and delight of the young artist may be more easily imagined than described. It was upon this violin that Paganini afterward performed in all his concerts, and the great virtuoso left it to the town of Genoa, where it is now preserved in a glass case in the Museum. An excellent engraving of it, from a photograph, was published in 1875 in George Hart's book on "The Violin."

At this period of his life, between the ages of seventeen and twenty, Nicolo Paganini was surrounded by numerous admirers, and led into all kinds of dissipation. He was naturally amiable and witty in conversation, though he has been reproached with selfishness. There can be no doubt that he was, at this period, constantly under the combined influences of flattery and unbounded ambition; nevertheless, in spite of all his successful performances at concerts, the style of life he was leading kept him so poor that he frequently took in hand all kinds of musical work to supply the wants of the moment. It is a curious coincidence that the fine violin which was presented to him by M. Livron, as we have just seen, was the cause of his abandoning, after a while, the allurements of the gaming-tables. Paganini tells us himself that a certain nobleman was anxious to possess this instrument, and had offered for it a sum equivalent to about four hundred dollars; but the artist would not sell it even if one thousand had been offered for it, although he was, at this juncture, in great need of funds to pay off a debt of honor, and sorely tempted to accept the proffered amount. Just at this point Paganini received an invitation to a friend's house where gambling was the order of the day. "All my capital," he says, "consisted of thirty francs, as I had disposed of my jewels, watch, rings, etc.; I nevertheless resolved on risking this last resource, and, if fortune proved fickle, to sell my violin and proceed to St. Petersburg, without instrument or baggage, with the view of reestablishing my affairs. My thirty francs were soon reduced to three, and I already fancied myself on the road to Russia, when luck took a sudden turn, and I won one hundred and sixty francs. This saved my violin and completely set me up. From that day forward I gradually gave up gaming, becoming more and more convinced that a gambler is an object of contempt to all well-regulated minds."

III.

Love-making was also among the diversions which Paganini began early to practice. Like nearly all great musicians, he was an object of great fascination to the fair sex, and his life had its full share of amorous romances. A strange episode was his retirement in the country chateau of a beautiful Bolognese lady for three years, between the years 1801 and 1804. Here, in the society of a lovely woman, who was passionately devoted to him, and amid beautiful scenery, he devoted himself to practicing and composition, also giving much study to the guitar (the favorite instrument of his inamorata), on which he became a wonderful proficient. This charming idyl in Paganini's life reminds one of the retirement of the pianist Chopin to the island of Majorca in the company of Mme. George Sand. It was during this period of his life that Paganini composed twelve of his finest sonatas for violin and guitar.

When our musician returned again to Genoa and active life in 1804, he devoted much time also to composition. He was twenty years of age, and wrote here four grand quartets for violin, tenor, violoncello, and guitar, and also some bravura variations for violin with guitar accompaniment. At this period he gave lessons to a young girl of Genoa, Catherine Calcagno, about seven years of age; eight years later, when only fifteen years old, this young lady astonished Italian audiences by the boldness of her style. She continued her artistic career till the year 1816, when she had attained the age of twenty-one, and all traces of her in the musical world appear to be lost; doubtless, at this period she found a husband, and retired completely from public life.

In 1805 Paganini accepted the position of director of music and conductor of the opera orchestra at Lucca, under the immediate patronage of the Princess Eliza, sister of Napoleon and wife of Bacciochi. The prince took lessons from him on the violin, and gave him whole charge of the court music. It was at the numerous concerts given at Lucca during this period of Paganini's early career that he first elaborated many of those curious effects, such as performances on one string, harmonic and pizzicato passages, which afterward became so characteristic of his style.

But the demon of unrest would not permit Paganini to remain very long in one place. In 1808 he began his wandering career of concert-giving afresh, performing throughout northern Italy, and amassing considerable money, for his fame had now become so widespread that engagements poured on him thick and fast. The lessons of his inconsiderate past had already made a deep impression on his mind, and Paganini became very economical, a tendency which afterward developed into an almost miserly passion for money-getting and -saving, though, through his whole life, he performed many acts of magnificent generosity. He had numerous curious adventures, some of which are worth recording. At a concert in Leghorn he came on the stage, limping, from the effects of a nail which had run into his foot. This made a great laugh. Just as he began to play, the candles fell out of his music desk, and again there was an uproar. Suddenly the first string broke, and there was more hilarity; but, says Paganini, naively, "I played the piece on three strings, and the sneers quickly changed into boisterous applause." At Ferrara he narrowly escaped an enraged audience with his life. It had been arranged that a certain Signora Marcolini should take part in his concert, but illness prevented her singing, and at the last moment Paganini secured the services of Signora Pallerini, who, though a danseuse, possessed an agreeable voice. The lady was very nervous and diffident, but sang exceedingly well, though there were a few in the audience who were inconsiderate enough to hiss. Paganini was furious at this insult, and vowed to be avenged. At the end of the concert he proposed to amuse the audience by imitating the noises of various animals on his violin. After he had reproduced the mewing of a cat, the barking of a dog, the crowing of a cock, etc., he advanced to the footlights and called out, "Questo e per quelli che han fischiato" ("This is for those who hissed"), and imitated in an unmistakable way the braying of the jackass. At this the pit rose to a man, and charged through the orchestra, climbed the stage, and would have killed Paganini, had he not fled incontinently, "standing not on the order of his going, but going at once." The explanation of this sensitiveness of the audience is found in the fact that the people of Ferrara had a general reputation for stupidity, and the appearance of a Ferrarese outside of the town walls was the signal for a significant hee-haw. Paganini never gave any more concerts in that town.

As he approached his thirtieth year his delicate and highly strung organization, already undermined by the excesses of his early youth, began to give way. He was frequently troubled with internal inflammation, and he was obliged to regulate his habits in the strictest fashion as to diet and hours of sleep. Even while comparatively well, his health always continued to be very frail.

Paganini composed his remarkable variations called "Le Streghe" ("The Witches") at Milan in 1813. In this composition, the air of which was taken from a ballet by Sussmayer, called "Il Noce de Benevento," at the part where the witches appear in the piece as performed on the stage, the violinist introduced many of his most remarkable effects. He played this piece for the first time at La Scala theatre, and he was honored with the most tumultuous enthusiasm, which for a long time prevented the progress of the programme. Paganini always had a predilection for Milan afterward, and said he enjoyed giving concerts there more than at any other city in Europe. He gave no less than thirty-seven concerts here in 1813. In this city, three years afterward, occurred his interesting musical duel with Lafont, the well-known French violinist. Paganini was then at Genoa, and, hearing of Lafont's presence at Milan, at once hastened to that city to hear him play. "His performance," said Pagani-ni, "pleased me exceedingly." When the Italian violinist, a week later, gave a concert at La Scala, Lafont was in the audience, and the very next day he proposed that Paganini and himself should play together at the same concert. "I excused my-self," said Paganini, "alleging that such experiments were impolitic, as the public invariably looked upon these matters as duels, in which there must be a victim, and that it would be so in this case; for, as he was acknowledged to be the best of the French violinists, so the public indulgently considered me to be the best player in Italy. Lafont not looking at it in this light, I was obliged to accept the challenge. I allowed him to arrange the programme. We each played a concerto of our own composition, after which we played together a duo concertante by Kreutzer. In this I did not deviate in the least from the composer's text while we played together, but in the solo parts I yielded freely to my own imagination, and introduced several novelties, which seemed to annoy my adversary. Then followed a 'Russian Air,' with variations, by Lafont, and I finished the concert with my variations called 'Le Streghe.' Lafont probably surpassed me in tone; but the applause which followed my efforts convinced me that I did not suffer by comparison." There seems to be no question that the victory remained with Paganini. A few years later Paganini played in a similar contest with the Polish violinist Lipinski, at Placentia. The two artists, however, were intimate friends, and there was not a spark of rivalry or jealousy in their generous emulation. In fact, Paganini appears to have been utterly without that conceit in his own extraordinary powers which is so common in musical artists. Heine gives an amusing illustration of this. He writes: "Once, after listening to a concert by Paganini, as I was addressing him with the most impassioned eulogies on his violin-playing, he interrupted me with the words, 'But how were you pleased to-day with my compliments and reverences?'" The musician thought more of his genuflexions than of his musical talent.

IV.

In the year 1817 Rossini, Meyerbeer, and Paganini were at Rome during Carnival time, and the trio determined on a grand frolic. Rossini had composed a very clever part-song, "Carnavale, Carnavale," known in English as "We are Poor Beggars," and the three great musicians, having disguised themselves as beggars, sang it with great effect through the streets. Rossini during this Carnival produced his "Cenerentola," and Paganini gave a series of concerts which excited great enthusiasm. Shortly after this, Paganini's health gave way completely at Naples, and the landlord of the hotel where he was stopping got the impression that his sickness was infectious. In the most brutal manner he turned the sick musician into the street. Fortunately, at this moment a violoncello player, Ciandelli, who knew Paganini well, was passing by, and came to the rescue, and his anger was so great, when he saw what had happened to the great violinist, that he belabored the barbarous landlord unmercifully with a stick, and conveyed the invalid to a comfortable lodging where he was carefully attended to. Some time subsequently Paganini had an opportunity of repaying this kindness, for he gave Ciandelli some valuable instruction, which enabled him in the course of a few years to become transformed from a very indifferent performer into an artist of considerable eminence.

At the age of thirty-six Paganini again found himself at Milan, and there organized a society of musical amateurs, called "Gli Orfei." He conducted several of their concerts. But either the love of a roving life or the necessity of wandering in order to fill his exchequer kept him constantly on the move; and, though during these travels he is said to have met with many extraordinary adventures, very little reliance can be placed upon the accounts that have come down to us, the more so when we consider that Paga-nini's mode of life was, as we shall see presently, become by this time extremely sober. It was not until he was forty-four years old that he finally quitted Italy to make himself better known in foreign countries. He had been encouraged to visit Vienna by Prince Metternich, who had heard and admired his playing at Rome in 1817, and had repeatedly made plans to visit Germany, but his health had been so wretched as to prevent his departure from his native country. But a sojourn in the balmy climate of Sicily for a few months had done him so much good that in 1828 he put his long-deferred plans into execution. The first concert in March of that year made an unparalleled sensation. He gave a great number of concerts in Vienna, among them several for the poor. A fever seized all classes of society. The shop windows were crowded with goods *a la Paganini*; a good stroke at billiards was called *un coup a la Paganini*; dishes Avere named after him; his portrait was enameled on snuff-boxes, and the Viennese dandies carried his bust on the head of their walking-sticks. A cabman wheedled out of the reluctant violinist permission to print on his cab, *Cabriolet de Paganini*. By this cunning device, Jehu so augmented his profits that he was able to rent a large house and establish a hotel, in which capacity Paganini found him when he returned again to Vienna.

Among the pleasant stories told of him is one similar to an incident previously related of Viotti. One day, as he was walking in Vienna, Paganini saw poor little Italian boy scraping some Neapolitan songs before the windows of a large house. A celebrated composer who accompanied the artist remarked to him, "There is one of your compatriots." Upon which Paganini evinced a desire to speak to the lad, and went across the street to him for that purpose. After ascertaining that he was a poor beggar-boy from the other side of the Alps, and that he supported his sick mother, his only relative, by his playing, the great violinist appeared touched. He literally emptied his pockets into the boy's hand, and, taking the violin and bow from him, began the most grotesque and extraordinary performance possible. A crowd soon collected, the great virtuoso was at once recognized by the bystanders, and when he brought the performance to an end, amid the cheers and shouts of all assembled, he handed round the boy's hat, and made a considerable collection of coin, in which silver pieces were very conspicuous. He then handed the sum to the young Italian, saying, "Take that to your mother," and, rejoining his companion, walked off with him, saying, "I hope I've done a good turn to that little animal." At Berlin, where he soon afterward astonished his crowded audiences by his marvelous playing, the same fanatical enthusiasm ensued; and, with the exception of Palermo, Naples (where he seems to have had many detractors), and Prague, his visits to the various cities of Europe were one continued triumph. People tried in vain to explain his method of playing, professors criticised him, and pamphlets were published which endeavored to make him out a quack or a charlatan. It was all to no purpose. Nothing could arrest his onward course; triumph succeeded triumph wherever he appeared; and, though no one could understand him, every one admired him, and he had only to touch his violin to enchant thousands. A curious scene occurred at Berlin, at a musical evening party to which Paganini was invited. A young and presumptuous professor of the violin performed there several pieces with very little effect; he was not aware of the presence of the Genoese giant, whom he did not know even by sight. Others, however, quickly recognized him, and he was asked to play, which he at first declined, but finally consented to do after urgent solicitation. Purposely he played a few variations in wretchedly bad style, which caused a suppressed laugh from those ignorant of his identity. The young professor came forward again and played another selection in a most pretentious and pointed way, as if to crush the daring wretch who had ventured to compete with him. Paganini again took up the instrument, and played a short piece with such touching pathos and astonishing execution, that the audience sat breathless till the last dying cadence wakened them into thunders of applause, and hearts thrilled as the name "Paganini" crept from mouth to mouth. The young professor had already vanished from the room, and was never again seen in the house where he had received so severe a lesson.

Paganini repeated his triumphs again the following year, performing in Vienna and the principal cities of Germany, and everywhere arousing similar feelings of admiration. Orders and medals were bestowed on him, and his progress was almost one of royalty. His first concert in Paris was given on March 9, 1831, at the opera-house. He was then forty-seven years old, and Castil-Blaze described him as being nearly six feet in height, with a long, pallid face, brilliant eyes, like those of an eagle, long curling black hair, which fell down over the collar of his coat, a thin and cadaverous figure--altogether a personality so gaunt and delicate as to be more like a shadow than a man. The eyes sparkled with a strange phosphorescent gleam, and the long bony fingers were so flexible as to be likened only to "a handkerchief tied to the end of a stick." Petis describes the impression he created at his first concert as amounting to a "positive and universal frenzy." Being questioned as to why he always performed his own compositions, he replied "that, if he played other compositions than his own, he was obliged to arrange them to suit his own peculiar style, and it was less trouble to write a piece of his own." Indeed, whenever he attempted to interpret the works of other composers, he failed to produce the effects which might have been expected of him. This was especially the case in the works of Beethoven.

V.

When Paganini appeared in England, of course there was a prodigious curiosity to see and hear the great player. All kinds of rumors were in the public mouth about him, and many of the lower classes really believed that he had sold himself to the evil one. The capacious area of the opera-house was densely packed, and the prices of admission were doubled on the opening night. The enthusiasm awakened by the performance can best be indicated by quoting from some of the contemporary accounts. The concert opened with Beethoven's Second Symphony, performed by the Philharmonic Society, and it was followed by Lablache, who sang Rossini's "Largo al factotum." "A breathless silence then ensued," writes Mr. Gardiner, an amateur of Leicester, who at the peril of his ribs had been struggling in the crowd for two hours to get admission, "and every eye watched the action of this extraordinary violinist as he glided from the side scenes to the front of the stage. An involuntary cheering burst from every part of the house, many persons rising from their seats to view the specter during the thunder of this unprecedented applause, his gaunt and extraordinary appearance being more like that of a devotee about to suffer martyrdom than one to delight you with his art. With the tip of his bow he set off the orchestra in a grand military movement with a force and vivacity as surprising as it was new. At the termination of this introduction, he commenced with a soft, streamy note of celestial quality, and with three or four whips of his bow elicited points of sound that mounted to the third heaven, and as bright as stars.... Immediately an execution followed which was equally indescribable. A scream of astonishment and delight burst from the audience at the novelty of this effect.... etc." This *naive* account may serve to show the impression created on the minds of those not trained to guard their words with moderation.

"Nothing can be more intense in feeling," said a contemporary critic, "than his conception and delivery of an adagio passage. His tone is, perhaps, not quite so full and round as that of a De Beriot or Baillot, for example; it is delicate rather than strong, but this delicacy was probably never possessed equally by another player." "There is no trick in his playing," writes another critic; "it is all fair scientific execution, opening to us a new order of sounds.... All his passages seem free and unpremeditated, as if conceived on the instant. One has no impression of their having cost him either forethought or labor.... The word difficulty has no place in his vocabulary.... etc." Paganini's lengthened tour through London and the provinces was everywhere attended with the same success, and brought him in a golden harvest, for his reputation had now grown so portentous that he could exact the greatest terms from managers.

Paganini avowed himself as not altogether pleased with England, but, under the surface of such complaints as the following, one detects the ring of gratified vanity. He writes in a MS. letter, dated from London in 1831, of the excessive and noisy admiration to which he was subjected in the London streets, which left him no peace, and actually blocked his passage to and from the theatre. "Although the public curiosity to see me," says he, "is long since satisfied; though I have played in public at least thirty times, and my likeness has been reproduced in all possible styles and forms, yet I can never leave my home without being mobbed by people who are not content with following and jostling me, but actually get in front of me, and prevent my going either way, address me in English of which I don't know a word, and even feel me as if to find out if I am made of flesh and blood. And this is not only among the common people, but among the upper classes." Paganini repeated his visit to England during the next season, playing his final farewell concert at the Victoria Theatre, London, June 17, 1832. The two following years our artist lived in Paris, and was the great lion of musical and social circles. People professed to be as much charmed with his lack of pretension, his *naive* and simple manners, as with his musical genius. Yet no man was more exacting of his rights as an artist. One day a court concert was announced at the Tuilleries, at which Paganini was asked to play. He consented, and went to examine the room the day before. He objected to the numerous curtains, so hung as to deaden the sound, and requested the superintendent to see that they were changed. The supercilious official ignored the artist's wish, and the offended Paganini determined not to play. When the hour of the concert arrived, there was no violinist. The royalties and their attendants were all seated; murmurs arose, but still no Paganini. At last an official was sent to the hotel of the artist, only to be informed that *the great violinist had not gone out, but that he went to bed very early*. It was during his residence in Paris in the winter of 1834 that he proposed to Berlioz, for whom he had the most cordial esteem and admiration, to write a concerto for his Stradiuarius violin, which resulted in the famous symphony "Harold en Italie." Four years after this he bestowed the sum of twenty thousand francs on Berlioz, who was then in pressing need, delicately disguising the donation as a testimonial of his admiration for the "Symphonie Fantastique." Though the eagerness of Paganini to make money urged him to labor for years while his health was exceedingly frail, and though he was justly stigmatized as penurious in many ways, he was capable of princely generosity on occasions which appealed strongly to the ardent sympathies which lay at the bottom of his nature.

Paganini made a great fortune by the exercise of his art, and in 1834 purchased, among other property in his native country, a charming country seat called Villa Gajona, near Parma. Here he spent two years in comparative quiet, though still continuing to give concerts. At this period and for some time previous many music-sellers had striven to buy the copyright of his works. But Paganini put a price on it which was prescriptive, the probability being that he did not wish his compositions to pass out of his hands till he had given up his career on the concert stage. He was willing that they should be arranged for the piano, but not published as violin music.

After his return to Italy Paganini gave several most successful concerts, among others, one for the poor at Placentia, on the 14th of November, 1834, and another at the court of the Duchess of Parma, in the December following. But his health was already giving way most visibly. Phthisis of the larynx, which rendered him a mere shadow of his former self, and sometimes almost deprived him of speech, had been gaining ground since his return to his native climate. In 1836, however, he was better, and some unscrupulous Parisian speculators induced him to lend his name to a joint-stock undertaking, a sort of gambling-room and concert-hall, which they called the Casino Paganini. This was duly opened in a fashionable part of Paris in 1837; but, as the Government would not allow the establishment to be used as a gambling-house, and the concerts did not pay the expenses, it became a great failure, and the illustrious artist actually suffered loss by it to the extent of forty thousand francs.

One of his last, if not his very last, concert was given with the guitar-player, Signor Legnani, at Turin, on the 9th of June, 1837, for the benefit of the poor. He was then on his way to fulfill his engagements at the fatal Parisian casino, which opened with much splendor in the November following. But his health had again broken down, and the fatigue of the journey had told upon him so much that he was unable to appear at the casino. When the enterprise was found to be a failure, a pettifogging lawsuit was carried on against him, and, according to Fetis, who is very explicit on this subject, the French judges condemned him to pay the aforesaid forty thousand francs, and to be deprived of his liberty until that amount was paid--all this without hearing his defense!

The career of Paganini was at this critical period fast drawing to a close. His medical advisers recommended him to return at once to the South, fearing that the winter would kill him in Paris. He died at Nice on May 27, 1840, aged fifty-six years. He left to his legitimized son Achille, the offspring of his *liaison* with the singer Antonia Bianchi, a fortune of eighty thousand pounds, and the title of baron, of which he had received the patent in Germany. His beautiful Guarnerius violin, the vehicle of so many splendid artistic triumphs, he bequeathed to the town of Genoa, where he was born. Though Paganini was superstitious, and died a son of Holy Church, he did not leave any money in religious bequests, nor did he even receive the last sacraments. The authorities of Rome raised many difficulties about the funeral, and it was only after an enormous amount of trouble and expense that Achille was able to have a solemn service to the memory of his father performed at Parma. It was five years after Paganini's death that this occurred, and permission was obtained to have the body removed to holy ground in the village churchyard near the Villa Gajona. During this long period the dishonored remains of the illustrious musician were at the hospital of Nice, where the body had been embalmed, and afterward at a country place near Genoa, belonging to the family. The superstitious peasantry believed that strange noises were heard about the grave at night-- the wailings of the unsatisfied spirit of Paganini over the unsanctified burial of its earthly shell. It was to end these painful stories that the young baron made a final determined effort to placate the ecclesiastical authorities.

VI.

The singular personality of Paganini displayed itself in his private no less than in his artistic life, and a few out of the many anecdotes told of him will be of interest, as throwing fresh light on the man. Paganini was accused of being selfish and miserly, of caring little even for his art, except as a means of accumulating money. While there is much in his life to justify such an indictment, it is no less true that he on many occasions displayed great generosity. He was always willing to give concerts for the benefit of his fellow-artists and for other charitable purposes, and on more than one occasion bestowed large sums of money for the relief of distress. We may assume that he was niggardly by habit and generous by impulse. Utterly ignorant of everything except the art of music, bred under the most unfortunate and demoralizing conditions, the fact that his character was, on the whole, so *naïve* and upright, speaks eloquently for the native qualities of his disposition. His eccentricities, perhaps, justified the unreasoning vulgar in believing that he was slightly crazed. His appearance and manner on the platform were fantastic in the extreme, and rarely failed to provoke ridicule, till his magic bow turned all other emotions into one of breathless admiration. He talked to himself continually when alone, a habit which was partly responsible for the popular belief that he was always attended by a familiar demon. When a stranger was introduced to him, his corpse-like face became galvanized into a ghastly smile, which produced a singular impression, half fascinating, half repulsive. He was taciturn in society, except among his intimates, when his buoyant spirits bubbled out in the most amusing jokes and anecdotes expressed in a polyglot tongue, for he never knew any language well except his own. Naturally irritable, his quick temper was inflamed by intestinal disease, which racked him with a suffering that was aggravated by a nostrum, in the use of which he indulged freely. Indeed, it was said by his friends that his death was accelerated by his devotion to medical quackery, from a belief in which no arguments could wean him.

To his fellow-artists he was always polite and attentive, though they annoyed him by their persistent curiosity as to the means by which he produced his unrivaled effects--effects which the established technique of violin-playing could not explain. An Englishman named George Harris, who was an *attache* of the Hanoverian court, attended Paganini for a year as his private secretary, and he asserts that Paganini was never seen to practice a single note of music in private. His astonishing dexterity was kept up to its pitch by the numerous concerts which he gave, and by his exquisitely delicate organization. He was accustomed to say that his whole early life had been one of prodigious and continual study, and that he could afford to repose in after years. Paganini's knowledge of music was profound and exact, and the most difficult music was mere child's play to him. Pasini, a well-known painter, living at Parma, did not believe the stories told of Paganini's ability to play the most difficult music at sight. Being the possessor of a valuable Stradiuarius violin, he challenged our artist to play, at first hand, a manuscript concerto which he placed before him. "This instrument shall be yours," he said, "if you can play, in a masterly manner, that concerto at first sight." The Genoese took the violin in his hand, saying, "In that case, my friend, you may bid adieu to it at once," and he immediately threw Pasini into ecstatic admiration by his performance of the piece. There is little doubt that this is the Stradiuarius instrument left by Paganini to his son, and valued at about six hundred pounds sterling.

Of Antonia Bianchi, the mother of his son Achille, Paganini tells us that, after many years of a most devoted life, the lady's temper became so violent that a separation was necessary. "Antonia was constantly tormented," he says, "by the most fearful jealousy. One day she happened to be behind my chair when I was writing some lines in the album of a great pianiste, and, when she read the few amiable words I had composed in honor of the artist to whom the book belonged, she tore it from my hands, demolished it on the spot, and, so fearful was her rage, would have assassinated me."

He was very fond of his little son Achille. A French gentleman tells us that he called once to take Paganini to dine with him. He found the artist's room in great disorder. A violin on the table with manuscript music, another upon a chair, a snuff-box on the bed along with his child's toys, music, money, letters, articles of dress-- all *pele-mele*; nor were the tables and chairs in their proper places. Everything was in the most conspicuous confusion. The child was out of temper; something had vexed him; he had been told to wash his hands; and, while the little one gave vent to the most violent bursts of temper, the father stood as calm and quiet as the most accomplished of nurses. He merely turned quietly to his visitor, and said, in melancholy accents: "The poor child is cross; I do not know what to do to amuse him; I have played with him ever since morning, and I can not stand it any longer."

"It was rather amusing," says the same writer, "to see Paganini in his slippers doing battle with his child, who came about up to his knees. The little one advanced boldly with his wooden sword, while the father retired, crying out, 'Enough, enough! I am already wounded.' But it was not enough; the young Achilles was never satisfied until his father, completely vanquished, fell heavily on the bed."

In the early part of the present century the facilities for travel were far less convenient than at the present time, and it was always an arduous undertaking to one in Paganini's frail condition of health. He was, however, generally cheerful while jolting along in the post-chaise, and chatted incessantly as long as his voice held out. Harris tells us that the artist was in the habit of getting out when the horses were changed, to stretch his long limbs after the confinement of the carriage. Often he extended his promenades when he became interested in the town through which he was passing, and would not return till long after the fresh horses had been harnessed, thereby causing much annoyance to the driver. On one occasion Jehu swore, if it occurred again, he would drive on, and leave his passenger behind, to get along as best he could. The secretary, Harris, was enjoying a nap, and the driver was true to his resolution at the next stopping-place, leaving Paganini behind. This made much trouble, and a special coach had to be sent for the enraged artist, who was found sputtering oaths in half a dozen languages. Paganini refused to pay for the carriage, and it was only by force of law that he reluctantly settled the bill.

His baggage was always of the plainest description; in fact, ludicrously simple. A shabby box contained his precious Guarnerius fiddle, and served also as a portmanteau wherein to pack his jewelry, his linen, and sundry trifles. In addition to this he carried a small traveling-bag and a hat-box. Mr. Harris tolls us that Paganini was in eating and drinking exceedingly frugal. Table indulgence was forbidden him by the condition of his health, as any deviation from the strictest diet resulted in great suffering. He was a thorough Italian in all his habits and ideas. Among other traits was a great disdain for the lower classes, though he was by no means subservient to people of rank and wealth. It was his habit, when an inferior addressed him, to inquire of his companion, "What does this animal want with me?" If he was pleased with his coachman, he would say, "That animal drives well." This seemed not so much the vulgar arrogance of a small nature, elevated above the class in life from which it sprang, as that pride of great gifts which made the freemasonry of genius the measure by which he judged all others, noble and simple. Like all men of highly nervous constitution, he was keenly susceptible to both enjoyment and suffering. He was so sensitive to atmospheric changes that his irritability was excessive during a thunderstorm. He would then remain silent for hours together, while his eyes rolled and his limbs twitched convulsively. Such fragile, nervous, highly sensitive organizations are not unfrequently characteristic of men of great genius, and in the great Italian violinist it was developed in an abnormal degree.

The circumstances accompanying the last scenes of Paganini's life are very interesting. He had been intimate with most of the great people of Europe, among them Lord Byron, Sir Clifford Constable, Lord Holland, Rossini, Ugo Fascolo, Monti, Prince Jerome, the Princess Eliza, and most of the great painters, poets, and musicians of his age. For Lord Byron he had a most ardent and exaggerated admiration. Paganini had stopped at Nice on his way from Paris, detained by extreme debility, for his last hours were drawing near. Under the blue sky and balmy air of this Mediterranean paradise the great musician somewhat recovered his strength at first. One night he sat by his bedroom window, surrounded by a circle of intimate friends, watching the glories of the Italian sunset that emblazoned earth, air, and sky, with the richest dyes of nature's palette. A soft breeze swept into the room, heavy with the perfumes of flowers, and the twittering of the birds in the green foliage mingled with the hum of talk from the throngs of gay promenaders sauntering on the beach. For a while Paganini sat silently absorbed in watching the joyous scene, when suddenly his eyes turned on the picture of Lord Byron that hung on the wall. A flash of enthusiasm lightened his face, as if a great thought were struggling to the surface, and he seized his violin to improvise. The listeners declared that this "swan song" was the most remarkable production of his life. He illustrated the stormy and romantic career of the English poet in music. The accents of doubt, irony, and despair mingled with the cry of liberty and the tumult of triumph. Paganini had scarcely finished this wonderful musical picture when the bow fell from the icy fingers that refused any longer to perform their function, and the player sank into a dead swoon.

The shock had been too great, and Paganini never quitted his bed afterward. The day before his death he seemed a little better, and directed his servant to buy a pigeon for him, as he had a slight return of appetite. On the last evening of his life he seemed very tranquil, and ordered the curtains to be drawn that he might look out of the window at the beautiful night. The full moon was sailing through the skies, flooding everything with splendor. Paganini gazed eagerly, gave a long sigh of pleasure, and fell back on his pillow dead.

VII.

Paganini was the first to develop the full resources of the violin as a solo instrument. He departed entirely from the traditions of violin-playing as practiced by earlier masters, as he believed that great fame could never be acquired in pursuing their methods. A work of Locatelli, one of the cleverest pupils of Corelli, and a great master of technique, first seems to have inspired him with a conception of the more brilliant possibilities of the violin. What further favored Paganini's new departure was that he lived in an age when the artistic mind, as well as thought in other directions, felt the desire of innovation. The French Revolution stirred Europe to its deepest roots, intellectually as well as politically. At a very early date in his career Paganini seems to have begun experimenting with the new effects for which he became famous, though these did not reach their full fruitage until just before he left Italy on his first general tour. Fetis says: "In adopting the ideas of his predecessors, in resuscitating forgotten effects, in superadding what his genius and perseverance gave birth to, he arrived at that distinctive character of performance which contributed to his ultimate greatness. The diversity of sounds, the different methods of tuning his instrument, the frequent employment of harmonics, single and double, the simultaneous pizzicato and bow passages, the various staccato effects, the use of double and even triple notes, a prodigious facility in executing wide intervals with unerring precision, together with an extraordinary knowledge of all styles of bowing--such were the principal features of Paganini's talent, rendered all the more perfect by his great execution, exquisitely nervous sensibility, and his deep musical feeling." In a word, Paganini possessed the most remarkable creative power in the technical treatment of an instrument ever given to a player. Franz Liszt as a pianist approaches him more nearly in this respect than any other virtuoso, but the field open to the violinist was far greater and wider than that offered to the great Hungarian pianist. It was not, however, mere perfection of technical power that threw Europe into such paroxysms of admiration; it was the irresistible power of a genius which has never been matched, and which almost justified the vulgar conclusion that none but one possessed with a demon could do such things. Paganini possessed the oft-quoted attribute of genius, "the power of taking infinite pains," but behind this there lay superlative gifts of mind, physique, and temperament. He completely dazzled the greatest musical artists as well as the masses. "His constant and daring flights," writes Moscheles, "his newly discovered flageolet tones, his gift of fusing and beautifying objects of the most diverse kinds--all these phases of genius so completely bewilder my musical perceptions that for days afterward my head is on fire and my brain reels." His tone lacked roundness and volume. His use of very thin strings, made necessary by his double harmonics and other specialties, necessarily prevented a broad, rich tone. But he more than compensated for this defect by the intense expression, "soft and melting as that of an Italian singer," to use the language of Moscheles again, which characterized the quality of sound he drew from his instrument. Spohr, a very great player, but, with all his polish, precision, and classical beauty of style, somewhat phlegmatic and conventional withal, critcised Paganini as lacking in good taste. He could never get in sympathy with the bent of individuality, the Southern passion and fire, and the exceptional gifts of temperament which made Paganini's idiosyncrasies of style as a player consummate beauties, where imitations of these effects on the part of others would be gross exaggeration. Spohr developed the school of Viotti and Rode, and in his attachment to that school could see no artistic beauty in any deviation. Paganini's peculiar method of treating the violin has never been regarded as a safe school for any other violinist to follow. Without Paganini's genius to give it vitality, his technique would justly be charged with exaggeration and charlatanism. Some of the modern French players, who have been strongly influenced by the great Italian, have failed to satisfy serious musical taste from this cause. On the German violinists he has had but little influence, owing to the powerful example of Spohr and the musical spirit of the great composers, which have tended to keep players within the strictly legitimate lines of art. Some of the principal compositions of Paganini are marked by great originality and beauty, and are violin classics. Schumann and Liszt have transcribed several of them for the piano, and Brahms for the orchestra. But the great glory of Paganini was as a virtuoso, not as a composer, and it has been generally agreed to place him on the highest pedestal which has yet been reached in the executive art of the violin.

DE BERIOT

De Beriot's High Place in the Art of the Violin and Violin Music.--The Scion of an Impoverished Noble Family.--Early Education and Musical Training.--He seeks the Advice of Viotti in Paris.--Becomes a Pupil of Kobrechts and Baillot successively.--De Beriot finishes and perfects his Style on his Own Model.--Great Success in England.--Artistic Travels in Europe.--Becomes Soloist to the King of the Netherlands.--He meets Malibran, the Great Cantatrice, in Paris.--Peculiar Circumstances which drew the Couple toward Each Other.--They form a Connection which only ends with Malibran's Life.--Sketch of Malibran and her Family.--The Various Artistic Journeys of Malibran and De Beriot.--Their Marriage and Mme. de Beriot's Death.--De Beriot becomes Professor in the Brussels Conservatoire.--His Later Life in Brussels.--His Son Charles Malibran de Beriot.--The Character of De Beriot as Composer and Player.

I.

Among the great players contemporary with Paganini, the name of Charles Auguste de Beriot shines in the musical horizon with the luster of a star of the first magnitude. His influence on music has been one of unmistakable import, for he has perpetuated his great talents through the number of gifted pupils who graduated from his teachings and gathered an inspiration from an artist-master, in whom were united splendid gifts as a player, an earnest musical spirit, depth and precision of science, the chivalry of high birth and breeding, and a width of intellectual culture which would have dignified the *litterateur* or scholar. De Beriot was for many years the chief of the violin department at the Brussels

Conservatoire, where, even before the revolution of 1830, there was one of the finest schools of instruction for stringed instruments to be found in Europe. When in the full ripeness of his fame as a virtuoso and composer, De Beriot was called on to take charge of the violin section of this great institution, and his influence has thus been transmitted in the world of art in a degree by no means limited to his direct greatness as an executant.

De Beriot was born at Louvain, in 1802, of a noble family, which had been impoverished through the crash and turmoil of the French Revolution. Left an orphan at the age of nine years, without inheritance except that of a high spirit and family pride, he would have fared badly in these early years, had it not been for the kindness of M. Tiby, a professor of music, who perceived the child's latent talent, and he acquired skill in playing so rapidly that he was able to play one of Viotti's concertos at the age of nine. His hearers, many of whom were connoisseurs, were delighted, and prophesied for him the great career which made the name of De Beriot famous. Naturally of a contemplative and thoughtful mind, he lost no time in studying not only the art of violin-playing but also acquiring proficiency in general branches of knowledge. His theories of an art ideal even at that early age were far more lofty and earnest than that which generally guides the aspirations of musicians. De Beriot, in after years, attributed many of the elevated ideas which from this time guided his life to the influence of the well-known scholar and philosopher Jacotot, who, though a poor musician himself, had very clear ideas as to the aesthetic and moral foundations on which art success must be built. The text-book, Jacotot's "Method," fell early into the young musician's hand, and imbued him with the principles of self-reliance, earnestness, and patience which helped to model his life, and contributed to the remarkable proficiency in his art on which his fame rests. Two golden principles were impressed on De Beriot's mind from these teachings: "All obstacles yield to unwearied pursuit," and "We are not ordinarily willing to do all that we are really able to accomplish." In after years De Beriot met Jacotot, and had the pleasure of acknowledging the deep obligation under which he felt himself bound.

In 1821 young Charles de Beriot had attained the age of nineteen, and it was determined that he should leave his native town and go to Paris, where he could receive the teachings of the great masters of the violin. At this time he was a handsome youth with a strongly knit figure, somewhat above the middle height, with fine, dark eyes and hair, a florid complexion, and very gentlemanly appearance. Good blood and breeding displayed themselves in every movement, and ardent hope shone in his face. He resided for several months in Brussels, which was afterward to be his home, and associated with the scenes of his greatest usefulness, and then pursued his eager way to Paris with a letter of introduction to Viotti, then director of music at the Grand Opera. De Beriot's ambition was to play before the veteran violinist of Europe, and to feed his own hopes on the great master's praise and encouragement.

"You have a fine style," said Viotti; "give yourself up to the business of perfecting it; hear all men of talent; profit by everything, but imitate nothing." There was at this time in Brussels a violinist named Robrechts, a former pupil of Viotti, and one of the last artists who derived instruction directly from the celebrated Italian. Andreas Robrechts was born at Brussels on the 18th of December, 1797, and made rapid progress as a musician under Planken, a professor, who, like the late M. Wery, who succeeded him, formed many excellent pupils. He then entered himself at the Conservatoire of Paris in 1814, where he received some private lessons from Baillot, while the institution itself was closed during the occupation by the allied armies.

Viotti, hearing the young Robrechts play, was so struck with his magnificent tone and broad style that he undertook to give him finishing lessons, with the approbation of Baillot. This was soon arranged, and for many years the two violinists were inseparable. He even accompanied Viotti in his journey to London, where they were heard more than once in duets. The illustrious Italian had recognized in Robrechts the pupil who most closely adhered to his style of playing, and one of the few who were likely to diffuse it in after years.

In 1820 Robrechts returned to Brussels, where he was elected first violin solo to the king, Wil-helm I. It was shortly after this that De Beriot took lessons from him, and he it was who gave him the letter of introduction to Viotti. The same excellent professor also gave instructions to the young Artot. He died in 1860, the last direct representative of the great Viotti school.

It will now be seen where De Beriot acquired the first principles of that large, bold, and exquisitely charming style that in after life characterized both his performances and his compositions.

II.

Arriving at Paris, and believing probably that the classical style of Robrechts, from whom he had had instruction in Brussels, did not lead him swiftly forward enough in the path he would travel, he sought Viotti, as we have related above, and by his advice entered himself in the violin class of the Conservatoire, which was directed by Baillot, an eminent player of the Viotti school, though never a direct pupil of the latter master. De Beriot, however, did not remain long in the class, but applied himself most assiduously to the study of the violin in his own way. This is what Paganini had done, and through this course had been able to form a style so peculiarly his own. It is not probable that De Beriot at this time knew much about Paganini; certainly he had never heard him. Paganini was at first looked on as a mere comet of extraordinary brilliancy, without much soundness or true genius, and many who afterward became his most ardent admirers began with sneering at his pretensions. De Beriot was in later years undoubtedly powerfully influenced by Paganini, but at the time of which we speak the young violinist appears to have been determined to evolve a style and character in art out of his own resources purely. He was carrying out Viot-ti's advice.

At this time our young artist was the possessor of a very fine instrument by Giovanni Magini, a celebrated maker of the Brescian school, and a pupil of Gaspar de Salo. Many of the violins of this make are of an excellence hardly inferior to the Strads of the best period, and De Beriot seems to have preferred this violin during the whole of his career, though he afterward owned instruments of the most celebrated makers.

Very soon De Beriot made his public appearance in concerts, and was brilliantly successful from the outset. The range of his ambition may be seen from the fact that he had enough confidence in his own genius from the very first to play his own music, and it was conceded to possess great freshness and originality. These early "Airs Varie" consisted of an introduction, a theme, followed by three or four variations, and a brilliant finale.

The young artist preceded Paganini in London several years, as he made his first appearance before an English audience in 1826. It was fortunate, perhaps, for De Beriot that such was the case, as it is more than probable that, after the dazzling and electric displays of the Geneose player, the more sedate and simple style which then characterized De Beriot would have failed to please. As it was, he was most cordially admired, and was generally recognized by English connoisseurs, as well as by the general public, as one of the most accomplished players who had ever visited England. The pecuniary results of these concerts were large, and sufficient to relieve De Beriot, who had formerly been rather straitened in his means, from the friction and embarrassment which poverty so often imposes on struggling talent. There was a peculiar charm in De Beriot's style which was permanently characteristic of him, though his technical method did not always remain the same. In addition to very facile execution and a rich, mellow tone, he possessed the most refined taste. His playing impressed people less as that of a great professional violinist than that of the marvelously accomplished amateur, the gentleman of leisure and culture, who performed with the easy, sparkling grace of one who took no thought of whether he played well or not, but did great feats on his instrument because he could not help it. Such was also the characteristic of Mario as a singer, and there seems to have been many features of resemblance between these two fine artists, though moving in different fields of art.

After traveling through Europe for several years, giving concerts with great success, he was presented to King Wilhelm of the then united kingdom of the Netherlands. This monarch, though quite ignorant of music, was an enthusiastic patron of art, and, believing that De Beriot was destined to be a great ornament of his native country (for he was born in Belgium, though his parents were from France), bestowed on the artist a pension of two thousand florins a year, and the title of first violin solo to his majesty. But this honor was soon rudely snatched from De Beriot's grasp. The revolution of 1830, which began with the excitement inflamed in Brussels by the performance of Auber's revolutionary opera, "La Muette di Portici," better known as "Masaniello," dissolved the kingdom, and Belgium parted permanently from Holland. It was, perhaps, owing to this apparent misfortune that De Beriot made an acquaintance which culminated in the most interesting episode of his life. He lost his official position at Brussels, but he met Mme. Malibran.

III.

De Beriot returned to Paris, where Sontag and Malibran were engaged in ardent artistic rivalry, about equally dividing the suffrages of the French public. Mlle. Sontag was a beautiful, fair-haired, blue-eyed woman, in the very flush of her youth, with an expression of exquisite sweetness and mildness. De Beriot became madly enamored of her at once, and pressed his suit with vehemence, but without success. Henrietta Sontag was already the betrothed of Count Rossi, whom she soon afterward married, though the engagement was then a secret. The lady's firm refusal of the young Belgian artist's overtures filled him with a deep melancholy, which he showed so unmistakably that he became an object of solicitude to all his friends. Among those was Mme. Malibran, whose warm sympathies went out to an artist whose talents she admired. Malibran, living apart from her husband, was obliged to be careful in her conduct, to avoid giving food for the scandal of a censorious world, but this did not prevent her from exhibiting the utmost pity and kindness in her demeanor toward De Beriot. The violinist was soothed by this gentle and delightful companion, and it was not long before a fresh affection, even stronger than the other, sprang up in his susceptible nature for the woman whose ardent Spanish frankness found it difficult to conceal the fact that she cherished sentiments different from mere friendship.

The splendid career of Mme. Malibran shines almost without a rival in the records of the lyric stage, and her influence on De Beriot, first her lover and afterward her husband, was most marked. Maria Garcia, afterward Mme. Malibran, was one of a family of very eminent musicians. She was trained by her father, Manuel Garcia, who, in addition to being a tenor singer of world-wide reputation, was a composer of some repute, and the greatest teacher of his time. Her sister, Pauline Garcia, in after years became one of the greatest dramatic singers who ever lived, and her brother Manuel also attained considerable eminence as singer, song-composer, and teacher. The whole family were richly dowered with musical gifts, and Maria was probably one of the most versatile and accomplished musical artists of any age. At the age of thirteen she was a professed musician, and at fifteen, when she came with her parents to London, she obtained a complete triumph by accidentally performing in Rossini's "Il Barbiere," to supply the place of a prima donna who was unable to appear.

We can not tarry here to enter into the details of her interesting life. Her father having taken her to America, where she fulfilled a number of engagements with an increasing success, she finally espoused there a rich merchant named Malibran, much older than herself. It was a most ill-advised marriage, and, to make matters worse, the merchant failed very soon afterward. Some go so far as to say that he foresaw this catastrophe before he contracted his marriage, in the hope of regaining his fortune by the proceeds of the singer's career. However that may be, a separation took place, and Mme. Malibran returned to Paris in 1827. Her singing in Italian opera was everywhere a source of the most enthusiastic ovation, and, as she rose like a star of the first magnitude in the world of song, so the young De Beriot was fast earning his laurels as one of the greatest violinists of the day. In 1830 an indissoluble friendship united these two kindred spirits, and in 1832 De Beriot, Lablache, the great basso, and Mme. Malibran set out for a tour in Italy, where the latter had operatic engagements at Milan, Rome, and Naples, and where they all three appeared in concerts with the most *eclatant* success--as may well be imagined.

At Bologna, in 1834, it is difficult to say whether the cantatrice, or the violinist, or the inestimable basso, produced the greatest sensation; but her bust in marble was there and then placed under the peristyle of the Opera-house.

Henceforward De Beriot never quitted her, and their affection seems to have increased as time wore on. In the year following she appeared in London, where she gave forty representations at Drury Lane, performing in "La Sonnambula," "The Maid of Artois," etc., for which she received the sum of three thousand two hundred pounds. De Beriot would not have made this amount probably with his violin in a year.

After a second journey to Italy, in which Mme. Malibran renewed the enthusiasm which she had first created in the public mind, and a series of brilliant concerts which also added to De Beriot's prestige, they returned to Paris to wait for the divorce of Mme. Malibran from her husband, which had been dragging its way through the courts. The much longed for release came in 1836, and the union of hearts and lives, whose sincerity and devotion had more than half condoned its irregularity, was sanctified by the Church. The happiness of the artistic pair was not destined to be long. Only a month afterward Mme. de Beriot, who was then singing in London, had a dangerous fall from her horse. Always passionately fond of activity and exercise, she was an excellent horsewoman, and was somewhat reckless in pursuing her favorite pursuit. The great singer was thrown by an unruly and badly trained animal, and received serious internal injuries. Her indomitable spirit would not, however, permit her to rest. She returned to the Continent after the close of the London season, to give concerts, in spite of her weak health, and gave herself but little chance of recovery, before she returned again to England in September to sing at the Manchester festival, her last triumph, and the brilliant close of a short and very remarkable life. She was seized with sudden and severe illness, and died after nine days of suffering. During this period of trial to De Beriot, he never left the bedside of his dying wife, but devoted himself to ministering to her comfort, except once when she insisted on his fulfilling an important concert engagement. Racked with pain as she was, her greatest anxiety was as to his artistic success, fearing that his mental anguish would prevent his doing full justice to his talents. It is said that her friends informed her of the vociferous applause which greeted his playing, and a happy smile brightened her dying face. She died September 22, 1836, at the age of twenty-eight, but not too soon to have attained one of the most dazzling reputations in the history of the operatic stage. M. de Beriot was almost frantic with grief, for a profound love had joined this sympathetic and well-matched pair, and their private happiness had not been less than their public fame.[1]

The news of this calamity to the world of music spread swiftly through the country, and was known in Paris the next day, where M. Mali-bran, the divorced husband of the dead singer, was then living. As the fortune which Mme. de Beriot had made by her art was principally invested in France, and there were certain irregularities in the French law which opened the way for claims of M. Malibran on her estate, De Beriot was obliged to hasten to Paris before his wife's funeral to take out letters of administration, and thus protect the future of the only child left by his wife, young Charles de Beriot, who afterward became a distinguished pianist, though never a professional musician. As the motives of this sudden disappearance

1   For a full sketch of Mme. Malibran de Beriot's artistic and personal career, the reader is referred to "Great Singers, Malibran to Tietjens," Appletons' "Handy-Volume Series."

were not known, De Beriot was charged with the most callous indifference to his wife. But it is now well known that his action was guided by a most imperative necessity, the welfare of his infant son, all that was left him of the woman he had loved so passionately. The remains of Mme. de Beriot were temporarily interred in the Collegiate Church in Manchester, but they were shortly afterward removed to Laeken, near Brussels. Over her tomb in the Laeken churchyard the magnificent mausoleum surmounted with her statue was erected by De Beriot. The celebrated sculptor Geefs modeled it, and the work is regarded as one of the *chefs-d'ouvre* of the artist.

IV.

M. de Beriot did not recover from this shock for more than a year, but remained secluded at his country place near Brussels. It was not till Pauline Garcia (subsequently Mme. Viardot) made her *debut* in concert in 1837, that De Beriot again appeared in public before one of the most brilliant audiences which had ever assembled in Brussels. In honor of this occasion the Philharmonic Society of that city caused two medals to be struck for M. de Beriot and Mlle. Garcia, the molds of which were instantly destroyed. The violinist gave a series of concerts assisted by the young singer in Belgium, Germany, and France, and returned to Brussels again on the anniversary of their first concert, where they appeared in the Theatre de la Renaissance before a most crowded and enthusiastic audience. Among the features of the performance which called out the warmest applause was Panseron's grand duo for voice and violin, "Le Songe de Tartini," Mlle. Garcia both singing and playing the piano-forte accompaniment with remarkable skill. Two years afterward Mile. Garcia married M. Viardot, director of the Italian Opera at Paris, and De Beriot espoused Mlle. Huber, daughter of a Viennese magistrate, and ward of Prince Dietrischten Preskau, who had adopted her at an early age.

De Beriot became identified with the Royal Conservatory of Music at Brussels in the year 1840, and thenceforward his life was devoted to composition and the direction of the violin school. He gave much time and care to the education of his son Charles, who, in addition to a wonderful resemblance to his mother, appears to have inherited much of the musical endowment of both parents. Had not an ample fortune rendered professional labor unnecessary, it is probable that the son of Malibran and De Beriot would have attained a musical eminence worthy of his lineage; but he is even now celebrated for his admirable performances in private, and his musical evenings are said to be among the most delightful entertainments in Parisian society, gathering the most celebrated artists and *litterateurs* of the great capital.

De Beriot ceased giving public concerts after taking charge of the violin classes of the Brussels Conservatoire, though he continued to charm select audiences in private concerts. Many of his pupils became distinguished players, among whom may be named Monasterio, Standish, Lauterbach, and, chief of all, Henri Vieuxtemps, with whose precocious talents he was so much pleased that he gave him lessons gratuitously. During his life at Brussels, and indeed during the whole of his career, De Beriot enjoyed the friendship and esteem of many of the most distinguished men of the day, among his most intimate friends and admirers having been Prince de Chimay, the Russian Prince Youssoupoff, and King Leopold I, of Belgium. The latter part of his life was not un-laborious in composition, but otherwise of affluent and elegant ease. During the last two years his eyesight failed him, and he gradually became totally blind. He died, April 13, 1870, at the age of sixty-eight, while visiting his friend Prince Youssoupoff at St. Petersburg, of the brain malady which had long been making fatal inroads on his health.

In originality as a composer for the violin, probably no one can surpass De Beriot except Paganini, who exerted a remarkable modifying influence on him after he had formed his own first style. His works are full of grace and poetic feeling, and worked out with an intellectual completeness of form which gives him an honorable distinction even among those musicians marked by affluence of ideas. These compositions are likely to be among the violin classics, though some of the violinists of the Spohr school have criticised them for want of depth. He produced seven concertos, eleven *airs varies*, several books of studies, four trios for piano, violin, and 'cello, and, together with Osborne, Thalberg, and other pianists, a number of brilliant duos for piano and violin. His book of instruction for the violin is among the best ever written, though somewhat diffuse in detail. He may be considered the founder of the Franco-Belgian school of violinists, as distinguished from the classical French school founded by Viotti, and illustrated by Rode and Baillot. His early playing was molded entirely in this style, but the dazzling example of Paganini, in course of time, had its effect on him, as he soon adopted the captivating effects of harmonics, arpeggios, pizzicatos, etc., which the Genoese had introduced, though he stopped short of sacrificing his breadth and richness of tone. He combined the Paganini school with that of Viotti, and gave status to a peculiar *genre* of players, in which may be numbered such great virtuosos as Vieuxtemps and Wieniawski, who successively occupied the same professional place formerly illustrated by De Beriot, and the latter of whom recently died. De Beriot's playing was noted for accuracy of intonation, remarkable deftness and facility in bowing, grace, elegance, and piquancy, though he never succeeded in creating the unbounded enthusiasm which everywhere greeted Paganini.

OLE BULL.

The Birth and Early Life of Ole Bull at Bergen, Norway.--His Family and Connections.--Surroundings of his Boyhood.--Early Display of his Musical Passion.--Learns the Violin without Aid.--Takes Lessons from an Old Musical Professor, and soon surpasses his Master.--Anecdotes of his Boyhood.--His Father's Opposition to Music as a Profession.--Competes for Admittance to the University at Christiania.--Is consoled for Failure by a Learned Professor.--"Better be a Fiddler than a Preacher."--Becomes Conductor of the Philharmonic Society at Bergen.--His first Musical Journey.--Sees Spohr.--Fights a Duel.--Visit to Paris.--He is reduced to Great Pecuniary Straits.--Strange Adventure with Vidocq, the Great Detective.--First Appearance in Concert in Paris.--Romantic Adventure leading to Acquaintance.--First Appearance in Italy.--Takes the Place of Do Beriot by Great Good Luck.--Ole Bull is most enthusiastically received.--Extended Concert Tour in Italy and France.--His *Debut* and Success in England.--One Hundred and Eighty Concerts in Six Months.--Ole Bull's Gaspar di Salo Violin, and the Circumstances under which he acquired it.--His Answer to the King of Sweden.--First Visit and Great Success in America in 1843.--Attempt to establish a National Theatre.--The Norwegian Colony in Pennsylvania.--Latter Years of Ole Bull.--His Personal Appearance.--Art Characteristics.

I.

The life of Olaus Bull, or Ole Bull, as he is generally known to the world, was not only of much interest in its relation to music, but singularly full of vicissitude and adventure. He was born at Bergen, Norway, February 5, 1810, of one of the leading families of that resort of shippers, timber-dealers, and fishermen. His father, John Storm Bull, was a pharmaceutist, and among his ancestors he numbered the Norwegian poet Edward Storm, author of the "Sinclair Lay," an epic on the fate of Colonel Sinclair, who with a thousand Hebridean and Scotch pirates, made a descent on the Norwegian coast, thus emulating the Vikingr forefathers of the Norwegians themselves. The peasants slew them to a man by rolling rocks down on them from the fearful pass of the Gulbrands Dahl, and the event has been celebrated both by the poet's lay and the painter's brush. By the mother's side Ole Bull came of excellent Dutch stock, three of his uncles being captains in the army and navy, and another a journalist of repute. A passion for music was inherent in the family, and the editor had occasional quartet parties at his house, where the works of Haydn, Mozart, and Beethoven were given, much to the delight of young Ole, who was often present at these festive occasions.

The romantic and ardent imagination of the boy was fed by the weird legends familiar to every Norwegian nursery. The Scheherezade of this occasion was the boy's own grandmother, who told him with hushed breath the fairy folk-lore of the mysterious Huldra and the Fossikal, or Spirit of the Waterfall, and Ole Bull, with his passion for music, was wont to fancy that the music of the rushing waters was the singing of the violins played by fairy artists. From an early age this Greek passion for personifying all the sights and sounds of nature manifested itself noticeably, but always in some way connected with music. He would fancy even that he could hear the bluebells and violets singing, and perfume and color translated themselves into analogies of sound. This poetic imagination grew with his years and widened with his experience, becoming the cardinal motive of Ole Bull's art life. For a long time the young boy had longed for a violin of his own, and finally his uncle who gave the musical parties presented him with a violin. Ole worked so hard in practicing on his new treasure that he was soon able to take part in the little concerts.

There happened to be at this time in Bergen a professor of music named Paulsen, who also played skillfully on the violin. Originally from Denmark, he had come to Bergen on business, but, finding the brandy so good and cheap, and his musical talent so much appreciated, he postponed his departure so long that he became a resident. Paulsen, it was said, would show his perseverance in playing as long as there remained a drop in the brandy bottle before him, when his musical ambition came to a sudden close. When the old man, for he was more than sixty when young

Ole Bull first knew him, had worn his clothes into a threadbare state, his friends would supply him with a fresh suit, and at intervals he gave concerts, which every one thought it a religious duty to attend. It was to this Dominie Sampson that Ole Bull was indebted for his earliest musical training; but it seems that the lad made such swift progress that his master soon had nothing further to teach him. Poor old Paulsen was in despair, for in his bright pupil he saw a successful rival, and, fearing that his occupation was gone, he left Bergen for ever.

In spite of the boy's most manifest genius for music, his father was bent on making him a clergyman, going almost to the length of forbidding him to practice any longer on the dearly loved fiddle, which had now become a part of himself; but Ole persevered, and played at night softly, in constant fear that the sounds would be heard. But his mother and grandmother sympathized with him, and encouraged his labors of love in spite of the paternal frowns. The author of a recent article in an American magazine relates an interview with Ole Bull, in which the aged artist gave some interesting facts of that early period in his life. His father's assistant, who was musical, occasionally received musical catalogues from Copenhagen, and in one of these the boy first saw the name of Paganini, and reference to his famous "Caprices." One evening his father brought home some Italian musicians, and Ole Bull heard from them all they knew of the great player, who was then turning the musical world topsy-turvy with a fever of excitement. "I went to my grandmother. 'Dear grandmother,' I said, 'can't I get some of Paganini's music?' 'Don't tell any one,' said that dear old woman, 'but I will try and buy a piece of his for you if you are a good child.' And she did try, and I was wild when I got the Paganini music. How difficult it was, but oh, how beautiful! That garden-house was my refuge. Maybe--I am not so sure of it--the cats did not go quite so wild as some four years before. One day--a memorable one--I went to a quartet party. The new leader of our philharmonic was there, a very fine violinist, and he played for us a concerto of Spohr's. I knew it, and was delighted with his reading of it. We had porter to drink in another room, and we all drank it, but before they had finished I went back to the music-room, and commenced trying the Spohr. I was, I suppose, carried away with the music, forgot myself, and they heard me.

"'This is impudence,' said the leader. 'And do you think, boy, that you can play it?' 'Yes,' I said, quite honestly. I don't to this day see why I should have told a story about it--do you? 'Now you shall play it,' said somebody. 'Hear him! hear him!' cried my uncle and the rest of them. I did try it, and played the allegro. All of them applauded save the leader, who looked mad.

"'You think you can play anything, then?' asked the leader. He took a caprice of Paganini's from a music stand. 'Now you try this,' he said, in a rage. 'I will try it,' I said. 'All right; go ahead.'

"Now it just happened that this caprice was my favorite, as the cats well knew. I could play it by memory, and I polished it off. When I did that, they all shouted. The leader before had been so cross and savage, I thought he would just rave now. But he did not say a word. He looked very quiet and composed like. He took the other musicians aside, and I saw that he was talking to them. Not long afterward this violinist left Bergen. I never thought I would see him again. It was in 1840, when I was traveling through Sweden on a concert tour, of a snowy day, that I met a man in a sleigh. It was quite a picture: just near sunset, and the northern lights were shooting in the sky; a man wrapped up in a bear-skin a-tracking along the snow. As he drew up abreast of me and unmuffled himself, he called out to my driver to stop. It was the leader, and he said to me, 'Well, now that you are a celebrated violinist, remember that, when I heard you play Paganini, I predicted that your career would be a remarkable one.' 'You were mistaken,' I cried, jumping up; 'I did not read that Paganini at sight; I had played it before.' 'It makes no difference; good-by,' and he urged on his horse, and in a minute the leader was gone."

II.

To please his father, Ole Bull studied assiduously to fit himself for the preliminary examination of the university, but he found time also to pursue his beloved music. At the age of eighteen he was entered at the University of Christiania as a candidate for admission, and went to that city somewhat in advance of the day of ordeal to finish his studies. He had hardly entered Christiania before he was seduced to play at a concert, which beginning gave full play to the music-madness beyond all self-restraint. As a result Ole Bull was "plucked," and at first he did not dare write to his father of this downfall of the hopes of the paternal Bull.

We are told that he found consolation from one of the very professors who had plucked him. "It's the best thing could have happened to you," said the latter, by way of encouragement.

"How so?" inquired Ole.

"My dear fellow," was the reply, "do you believe you are a fit man for a curacy in Finmarken or a mission among the Laps? Nature has made you a musician; stick to your violin, and you will never regret it."

"But my father, think of his disappointed hopes," said Ole Bull.

"Your father will never regret it either," answered the professor.

As good fortune ordered for the forlorn youth, his musical friends did not desert him, but secured for him the temporary position of director of the Philharmonic Society of Christiania, the regular incumbent being ill. On the death of the latter shortly afterward, Ole Bull was tendered the place. As the new duties were very well paid, and relieved the youth from dependence on his father's purse, further opposition to his musical career was withdrawn.

In the summer of 1829 Ole Bull made a holiday trip into Germany, and heard Dr. Spohr, then director of the opera at Cassel. "From this excursion," said one of Ole Bull's friends, "he returned completely disappointed. He had fancied that a violin-player like Spohr must be a man who, by his personal appearance, by the poetic character of his performance, or by the flash of genius, would enchant and overwhelm his hearers. Instead of this, he found in Spohr a correct teacher, exacting from the young Norwegian the same cool precision which characterized his own performance, and quite unable to appreciate the wild, strange melodies he brought from the land of the North." Spohr was a man of clock-work mechanism in all his methods and theories--young Ole Bull was all poetry, romance, and enthusiasm.

At Minden our young violinist met with an adventure not of the pleasantest sort. He had joined a party of students about to give a concert at that place, and was persuaded to take the place of the violinist of the party, who had been rather free in his libations, and became "a victim of the rosy god." Ole Bull was very warmly applauded at the concert, and so much nettled was the student whose failure had made the vacancy for Ole Bull's talent, that the latter received a challenge to fight a duel, which was promptly accepted. Ole Bull proved that he could handle a sword as well as a fiddle-bow, for in a few passes he wounded and disabled his antagonist.

He was advised, however, to leave that locality as soon as possible, and so he returned straight to Christiania, "feeling as if the very soil of Europe repelled him" (to use an expression from one of his letters).

Ole Bull remained in Norway for two years, but he felt that he must bestir himself, and go to the great centers of musical culture if he would find a proper development and field for the genius which he believed he possessed. His friends at Christiania idolized him, and were loath to let him go, but nothing could stay him, so with pilgrim's staff and violin-case he started on his journey. Scarcely twenty-one years of age, nearly penniless, with no letters of introduction to people who could help him, but with boundless hope and resolution, he first set foot in Paris in 1831. The town was agog over Paganini and Mme. Malibran, and of course the first impulse of the young artist was to hear these great people. One night he returned from hearing Malibran, and went to bed so late that he slept till nearly noon the next day. To his infinite consternation, he discovered that his landlord had decamped during the early morning, taking away the household furniture of any value, and even abstracting the modest trunk which contained Ole Bull's clothes and his violin. After such an overwhelming calamity as this, the Seine seemed the only resource, and the young Norwegian, it is said, had nearly concluded to find relief from his troubles in its turbid and sin-weighted waters. But it happened that the young man had still a little money left, enough to support him for a week, and he concluded to delay the fatal plunge till the last sou was gone. It was while he was slowly enjoying the last dinner which he was able to pay for, that he made the acquaintance of a remarkable character, to whom he confided his misery and his determination to find a tomb in the Seine.

III.

Said the stranger, after pondering a few moments over the simple but sad story of the young violinist, in whom he had taken a sudden interest:

"Well, I will do something for you, if you have courage and five francs."

"I have both."

"Then go to Frascate's at ten; pass through the first room, enter the second, where they play 'rouge-et-noir,' and when a new *taille* begins put your five francs on *rouge*, and leave it there."

This promise of an adventure revived Ole Bull's drooping spirits, and he was faithful in carrying out his unknown friend's instructions. At the precise hour the tall stalwart figure of the young Norwegian bent over the table at Frascate's, while the game of "rouge-et-noir" was being played. He threw his five francs on red; the card was drawn--red wins, and the five francs were ten. Again Ole Bull bet his ten francs on *rouge*, and again he won; and so he continued, leaving his money on the same color till a considerable amount of money lay before him. By this time the spirit of gaming was thoroughly aroused. Should he leave the money and trust to red turning up again, or withdraw the pile of gold and notes, satisfied with the kindness of Fortune, without further tempting the fickle goddess? He said to a friend afterward, in relating his feelings on this occasion:

"I was in a fear--I acted as if possessed by a spirit not my own; no one can understand my feelings who has not been so tried--left alone in the world, as if on the extreme verge of an abyss yawning beneath, and at the same time feeling something within that might merit a saving hand at the last moment."

Ole Bull stretched forth to grasp the money, when a white hand covered it before his. He seized the wrist with a fierce grasp, while the owner of it uttered a loud shriek, and loud threats came from the other players, who took sides in the matter, when a dark figure suddenly appeared on the scene, and spoke in a voice whose tones carried with them a magic authority which stilled all tumult at once. "Madame, leave this gold alone!"--and to Ole Bull: "Sir, take your money, if you please." The winner of an amount which had become very considerable lingered a few moments to see the further results of the play, and, much to his disgust, discovered that he would have possessed quite a little fortune had he left his pile undisturbed for one more turn of the cards. He was consoled, however, on arriving at his miserable lodgings, for he could scarcely believe that this stroke of good luck was true, and yet there was something repulsive in it to the fresh, unsophisticated nature of the man. He said in a letter to one of his friends, "What a hideous joy I felt--what a horrible pleasure it was to have saved one's own soul by the spoil of others!" The mysterious stranger who had thus befriended Ole Bull was the great detective Vidocq, whose adventures and exploits had given him a world-wide reputation. Ole Bull never saw him again.

In exploring Paris for the purchase of a new violin, he accidentally made the acquaintance of an individual named Labout, who fancied that he had found the secret of the old Cremona varnish, and that, by using it on modern-made violins, the instruments would acquire all the tone and quality of the best old fiddles of the days of the Stradiuarii and Amati. The inventor persuaded Ole Bull to appear at a private concert where he proposed to test his invention, and where the Duke and Duchesse de Montebello were to be present. The Norwegian's playing produced a genuine sensation, and the duke took the young artist under his patronage. The result was that Ole Bull was soon able to give a concert on his own account, which brought him a profit of about twelve hundred francs, and made him talked about among the musical *cognoscenti* of Paris. Of course every one at the time was Paganini mad, but Ole Bull secured more than a respectful hearing, and opened the way toward getting a solid footing for himself.

Among the incidents which occurred to him in Paris about this time was one which had a curiously interesting bearing on his life. Obliged to move from his lodgings on account of the death of the landlord and his wife of cholera, a disease then raging in Paris, Ole Bull was told of a noble but impoverished family who had a room to let on account of the recent death of the only son. The Norwegian violinist presented himself at the somewhat dilapidated mansion of the Comtesse de Faye, and was shown into the presence of three ladies dressed in deepest mourning. The eldest of them, on hearing his errand, haughtily declined the proposition, when the more beautiful of the two girls said, "Look at him, mother!" with such eagerness as to startle the ancient dame.

Ole Bull was surprised at this. The old lady put on her spectacles, and, as she riveted her eyes upon him, her countenance changed suddenly. She had found in him such a resemblance to the son she had lost that she at once consented to his residing in her house. Some time afterward Ole Bull became her son indeed, having married the fascinating girl who had exclaimed, "Look at him, mother!"

With the little money he had now earned he determined to go to Italy, provided with some letters of introduction; and he gave his first Italian concert at Milan in 1834. Applause was not wanting, but his performance was rather severely criticised in the papers. The following paragraph, reproduced from an Italian musical periodical, published shortly after this concert, probably represents very truly the state of his talent at that period:

"M. Ole Bull plays the music of Spohr, May-seder, Pugnani, and others, without knowing the true character of the music he plays, and partly spoils it by adding a color of his own. It is manifest that this color of his own proceeds from an original, poetical, and musical individuality; but of this originality he is himself unconscious. He has not formed himself; in fact, he has no style; he is an uneducated musician. *Whether he is a diamond or not is uncertain; but certain it is that the diamond is not polished*."

In a short time Ole Bull discovered that it was necessary to cultivate, more than he had done, his cantabile--this was his weakest point, and a most important one. In Italy he found masters who enabled him to develop this great quality of the violin, and from that moment his career as an artist was established. The next concert of any consequence in which he played was at Bologna under peculiar circumstances; and his reputation as a great violinist appears to date from that concert. De Beriot and Malibran were then idolized at Bologna, and just as Ole Bull arrived in that ancient town, De Beriot was about to fulfill an engagement to play at a concert given by the celebrated Philharmonic Society there. The engagement had been made by the Marquis di Zampieri, between whom and the Belgian artist there was some feeling of mutual aversion, growing out of a misunderstanding and a remark of the marquis which had wounded the susceptibilities of the other. The consequence was that on the day of the concert De Beriot sent a note, saying that he had a sore finger and could not play.

Marquis Zampieri was in a quandary, for the time was short. In his embarrassment he took council with Mme. Colbran Rossini, who was then at Bologna with her husband, the illustrious composer. It happened that Ole Bull's lodging was in the same palazzo, and Mme. Rossini had often heard the tones of the young artist's violin in his daily practicing; her curiosity had been greatly aroused about this unknown player, and now was the chance to gratify it. She told the noble *entrepreneur* that she had discovered a violinist quite worthy of taking De Beriot's place.

"Who is it?" inquired the marquis.

"I don't know," answered the wife of Rossini.

"You are joking, then?"

"Not at all, but I am sure there is a genius in town, and he lodges close by here," pointing to Ole Bull's apartment. "Take your net," she added, "and catch your bird before he has flown away." The marquis knocked at Ole Bull's door, and the delighted young artist soon concluded an engagement which insured him an appearance under the best auspices, for Mme. Malibran would sing at the same concert.

In a few hours Ole Bull was performing before a distinguished audience in the concert-hall of the Philharmonic Society. Among the pieces he played, all of his own composition, was his "Quartet for One Violin," in which his great skill in double and triple harmonics was admirably shown. Enthusiastic applause greeted the young virtuoso, and he was escorted home by a torchlight procession of eager and noisy admirers. This was Ole Bull's first really great success, though he had played in France and Germany. The Italians, with their quick, generous appreciation, and their demonstrative manner of showing admiration, had given him a reception of such unreserved approval as warmed his artistic ambition to the very core. Mme. Malibran, though annoyed at the mischance which glorified another at the expense of De Beriot, was too just and amiable not to express her hearty congratulations to the young artist, and De Beriot himself, when he was shortly afterward introduced to Ole Bull, treated him with most brotherly kindness and cordiality. Prince and Princess Poniatowsky also sent their cards to the now successful artist, and gave him letters of introduction to distinguished people which wore of great use in his concert tour. His career had now become assured, and the world received him with open arms.

The following year, 1835, contributed a catalogue of similar successes in various cities of Italy and France, culminating in a grand concert at Paris in the Opera-house, where the most distinguished musicians of the city gave their warmest applause in recognition of the growing fame and skill of Ole Bull, for he had already begun to illustrate a new field in music by setting the quaint poetic legends and folk-songs of his native land. His specialty as a composer was in the domain of descriptive music, his genius was for the picturesque. His vivid imagination, full of poetic phantasy, and saturated with the heroic traditions and fairy-lore of a race singularly rich in this inheritance from an earlier age, instinctively flowered into art-forms designed to embody this legendary wealth. Ole Bull's violin compositions, though dry and rigorous musicians object to them as lacking in depth of science, as shallow and sensational, are distinctly tone-pictures full of suggestiveness for the imagination. It was this peculiarity which early began to impress his audiences, and gave Ole Bull a separate place by himself in an age of eminent players.

IV.

In 1836 and 1837 Ole Bull gave one hundred and eighty concerts in England during the space of sixteen months. By this time he had become famous, and a mere announcement sufficed to attract large audiences. Subsequently he visited successively every town of importance in Europe, earning large amounts of money and golden opinions everywhere. For a long time our artist used a fine Guarnerius violin and afterward a Nicholas Amati, which was said to be the finest instrument of this make in the world. But the violin which Ole Bull prized in latter years above all others was the famous Gaspar di Salo with the scroll carved by Benvenuto Cellini. Mr. Barnett Phillips, an American *litterateur*, tells the story of this noble old instrument, as related in Ole Bull's words:

"Well, in 1839 I gave sixteen concerts at Vienna, and then Rhehazek was the great violin collector. I saw at his house this violin for the first time. I just went wild over it. 'Will you sell it?' I asked. 'Yes,' was the reply--'for one quarter of all Vienna.' Now Ehehazek was really as poor as a church mouse. Though he had no end of money put out in the most valuable instruments, he never sold any of them unless when forced by hunger. I invited Rhehazek to my concerts. I wanted to buy the violin so much that I made him some tempting offers. One day he said to me, 'See here, Ole Bull, if I do sell the violin, you shall have the preference at four thousand ducats.' 'Agreed,' I cried, though I knew it was a big sum.

"That violin came strolling, or playing rather, through my brain for some years. It was in 1841. I was in Leipsic giving concerts. Liszt was there, and so also was Mendelssohn. One day we were all dining together. We were having a splendid time. During the dinner came an immense letter with a seal--an official document. Said Mendelssohn, 'Use no ceremony; open your letter.' 'What an awful seal!' cried Liszt. 'With your permission,' said I, and I opened the letter. It was from Bhehazek's son, for the collector was dead. His father had said that the violin should be offered to me at the price he had mentioned. I told Liszt and Mendelssohn about the price. 'You man from Norway, you are crazy,' said Liszt. 'Unheard of extravagance, which only a fiddler is capable of,' exclaimed Mendelssohn. 'Have you ever played on it? Have you ever tried it?' they both inquired. 'Never,' I answered, 'for it can not be played on at all just now.'

"I never was happier than when I felt sure that the prize was mine. Originally the bridge was of boxwood, with two fishes carved on it--that was the zodiacal sign of my birthday, February--which was a good sign. Oh, the good times that violin and I have had! As to its history, Ehehazek told me that in 1809, when Innspruck was taken by the French, the soldiers sacked the town. This violin had been placed in the Innspruck Museum by Cardinal Aldobrandi at the close of the sixteenth century. A French soldier looted it, and sold it to Ehehazek for a trifle. This is the same violin that I played on, when I first came to the United States, in the Park Theatre. That was on Evacuation day, 1843. I went to the Astor House, and made a joke--I am quite capable of doing such things. It was the day when John Bull went out and Ole Bull came in. I remember that at the very first concert one of my strings broke, and I had to work out my piece on the three strings, and it was supposed I did it on purpose." Ole Bull valued this instrument as beyond all price, and justly, for there have been few more famous violins than the Treasury violin of Innspruck, under which name it was known to all the amateurs and collectors of the world.

During his various art wanderings through Europe, Ole Bull made many friends among the distinguished men of the world. A dominant pride of person and race, however, always preserved him from the slightest approach to servility. In 1838 he was presented to Carl Johann, king of Sweden, at Stockholm. The king had at that time a great feeling of bitterness against Norway, on account of the obstinate refusal of the people of that country to be united with Sweden under his rule. At the interview with Ole Bull the irate king let fall some sharp expressions relative to his chagrin in the matter.

"Sire," said the artist, drawing himself up to the fullness of his magnificent height, and looking sternly at the monarch, "you forget that I have the honor to be a Norwegian."

The king was startled by this curt rebuke, and was about to make an angry reply, but smoothed his face and answered, with a laugh:

"Well! well! I know you d--d sturdy fellows." Carl Johann afterward bestowed on Ole Bull the order of Gustavus Vasa.

V.

Ole Bull's first visit to America was in 1843, and the impression produced by his playing was, for manifest causes, even greater than that created in Europe. He was the first really great violinist who had ever come to this country for concert purposes, and there was none other to measure him by. There were no great traditions of players who had preceded him; there were no rivals like Spohr, Paganini, and De Beriot to provoke comparisons. In later years artists discovered that this country was a veritable El Dorado, and regarded an American tour as indispensable to the fulfillment of a well-rounded career. But, when Ole Bull began to play in America, his performances were revelations, to the masses of those that heard him, of the possibilities of the violin. The greatest enthusiasm was manifested everywhere, and, during the three years of this early visit, he gave repeated performances in every city of any note in America. The writer of this little work met Ole Bull a few years ago in Chicago, and heard the artist laughingly say that, when he first entered what was destined to be such a great city, it was little more than a vast mudhole, a good-sized village scattered over a wide space of ground, and with no building of pretension except Fort Dearborn, a stockade fortification.

Our artist returned to Europe in 1846, and for five years led a wandering life of concert-giving in England, France, Holland, Germany, Italy, and Spain, adding to his laurels by the recognition everywhere conceded of the increased soundness and musicianly excellence of his playing. It was indeed at this period that Ole Bull attained his best as a virtuoso. He had been previously seduced by the example of Paganini, and in the attempt to master the more strange and remote difficulties of the instrument had often laid himself open to serious criticism. But Ole Bull gradually formed a style of his own which was the outcome of his passion for descriptive and poetic playing, and the correlative of the mode of composition which he adopted. In still later years Ole Bull seems to have returned again to what might be termed claptrap and trickery in his art, and to have desired rather to excite wonder and curiosity than to charm the sensibilities or to satisfy the requirements of sound musical taste.

In 1851 Ole Bull returned home with the patriotic purpose of establishing a strictly national theatre. This had been for a long time one of the many dreams which his active imagination had conjured up as a part of his mission. He was one of the earliest of that school of reformers, of whom we have heard so much of late years, that urge the readoption of the old Norse language--or, what is nearest to it now, the Icelandic--as the vehicle of art and literature. In the attempt to dethrone Dansk from its preeminence as the language of the drama, Ole Bull signally failed, and his Norwegian theatre, established at Bergen, proved only an insatiable tax on money-resources earned in other directions.

The year succeeding this, Ole Bull again visited the United States, and spent five years here. The return to America did not altogether contemplate the pursuit of music, for there had been for a good while boiling in his brain, among other schemes, the project of a great Scandinavian colony, to be established in Pennsylvania under his auspices. He purchased one hundred and twenty-five thousand acres of land on the Susquehanna, and hundreds of sturdy Norwegians flocked over to the land of milk and honey thus auspiciously opened to them. Timber was felled, ground cleared, churches, cottages, school-houses built, and everything was progressing desirably, when the ambitious colonizer discovered that the parties who sold him the land were swindlers without any rightful claim to it. With the un-business-like carelessness of the man of genius, our artist had not investigated the claims of others on the property, and he thus became involved in a most perplexing and expensive suit at law. He attempted to punish the rascals who so nearly ruined him, but they were shielded behind the quips and quirks of the law, and got away scot free. Ole Bull's previously ample means were so heavily drained by this misfortune that he was compelled to take up his violin again and resume concert-giving, for he had incurred heavy pecuniary obligations that must be met. Driven by the most feverish anxiety, he passed from town to town, playing almost every night, till he was stricken down by yellow fever in New Orleans. His powerful frame and sound constitution, fortified by the abstemious habits which had marked his whole life of queer vicissitudes, carried him through this danger safely, and he finally succeeded in honorably fulfilling the responsibility which he had assumed toward his countrymen.

For many recent years Ole Bull, when not engaged in concert-giving in Europe or America, has resided at a charming country estate on one of the little islands off the coast of Norway. His numerous farewell concert tours are very well known to the public, and would have won him ridicule, had not the genial presence and brilliant talents of the Norwegian artist been always good for a renewed and no less cordial welcome. He frequently referred to the United States in latter years as the beloved land of his adoption. One striking proof of his preference was, at all events, displayed in his marriage to an American lady, Miss Thorpe, of Wisconsin, in 1870. One son was the fruit of this second marriage, and Mr. and Mrs. Ole Bull divided their time between Norway and the United States.

The magnificent presence of Ole Bull, as if of some grand old viking stepped out of his armor and dressed in modern garb, made a most picturesque personality. Those who have seen him can never forget him. The great stature, the massive, stalwart form, as upright as a pine, the white floating locks framing the ruddy face, full of strength and genial humor, lit up by keen blue eyes--all these things made Ole Bull the most striking man in *personnel* among all the artists who have been familiar to our public.

While Ole Bull will not be known in the history of art as a great scientific musician, there can be no doubt that his place as a brilliant and gifted solo player will stand among the very foremost. As a composer he will probably be forgotten, for his compositions, which made up the most of his concert programmes, were so radically interwoven with his executive art as a virtuoso that the two can not be dissevered. No one, unless he should be inspired by the same feelings which animated the breast of Ole Bull, could ever evolve from his musical tone-pictures of Scandinavian myth and folk-lore the weird fascination which his bow struck from the strings. Ole Bull, like Paganini, laid no claim to greatness in interpreting the violin classics. His peculiar title to fame is that of being, aside from brilliancy as a violin virtuoso, the musical exponent of his people and their traditions. He died at Bergen, Norway, on August 18, 1880, in the seventy-first year of his age, and his funeral services made one of the most august and imposing ceremonials held for many a long year in Norway.

MUZIO CLEMENTI

The Genealogy of the Piano-forte.--The Harpsichord its Immediate Predecessor.--Supposed Invention of the Piano-forte.--Silbermann the First Maker.--Anecdote of Frederick the Great.--The Piano-forte only slowly makes its Way as against the Clavichord and Harpsichord.--Emanuel Bach, the First Composer of Sonatas for the Piano-forte.--His Views of playing on the New Instrument.--Haydn and Mozart as Players.--Muzio Clementi, the Earliest Virtuoso, strictly speaking, as a Pianist.--Born in Rome in 1752.--Scion of an Artistic Family.--First Musical Training.--Rapid Development of his Talents.--Composes Contrapuntal Works at the Age of Fourteen.--Early Studies of the Organ and Harpsichord.--Goes to England to complete his Studies.--Creates an Unequaled Furore in London.--John Christian Bach's Opinion of Clementi.--Clementi's Musical Tour.--His Duel with Mozart before the Emperor.--Tenor of Clementi's Life in England.--Clementi's Pupils.--Trip to St. Petersburg.--Sphor's Anecdote of Him.--Mercantile and Manufacturing Interest in the Piano as Partner of Collard.--The Players and Composers trained under Clementi.--His Composition.--Status as a Player.--Character and Influence as an Artist.--Development of the Technique of the Piano, culminating in Clementi.

I.

Before touching the life of Clementi, the first of the great virtuosos who may be considered distinctively composers for and players on the pianoforte, it is indispensable to a clear understanding of the theme involved that the reader should turn back for a brief glance at the history of the piano and piano-playing prior to his time. Before the piano-forte came the harpsichord, prior to the latter the spinet, then the virginal, the clavichord, and monochord; before these, the clavieytherium. Before these instruments, which bring us down to modern civilized times, and constitute the genealogy of the piano-forte, we have the dulcimer and psaltery, and all the Egyptian, Grecian, and Roman harps and lyres which were struck with a quill or plectrum. No product of human ingenuity has been the outcome of a steady and systematic growth from age to age by more demonstrable stages than this most remarkable of musical instruments. As it is not the intention to offer an essay on the piano, but only to make clearer the conditions under which a great school of players began to appear, the antiquities of the topic are not necessary to be touched.

The modern piano-forte had as its immediate predecessor the harpsichord, the instrument on which the heroines of the novels of Fielding, Smollett, Richardson, and their contemporaries were wont to discourse sweet music, and for which Haydn and Mozart composed some delightful minor works. In the harpsichord the strings were set in vibration by points of quill or hard leather. One of these instruments looked like a piano, only it was provided with two keyboards, one above the other, related to each other as the swell and main keyboards of an organ. At last it occurred to lovers of music that all refinement of musical expression depended on touch, and that whereas a string could be plucked or pulled by machinery in but one way, it could be hit in a hundred ways. It was then that the notion of striking the strings with a hammer found practical use, and by the addition of this element the piano-forte emerged into existence. The idea appears to have occurred to three men early in the eighteenth century, almost simultaneously--Cristofori, an Italian, Marins, a Frenchman, and Schroter, a German. For years attempts to carry out the new mechanism were so clumsy that good harpsichords on the wrong principle were preferred to poor piano-fortes on the right principle. But the keynote of progress had been struck, and the day of the quill and leather jack was swiftly drawing to a close. A small hammer was made to strike the string, producing a marvelously clear, precise, delicate tone, and the "scratch" with a sound at the end of it was about to be consigned to oblivion for ever and a day.

Gottfried Silbermann, an ingenious musical instrument maker, of Freyhurg, Saxony, was the first to give the new principle adequate expression, about the year 1740, and his pianos excited a great deal of curiosity among musicians and scientific men. He followed the mechanism of Cristofori, the Italian, rather than of his own countrymen. Schroter and his instruments appear to have been ingenious, though Sebastian Bach, who loved his "well-tempered clavichord" (the most powerful instrument of the harpsichord class) too well to be seduced from his allegiance, pronounced them too feeble in tone, a criticism which he retracted in after years. Silbermann experimented and labored with incessant energy for many years, and he had the satisfaction before dying of seeing the piano firmly established in the affection and admiration of the musical world. One of the most authentic of musical anecdotes is that of the visit of John Sebastian Bach and his son to Frederick the Great, at Potsdam, in 1747. The Prussian king was an enthusiast in music, and himself an excellent performer on the flute, of which, as well as of other instruments, he had a large collection. He had for a long time been anxious for a visit from Bach, but that great man was too much enamored of his own quiet musical solitude to run hither and thither at the beck of kings. At last, after much solicitation, he consented, and arrived at Potsdam late in the evening, all dusty and travel-stained. The king was just taking up his flute to play a concerto, when a lackey informed him of the coming of Bach. Frederick was more agitated than he ever had been in the tumult of battle. Crying aloud, "Gentlemen, old Bach is here!" he rushed out to meet the king in a loftier domain than his own, and ushered him into the lordly company of powdered wigs and doublets, of fair dames shining with jewels, satins, and velvets, of courtiers glittering in all the colors of the rainbow. "Old Bach" presented a shabby figure amid all this splendor, but the king cared nothing for that. He was most anxious to hear the grand old musician play on the new Silbermann piano, which was the latest hobby of the Prussian monarch.

It is not a matter of wonder that the lovers of the harpsichord and clavichord did not take kindly to the piano-forte at first. The keys needed a greater delicacy of treatment, and the very fact that the instrument required a new style of playing was of course sufficient to relegate the piano to another generation. The art of playing had at the time of the invention of the piano attained a high degree of efficiency. Such musicians as Do-menico Scarlatti in Italy and John Sebastian Bach in Germany had developed a wonderful degree of skill in treating the *clavecin*, or spinet, and the clavichord, and, if we may trust the old accounts, they called out ecstasies of admiration similar to those which the great modern players have excited. With the piano-forte, however, an entirely new style of expression came into existence. The power to play soft or loud at will developed the individual or personal feeling of the player, and new effects were speedily invented and put in practice. The art of playing ceased to be considered from the merely objective point of view, for the richer resources of the piano suggested the indulgence of individuality of expression. It was left to Emanuel Bach to make the first step toward the proper treatment of the piano, and to adapt a style of composition expressly to its requirements, though even he continued to prefer the clavichord. The rigorous, polyphonic style of his illustrious father was succeeded by the lyrical and singing element, which, if fantastic and daring, had a sweet, bright charm very fascinating. He writes in one of his treatises: "Methinks music ought appeal directly to the heart, and in this no performer on the piano-forte will succeed by merely thumping and drumming, or by continual arpeggio playing. During the last few years my chief endeavor has been to play the piano-forte, in spite of its deficiency in sustaining the sound, so much as possible, in a singing manner, and to compose for it accordingly. This is by no means an easy task, if we desire not to leave the ear empty or to disturb the noble simplicity of the cantabile by too much noise."

Haydn and Mozart, who composed somewhat for the harpsichord (for until the closing years of the eighteenth century this instrument had not entirely yielded to the growing popularity of the piano-forte), distinguished themselves still more by their treatment of the latter instrument. They closely followed the maxims of Emanuel Bach. They aimed to please the public by sweet melody and agreeable harmony, by spontaneous elegance and cheerfulness, by suave and smooth simplicity. Their practice in writing for the orchestra and for voices modified their piano-forte style both as composers and players, but they never sacrificed that intelligible and simple charm which appeals to the universal heart to the taste for grand, complex, and eccentric effects, which has so dominated the efforts of their successors. Mozart's most distinguished contemporaries bear witness to his excellence as a player, and his great command over the piano-forte, and his own remarks on piano-playing are full of point and suggestion. He asserts "that the performer should possess a quiet and steady hand, with its natural lightness, smoothness, and gliding rapidity so well developed that the passages should flow like oil.... All notes, graces, accents, etc., should be brought out with fitting taste and expression.... In passages [technical figures], some notes may be left to their fate without notice, but is that right? Three things are necessary to a good performer"; and he pointed significantly to his head, his heart, and the tips of his fingers, as symbolical of understanding, sympathy, and technical skill. But it was fated that Clementi should be the Columbus in the domain of piano-forte playing and composition. He was the father of the school of modern piano technique, and by far surpassed all his contemporaries in the boldness, vigor, brilliancy, and variety of his execution, and he is entitled to be called first (in respect of date) of the great piano-forte virtuosos, Clementi wrote solely for this instrument (for his few orchestral works are now dead). The piano, as his sole medium of expression, became a vehicle of great eloquence and power, and his sonatas, as pure types of piano-forte compositions, are unsurpassed, even in this age of exuberant musical fertility.

II.

Muzio Clementi was born at Rome in the year 1752, and was the son of a silver worker of great skill, who was principally engaged on the execution of the embossed figures and vases employed in the Catholic worship. The boy at a very early age evinced a most decided taste for music, a predilection which delighted his father, himself an enthusiastic amateur, and caused him to bestow the utmost pains on the cultivation of the child's talents. The boy's first master was Buroni, choir-master a tone of the churches, and a relation of the family. Later, young Clementi took lessons in thorough bass from an eminent organist, Condicelli, and after a couple of years' application he was thought sufficiently advanced to apply for the position of organist, which he obtained, his age then being barely nine. He prosecuted his studies with great zeal under the ablest masters, and his genius for composition as well as for playing displayed a rapid development. By the time Clementi had attained the age of fourteen he had composed several contrapuntal works of considerable merit, one of which, a mass for four voices and chorus, gained great applause from the musicians and public of Rome.

During his studies of counterpoint and the organ Clementi never neglected his harpsichord, on which he achieved remarkable proficiency, for the piano-forte at this time, though gradually coming into use, was looked on rather as a curiosity than an instrument of practical value. The turning-point of Clementi's life occurred in 1767, through his acquaintance with an English gentleman of wealth, Mr. Peter Beckford, who evinced a deep interest in the young musician's career. After much opposition Mr. Beckford persuaded the elder Clementi to intrust his son's further musical education to his care. The country seat of Mr. Beckford was in Dorsetshire, England, and here, by the aid of a fine library, social surroundings of the most favorable kind, and indomitable energy on his own part, he speedily made himself an adept in the English language and literature. The talents of Clementi made him almost an Admirable Crichton, for it is asserted that, in addition to the most severe musical studies, he made himself in a few years a proficient in the principal modern languages, in Greek and Latin, and in the whole circle of the belles-lettres. His studies in his own art were principally based on the works of Corelli, Alexander Scarlatti, Handel's harpsichord and organ music, and on the sonatas of Paradies, a Neapolitan composer and teacher, who enjoyed high repute in London for many years. Until 1770 Clementi spent his time secluded at his patron's country seat, and then fully equipped with musical knowledge, and with an unequaled command of the instrument, he burst on the town as pianist and composer. He had already written at this time his "Opus No. 2," which established a new era for sonata compositions, and is recognized to-day as the basis for all modern works of this class.

Clementi's attainments were so phenomenal that he carried everything before him in London, and met with a success so brilliant as to be almost without precedent. Socially and musically he was one of the idols of the hour, and the great Handel himself had not met with as much adulation. Apropos of the great sonata above mentioned, with which the Clementi furore began in London, it is said that John Christian Bach, son of Sebastian, one of the greatest executants of the time, confessed his inability to do it justice, and Schroter, one of those sharing the honor of the invention of the piano-forte, and a leading musician of his age, said, "Only the devil and Clementi could play it." For seven years the subject of our sketch poured forth a succession of brilliant works, continually gave concerts, and in addition acted as conductor of the Italian opera, a life sufficiently busy for the most ambitious man. In 1780 Clementi began his musical travels, and gave the first concerts of his tour at Paris, whither he was accompanied by the great singer Pacchierotti. He was received with the greatest favor by the queen, Marie Antoinette, and the court, and made the acquaintance of Gluck, who warmly admired the brilliant player who had so completely revolutionized the style of execution on instruments with a keyboard. Here he also met Viotti, the great violinist, and played a ***duo concertante*** with the latter, expressly composed for the occasion. Clementi was delighted with the almost frantic enthusiasm of the French, so different from the more temperate approbation of the English. He was wont to say jocosely that he hardly knew himself to be the same man. From Paris Clementi passed, via Strasburg and Munich, where he was most cordially welcomed, to Vienna, the then musical Mecca of Europe, for it contained two world-famed men--"Papa" Haydn and the young prodigy Mozart. The Emperor Joseph II, a great lover of music, could not let the opportunity slip, for he now had a chance to determine which was the greater player, his own pet Mozart or the Anglo-Italian stranger whose fame as an executant had risen to such dimensions. So the two musicians fought a musical duel, in which they played at sight the most difficult works, and improvised on themes selected by the imperial arbiter. The victory was left undecided, though Mozart, who disliked the Italians, spoke afterward of Clementi, in a tone at variance with his usual gentleness, as "a mere mechanician, without a pennyworth of feeling or taste." Clementi was more generous, for he couldn't say too much of Mozart's "singing touch and exquisite taste," and dated from this meeting a considerable difference in his own style of play.

With the exception of occasional concert tours to Paris, Clementi devoted all his time up to 1802 in England, busy as conductor, composer, virtuoso, and teacher. In the latter capacity he was unrivaled, and pupils came to him from all parts of Europe. Among these pupils were John B. Cramer and John Field, names celebrated in music. In 1802 Clementi took the brilliant young Irishman, John Field, to St. Petersburg on a musical tour, where both master and pupil were received with unbounded enthusiasm, and where the latter remained in affluent circumstances, having married a Russian lady of rank and wealth. Field was idolized by the Russians, and they claim his compositions as belonging to their music. He is now distinctively remembered as the inventor of that beautiful form of musical writing, the nocturne. Spohr, the violinist, met Clementi and Field at the Russian capital, and gives the following amusing account in his "Autobiography": "Clementi, a man in his best years, of an extremely lively disposition and very engaging manners, liked much to converse with me, and often invited me after dinner to play at billiards. In the evening I sometimes accompanied him to his large piano-forte warehouse, where Field was often obliged to play for hours to display instruments to the best advantage to purchasers. I have still in recollection the figure of the pale overgrown youth, whom I have never since seen. When Field, who had outgrown his clothes, placed himself at the piano, stretching out his arms over the keyboard, so that the sleeves shrank up nearly to the elbow, his whole figure appeared awkward and stiff in the highest degree. But, as soon as his touching instrumentation began, everything else was forgotten, and one became all ear. Unfortunately I could not express my emotion and thankfulness to the young man otherwise than by the pressure of the hand, for he spoke no language but his mother tongue. Even at that time many anecdotes of the remarkable avarice of the rich Clementi were related, which had greatly increased in later years when I again met him in London. It was generally reported that Field was kept on very short allowance by his master, and was obliged to pay for the good fortune of having his instruction by many privations. I myself experienced a little sample of Clementi's truly Italian parsimony, for one day I found teacher and pupil with upturned sleeves, engaged at the wash-tub, washing their stockings and other linen. They did not suffer themselves to be disturbed, and Clementi advised me to do the same, as washing in St. Petersburg was not only very expensive, but the linen suffered much from the method used in washing it."

From the above it may be suspected that Clementi was not only player and composer, but man of business. He had been very successful in money-making in England from the start, and it was not many years before he accumulated a sufficient amount to buy an interest in the firm of Longman & Broderip, "manufacturers of musical instruments, and music sellers to their majesties." The failure of the house, by which he sustained heavy losses, induced him to try his hand alone at music publishing and piano-forte manufacturing; and his great success (the firm is still extant in the person of his partner's son, Mr. Col-lard) proves he was an exception to the majority of artists, who rarely possess business talents. Clementi met many reverses in his commercial career. In March, 1807, the warehouses occupied by Clementi's new firm were destroyed by fire, entailing a loss of about forty thousand pounds. But the man's courage was indomitable, and he retrieved his misfortunes with characteristic pluck and cheerfulness. After 1810 he gave up playing in public, and devoted himself to composing and the conduct of his piano-forte business, which became very large and valuable. Himself an inventor and mechanician, he made many important improvements in the construction of the piano, some of which have never been superseded.

III.

Clementi numbers among his pupils more great names in the art of piano-forte playing than any other great master. This is partly owing to the fact, it may be, that he began his career in the infancy of the piano-forte as an instrument, and was the first to establish a solid basis for the technique of the instrument. In addition to John Field and J. B. Cramer, previously mentioned, were Zeuner, Dussek, Alex. Kleugel, Ludwig Berger, Kalkbrenner, Charles Mayer, and Meyerbeer. These musicians not only added richly to the literature of the piano-forte, but were splendid exponents of its powers as virtuosos. But mere artistic fame is transitory, and it is in Clementi's contributions to the permanent history of piano-forte playing that we must find his chief claim on the admiration of posterity. He composed not a few works for the orchestra, and transcriptions of opera, but these have now receded to the lumber closet. The works which live are his piano concertos, of which about sixty were written for the piano alone, and the remainder as duets or trios; and, *par excellence*, his "Gradus ad Parnassum," a superb series of one hundred studies, upon which even to-day the solid art of piano-forte playing rests. Clementi's works must always remain indispensable to the pianist, and, in spite of the fact that piano technique has made such advances during the last half century, there are several of Clementi's sonatas which tax the utmost skill of such players as Liszt and Von Billow, to whom all ordinary difficulty is merely a plaything. As Viotti was the father of modern violin-playing, Clementi may be considered the father of virtuosoism on the piano-forte, and he has left an indelible mark, both mechanically and spiritually, on all that pertains to piano-playing. Compared with Clementi's style in piano-forte composition, that of Haydn and Mozart appears poor and thin. Haydn and Mozart regarded execution as merely the vehicle of ideas, and valued technical brilliancy less than musical substance. Clementi, on the other hand, led the way for that class of compositions which pay large attention to manual skill. His works can not be said to burn with that sacred fire which inspires men of the highest genius, but they are magnificently modeled for the display of technical execution, brilliancy of effect, and virile force of expression. The great Beethoven, who composed the greatest works for the piano-forte, as also for the orchestra, had a most exalted estimate of Clementi, and never wearied of playing his music and sounding his praises. No musician has probably exerted more far-reaching effects in this department of his art than Clementi, though he can not be called a man of the highest genius, for this lofty attribute supposes great creative imagination and rich resources of thought, as well as knowledge, experience, skill, and transcendent aptitude for a single instrument.

As far as a musician of such unique and colossal genius as Beethoven could be influenced by preceding or contemporary artists, his style as a piano-forte player and composer was more modified by Clementi than by any other. He was wont to say that no one could play till he knew Clementi by heart. He adopted many of the peculiar figures and combinations original with Clementi, though his musical mentality, incomparably richer and greater than that of the other, transfigured them into a new life. That Beethoven found novel means of expression to satisfy the importunate demands of his musical conceptions; that his piano works display a greater polyphony, stronger contrasts, bolder and richer rhythm, broader design and execution, by no means impair the value of his obligations to Clementi, obligations which the most arrogant and self-centered of men freely allowed. Beethoven's fancy was penetrated by all the qualities of tone which distinguish the string, reed, and brass instruments; his imagination shot through and through with orchestral color; and he succeeded in saturating his sonatas with these rich effects without sacrificing the specialty of the piano-forte. But in general style and technique he is distinctly a follower of Clementi. The most unique and splendid personality in music has thus been singled out as furnishing a vivid illustration of the influence exerted by Clementi in the department of the piano-forte.

Clementi lived to the age of eighty, and spent the last twelve years of his life in London uninterruptedly, his growing feebleness preventing him from taking his usual musical trips to the Continent. He retained his characteristic energy and freshness of mind to the last, and was held in the highest honor by the great circle of artists who had centered in London, for he was the musical patriarch in England, as Cherubini was in France at a little later date. He was married three times, had children in his old age, and only a few months before his death, Moscheles records in his diary, he was able to arouse the greatest enthusiasm by the vigor and brilliancy of his playing, in spite of his enfeebled physical powers. He died March 9, 1832, at Eversham, and his funeral gathered a great convocation of musical celebrities. His life covered an immense arch in the history of music.

At his birth Handel was alive; at his death Beethoven, Schubert, and Weber had found refuge in the grave from the ingratitude of a contemporary public. He began his career by practicing Scarlatti's harpsichord sonatas; he lived to be acquainted with the finest piano-forte works of all time. When he first used the piano, he practiced on the imperfect and feeble Silbermann instrument. When he died, the magnificent instruments of Erard, Broadwood, and Collard, to the latter of which his own mechanical and musical knowledge had contributed much, were in common vogue. Such was the career of Muzio Clementi, the father of piano-forte virtuosos. Had he lived later, he might have been far eclipsed by the great players who have since adorned the art of music. As Goethe says, through the mouthpiece of Wil-helm. Meister: "The narrowest man may be complete while he moves within the bounds of his own capacity and acquirements, but even fine qualities become clouded and destroyed if this indispensable proportion is exceeded. This unwholesome excess, however, will begin to appear frequently, for who can suffice to the swift progress and increasing requirements of the ever-soaring present time?" But, measured by his own day and age, Clementi deserves the pedestal on which musical criticism has placed him.

MOSCHELES.

Clementi and Mozart as Points of Departure in Piano-forte Playing.--Moscheles the most Brilliant Climax reached by the Viennese School.--His Child-Life at Prague.--Extraordinary Precocity.--Goes to Vienna as the Pupil of Salieri and Albrechts-burger.--Acquaintance with Beethoven.--Moscheles is honored with a Commission to make a Piano Transcription of Beethoven's "Fidelio."--His Intercourse with the Great Man.--Concert Tour.--Arrival in Paris.--The Artistic Circle into which he is received.--Pictures of Art-Life in Paris.--London and its Musical Celebrities.--Career as a Wandering Virtuoso.--Felix Mendelssohn becomes his Pupil.--The Mendelssohn Family.--Moscheles's Marriage to a Hamburg Lady.--Settles in London.--His Life as Teacher, Player, and Composer.--Eminent Place taken by Moscheles among the Musicians of his Age.--His Efforts soothe the Sufferings of Beethoven's Deathbed.--Friendship for Mendelssohn.--Moscheles becomes connected with the Leipzig Conservatorium.--Death in 1870.--Moscheles as Pianist and Composer.--Sympathy with the Old as against the New School of the Piano.--His Powerful Influence on the Musical Culture and Tendencies of his Age.

I.

The rivalry of Clementi and Mozart as exponents of piano-forte playing in their day was continued in their schools of performance. The original cause of this difference was largely based on the character of the instruments on which they played. Clementi used the English piano-forte, and Mozart the Viennese, and the style of execution was no less the outcome of the mechanical difference between the two vehicles of expression than the result of personal idiosyncrasies. The English instrument was speedily developed into the production of a richer, fuller, and more sonorous tone, while the Viennese piano-forte continued for a long time to be distinguished by its light, thin, sweet quality of sound, and an action so sensitive that the slightest pressure produced a sound from the key, so that the term "breathing on the keys" became a current expression, Clementi's piano favored a bold, masculine, brilliant style of playing, while the Viennese piano led to a rapid, fluent, delicate treatment. The former player founded the school which has culminated, through a series of great players, in the magnificent virtuosoism of Franz Liszt, while the Vienna school has no nearer representative than Tgnaz Moscheles, one of the greatest players in the history of the pianoforte, who, whether judged by his gifts as a concert performer, a composer for the instrument which he so brilliantly adorned, or from his social and intellectual prominence, must be set apart as peculiarly a representative man. There were other eminent players, such as Hummel, Czerny, and Herz, contemporary with Moscheles and belonging to the same *genre* as a pianist, but these names do not stand forth with the same clear and permanent luster in their relation to the musical art.

Ignaz Moscheles was born at Prague, May 30, 1794, his parents being well-to-do people of Hebrew stock. His father, a cloth merchant, was passionately fond of music, and was accustomed to say, "One of my children must become a thoroughbred musician." Ignaz was soon selected as the one on whom the experiment should be made, and the rapid progress he made justified the accident of choice, for all of the family possessed some musical talent. The boy progressed too fast, for he attempted at the age of seven to play Beethoven's "Sonata Pathetique." He was traveling on the wrong road, attempting what he could in no way attain, when his father took him to Dionys Weber, one of the best teachers of the time. "I come," said the parent, "to you as our first musician, for sincere truth instead of empty flattery. I want to find out from you if my boy has such genuine talent that you can make a really good musician of him." "Naturally, I was called on to play," says Moscheles, in his "Autobiography," "and I was bungler enough to do it with some conceit. My mother having decked me out in my Sunday best, I played my best piece, Beethoven's 'Sonata Pathetique.' But what was my astonishment on finding that I was neither interrupted by bravos nor overwhelmed by praise! and what were my feelings when Dionys Weber finally delivered himself thus:

"'Candidly speaking, the boy has talent, but is on the wrong road, for he makes bosh of great works which he does not understand, and to which he is utterly unequal. I could make something of him if you could hand him over to me for three years, and follow out my plan to the letter. The first year he must play nothing but Mozart, the second Clementi, and the third Bach; but only that: not a note as yet of Beethoven; and if he persists in using the circulating libraries, I have done with him for ever.'"

This scheme was followed out strictly, and Moscheles at the age of fourteen had acquired a sufficient mastery of the piano to give a concert at Prague with brilliant success. The young musician continued to pursue his studies assiduously under Weber's direction until his father's death, and his mother then determined to yield to his oft-repeated wish to try his musical fortunes in a larger field, and win his own way in life. So young Ignaz, little more than a child, went to Vienna, where he was warmly received in the hospitable musical circles of that capital. He took lessons in counterpoint from Albrechts-burger, and in composition from Salieri, and in all ways indicated that serene, tireless industry which marked his whole after-career. Moscheles spent eight years at Vienna, continually growing in estimation as artist and beginning to make his mark as a composer. His own reminiscences of the brilliant and gifted men who clustered in Vienna are very pleasant, but it is to Beethoven that his admiration specially went forth. The great master liked his young disciple much, and proposed to him that he should set the numbers of "Fidelio" for the piano, a task which, it is needless to say, was gladly accepted. Moscheles tells us one morning, when he went to see Beethoven, he found him lying in bed. "He happened to be in remarkably good spirits, jumped up immediately, and placed himself, just as he was, at the window looking out on the Schotten-bastei, with the view of examining the 'Fidelio' numbers which I had arranged. Naturally, a crowd of street-boys collected under the window, when he roared out, 'Now, what do these confounded boys want?' I laughed and pointed to his own figure. 'Yes, yes! You are quite right,' he said, and hastily put on a dressing-gown."

Moscheles's associations were even at this early period with all the foremost people of the age, and he was cordially welcome in every circle. He composed a good deal, besides giving concerts and playing in private select circles, and was recognized as being the equal of Hummel, who had hitherto been accepted as the great piano virtuoso of Vienna. The two were very good friends in spite of their rivalry. They, as well as all the Viennese musicians, were bound together by a common tie, very well expressed in the saying of Moscheles: "We musicians, whatever we be, are mere satellites of the great Beethoven, the dazzling luminary."

II.

In the autumn of 1816 Moscheles bade a sorrowful adieu to the imperial city, where he had spent so many happy years, to undertake an extended concert tour, armed with letters of introduction to all the courts of Europe from Prince Lichtenstein, Countess Hardigg, and other influential admirers. He proceeded directly to Leipzig, where he was warmly received by the musical fraternity of that city, especially by the Wiecks, of whose daughter Clara he speaks in highly eulogistic words. He played his own compositions, which already began to show that serene and finished beauty so characteristic of his after-writings. A similar success greeted him at Dresden, where, among other concerts, he gave one before the court. Of this entertainment Moscheles writes: "The court actually dined (this barbarous custom still prevails), and the royal household listened in the galleries, while I and the court band made music to them, and barbarous it really was; but, in regard to truth, I must add that royalty and also the lackeys kept as quiet as possible, and the former congratulated me, and actually condescended to admit me to friendly conversation." He continued his concerts in Munich, Augsburg, Amsterdam, Brussels, and other cities, creating the most genuine admiration wherever he went, and finally reached Paris in December, 1817.

Here our young artist was promptly received in the extraordinary world of musicians, artists, authors, wits, and social celebrities which then, as now, made Paris so delightful for those possessing the countersign of admission. Baillot, the violinist, gave a private concert in his honor, in which he in company with Spohr played before an audience made up of such artists and celebrities as Cherubini, Auber, Herold, Adam, Lesueur, Pacini, Paer, Habeneck, Plantade, Blangini, La-font, Pleyel, Ivan Muller, Viotti, Pellegrini, Boieldieu, Schlesinger, Manuel Garcia, and others. These areopagites of music set the mighty seal of their approval on Moscheles's genius. He was invited everywhere, to dinners, balls, and *fetes*, and there was no **salon** in Paris so high and exclusive which did not feel itself honored by his presence. His public concerts were thronged with the best and most critical audiences, and he by no means shone the less that he appeared in conjunction with other distinguished artists. He often entertained parties of jovial artists at his lodgings, and music, punch, and supper enlivened the night till 3 A.M. Whoever could play or sing was present, and good music alternated with amusing tricks played on the respective instruments. "Altogether," he writes, "it is a happy, merry time! Certainly, at the last state dinner of the Rothschilds, in the presence of such notabilities as Canning or Narischkin, I was obliged to keep rather in the background. The invitation to a large, brilliant, but ceremonious ball appears a very questionable way of showing me attention. The drive up, the endless queue of carriages, wearied me, and at last I got out and walked. There, too, I found little pleasure." On the other hand, he praises the performance of Gluck's opera at the house of the Erards. The "concerts spirituels" delight him. "Who would not," he says, "envy me this enjoyment? These concerts justly enjoy a world-wide celebrity. There I listen with the most solemn earnestness." On the other hand, there are cheerful episodes, and jovial dinners with Carl Blum and Schlesinger, at the Restaurant Lemelle. "Yesterday," he writes, "Schlesinger quizzed me about my slowness in eating, and went so far as to make the stupid bet with me, that he would demolish three dozen oysters while I ate one dozen, and he was quite right. On perceiving, however, that he was on the point of winning, I took to making faces, made him laugh so heartily that he couldn't go on eating; thus I won my bet." We find the following notice on the 20th of March: "I spent the evening at Ciceri's, son-in-law of Isabey, the famous painter, where I was introduced to one of the most interesting circles of artists. In the first room were assembled the most famous painters, engaged in drawing several things for their own amusement. In the midst of these was Cherubini, also drawing. I had the honor, like every one newly introduced, of having my portrait taken in caricature. Begasse took me in hand, and succeeded well. In an adjoining room were musicians and actors, among them Ponchard, Le-vasseur, Dugazon, Panseron, Mlle, de Munck, and Mme. Livere, of the Theatre Francais. The most interesting of their performances, which I attended merely as a listener, was a vocal quartet by Cherubini, performed under his direction. Later in the evening, the whole party armed itself with larger or smaller 'mirlitons' (reed-pipe whistles), and on these small monotonous instruments, sometimes made of sugar, they played, after the fashion of Russian horn music, the overture to 'Demophon,' two frying-pans representing the drums." On the 27th of March this "mirliton" concert was repeated at Ciceri's, and on this occasion Cherubini took an active part. Moscheles relates: "Horace Vernet entertained us with his ventriloquizing powers, M. Salmon with his imitation of a horn, and Dugazon actually with a 'mirliton' solo. Lafont and I represented the classical music, which, after all, held, its own." It was hard to tear himself from these gayeties; but he had not visited London, and he was anxious to make himself known at a musical capital inferior to none in Europe. He little thought that in London he was destined to find his second home. He plunged into the gayeties and enjoyments of the English capital with no less zest than he had already experienced in Paris. He found such great players as J. B. Cramer, Ferdinand Ries, Kalkbrenner, and Clementi in the field; but our young artist did not altogether lose by comparison. Among other distinguished musicians, Moscheles also met Kiesewetter, the violinist, the great singers Mara and Catalani, and Dragonetti, the greatest of double-bass players. Dragonetti was a most eccentric man, and of him Moscheles says: "In his *salon* in Liecester Square he has collected a large number of various kinds of dolls, among them a negress. When visitors are announced, he politely receives them, and says that this or that young lady will make room for them; he also asks his intimate acquaintances whether his favorite dolls look better or worse since their last visit, and similar absurdities. He is a terrible snuff-taker, helping himself out of a gigantic snuff-box, and he has an immense and varied collection of snuff-boxes. The most curious part of him is his language, a regular jargon, in which there is a mixture of his native Bergamese, bad French, and still worse English."

During the several months of this first English visit Moscheles made many acquaintances which were destined to ripen into solid friendships, and gave many concerts in which the most distinguished artists, vocal and instrumental, participated. Altogether, he appears to have been delighted with the London art and social world little less than he had been with that of Paris. He returned, however, to the latter city in August, and again became a prominent figure in the most fashionable and admired concerts. During this visit to Paris he writes in his diary: "Young Erard took me to-day to his piano-forte factory to try the new invention of his uncle Sebastian. This quicker action of the hammer seems to me so important that I prophesy a new era in the manufacture of piano-fortes. I still complain of some heaviness in the touch, and, therefore, prefer to play on Pape's and Petzold's instruments (Viennese pianos). I admired the Erards, but am not thoroughly satisfied, and urged him to make new improvements."

From 1815, when Moscheles began his career as a virtuoso in the production of his "Variationen fiber den Alexandermarsch," to 1826, he established a great reputation as a virtuoso and composer for the piano-forte. Though he played his own works at concerts with marked approbation, he also became distinguished as an interpreter of Mozart and Beethoven, for whom he had a reverential admiration. Moscheles often records his own sense of insignificance by the side of these Titans of music. A delightful characteristic of the man was his modesty about himself, and his genial appreciation of other musicians. Nowhere do those performers who, for example, came in active rivalry with himself, receive more cordial and unalloyed praise. Moscheles was entirely devoid of that littleness which finds vent in envy and jealousy, and was as frank and sympathetic in his estimate of others as he was ambitious and industrious in the development of his own great talents. In 1824 he gave piano-forte lessons to Felix Mendelssohn, then a youth of fifteen, at Berlin. He wrote of the Mendelssohn family: "This is a family the like of which I have never known. Felix, a boy of fifteen, is a phenomenon. What are all prodigies as compared with him? Gifted children, but nothing else. This Felix Mendelssohn is already a mature artist, and yet but fifteen years old! We at once settled down together for several hours, for I was obliged to play a great deal, when really I wanted to hear him and see his compositions, for Felix had to show me a concerto in C minor, a double concerto, and several motets; and all so full of genius, and at the same time so correct and thorough! His elder sister Fanny, also extraordinarily gifted, played by heart, and with admirable precision, fugues and passacailles by Bach. I think one may well call her a thorough 'Mus. Doc' (guter Musiker). Both parents give one the impression of being people of the highest refinement. They are far from overrating their children's talents; in fact, they are anxious about Felix's future, and to know whether his gift will prove sufficient to lead to a noble and truly great career. Will he not, like so many other brilliant children, suddenly collapse? I asserted my conscientious conviction that Felix would ultimately become a great master, that I had not the slightest doubt of his genius; but again and again I had to insist on my opinion before they believed me. These two are not specimens of the genus prodigy-parents (Wunderkinds Eltern), such as I most frequently endure." Moscheles soon came to the conclusion that to give Felix regular lessons was useless. Only a little hint from time to time was necessary for the marvelous youth, who had already begun to compose works which excited Moscheles's deepest admiration.

III.

In January, 1825, Moscheles, in the course of his musical wanderings, gave several concerts at Hamburg. Among the crowd of listeners who came to hear the great pianist was Charlotte Embden, the daughter of an excellent Hamburg family. She was enchanted by the playing of Moscheles, and, when she accidentally made the acquaintance of the performer at the house of a mutual acquaintance, the couple quickly became enamored of each other. A brief engagement of less than a month was followed by marriage, and so Moscheles entered into a relation singularly felicitous in all the elements which make domestic life most blessed. After a brief tour in the Rhenish cities, and a visit to Paris, Moscheles proceeded to London, where he had determined to make his home, for in no country had such genuine and unaffected cordiality boon shown him, and nowhere were the rewards of musical talent, whether as teacher, virtuoso, or composer, more satisfying to the man of high ambition. He made London his home for twenty years, and during this time became one of the most prominent figures in the art circles of that great city. Moscheles's mental accomplishments and singular geniality of nature contributed, with his very great abilities as a musician, to give him a position attained by but few artists. He gave lessons to none but the most talented pupils, and his services were sought by the most wealthy families of the English capital, though the ability to pay great prices was by no means a passport to the good graces of Moscheles. Among the pupils who early came under the charge of this great master was Thalberg, who even then was a brilliant player, but found in the exact knowledge and great experience of Moscheles that which gave the crowning finish to his style. Busy in teaching, composing, and public performance; busy in responding to the almost incessant demands made by social necessity on one who was not only intimate in the best circles of London society, but the center to whom all foreign artists of merit gravitated instantly they arrived in London; busy in confidential correspondence with all the great musicians of Europe, who discussed with the genial and sympathetic Moscheles all their plans and aspirations, and to whom they turned in their moments of trouble, he was indeed a busy man; and had it not been for the loving labors of his wife, who was his secretary, his musical copyist, and his assistant in a myriad of ways, he would have been unequal to his burden. Moscheles's diary tells the story of a man whose life, though one of tireless industry, was singularly serene and happy, and without those salient accidents and vicissitudes which make up the material of a picturesque life.

He made almost yearly tours to the Continent for concert-giving purposes, and kept his friendship with the great composers of the Continent green by personal contact. Beethoven was the god of his musical idolatry, and his pilgrimage to Vienna was always delightful to him. When Beethoven, in the early part of 1827, was in dire distress from poverty, just before his death, it was to Moscheles that he applied for assistance; and it was this generous friend who promptly arranged the concert with the Philharmonic Society by which one hundred pounds sterling was raised to alleviate the dying moments of the great man whom his own countrymen would have let starve, even as they had allowed Schubert and Mozart to suffer the direst want on their deathbeds.

An adequate record of Moscheles's life during the twenty years of his London career would be a pretty full record of all matters of musical interest occurring during this time. In 1832 he was made one of the directors of the Philharmonic Society, and in 1837-'38 he conducted with signal success Beethoven's "Ninth Symphony." When Sir Henry Bishop resigned, in 1845, Moscheles was made the conductor, and thereafter wielded the baton over this orchestra, the noblest in England. Among the yearly pleasures to which our pianist looked forward with the greatest interest were the visits of Mendelssohn, between whom and Moscheles there was the most tender friendship. Whole pages of his diary are given up to an account of Mendelssohn's doings, and to the most enthusiastic expression of his love and admiration for one of the greatest musical geniuses of modern times.

We can not attempt to follow up the placid and gentle current of Moscheles's life, flowing on to ever-increasing honor and usefulness, but hasten to the period when he left England in 1846, to become associated with Mendelssohn in the conduct of the Leipzig Conservatorium, then recently organized. Mendelssohn lived but a few months after achieving this great monument of musical education, but Moscheles remained connected with it for nearly twenty years, and to his great zeal, knowledge, and executive skill is due in large measure the solid success of the institution. Mendelssohn's early death, while yet in the very prime of creative genius, was a stunning blow to Moscheles; more so, perhaps, than would have occurred from the loss of any one except his beloved wife, the mother of his five children. Our musician died himself, in Leipzig, March 10, 1870, and his passage from this world was as serene and quiet as his passage through had been. He lived to see his daughters married to men of high worth and position, and his sons substantially placed in life. Perhaps few distinguished musicians have lived a life of such monotonous happiness, unmarked by those events which, while they give romantic interest to a career, make the gift at the expense of so much personal misery.

IV.

As a pianist Moscheles was distinguished by an incisive, brilliant touch, wonderfully clear, precise phrasing, and close attention to the careful accentuation of every phase of the composer's meaning. Of the younger composers for the piano, Mendelssohn and Schumann were the only ones with whose works he had any sympathy, though he often complains of the latter on account of his mysticism. His intelligence had as much if not more part in his art work than his emotions, and to this we may attribute that fine symmetry and balance in his own compositions, which make them equal in this respect to the productions of Mendelssohn. Chopin he regarded with a sense of admiration mingled with dread, for he could by no means enter into the peculiar conditions which make the works of the Polish composer so unique. He wrote of Chopin's "Etudes," in 1838: "My thoughts and consequently my fingers ever stumble and sprawl at certain crude modulations, and I find Chopin's productions on the whole too sugared, too little worthy of a man and an educated musician, though there is much charm and originality in the national color of his motive." When he heard Chopin play in after-years, however, he confessed the fascination of the performance, and bewailed his own incapacity to produce such effects in execution, though himself one of the greatest pianists in the world. So, too, Moscheles, though dazzled by Liszt's brilliant virtuosoism and power of transforming a single instrument into an orchestra, shook his head in doubt over such performances, and looked on them as charlatanism, which, however magnificent as an exhibition of talent, would ultimately help to degrade the piano by carrying it out of its true sphere. Moscheles himself was a more bold and versatile player than any other performer of his school, but he aimed assiduously to confine his efforts within the perfectly legitimate and well-established channels of pianism.

As an extemporaneous player, perhaps no pianist has ever lived who could surpass Moscheles. His improvisation on themes suggested by the audience always made one of the most attractive features of his concerts. His profound musical knowledge, his strong sense of form, the clearness and precision with which he instinctively clothed his ideas, as well as the fertility of the ideas themselves, gave his improvised pieces something of the same air of completeness as if they were the outcome of hours of laborious solitude. His very lack of passion and fire were favorable to this clear-cut and symmetrical expression. His last improvisation in public, on themes furnished by the audience, formed part of the programme of a concert at London, in 1865, given by Mme. Jenny Lind Goldschmidt, in aid of the sufferers by the war between Austria and Prussia, where he extemporized for half an hour on "See the Conquering Hero Comes," and on a theme from the andante of Beethoven's C Minor Symphony, in a most brilliant and astonishing style.

Aside from his greatness as a virtuoso and composer for the piano-forte, whose works will always remain classics in spite of vicissitudes of public opinion, even as those of Spohr will for the violin, the influence of Moscheles in furtherance of a solid and true musical taste was very great, and worthy of special notice. Perhaps no one did more to educate the English mind up to a full appreciation of the greatest musical works. As teacher, conductor, player, and composer, the life of Ignaz Moscheles was one of signal and permanent worth, and its influences fertilized in no inconsiderable streams the public thought, not only of his own times, but indirectly of the generation which has followed. It is not necessary to attribute to him transcendent genius, but lie possessed, what was perhaps of equal value to the world, an intellect and temperament splendidly balanced to the artistic needs of his epoch. The list of Moscheles's numbered compositions reaches Op. 142, besides a large number of ephemeral productions which he did not care to preserve.

THE SCHUMANNS AND CHOPIN.

Robert Schumann's Place as a National Composer.--Peculiar Greatness as a Piano-forte Composer.--Born at Zwickau in 1810.--His Father's Aversion to his Musical Studies.--Becomes a Student of Jurisprudence in Leipzig.--Makes the Acquaintance of Clara Wieck.--Tedium of his Law Studies.--Vacation Tour to Italy.--Death of his Father, and Consent of his Mother to Schumann adopting the Profession of Music.--Becomes Wieck's Pupil.--Injury to his Hand which prevents all Possibilities of his becoming a Great Performer.--Devotes himself to Composition.--The Child, Clara Wieck--Remarkable Genius as a Player.--Her Early Training.--Paganini's Delight in her Genius.--Clara Wieck's Concert Tours.--Schumann falls deeply in Love with her, and Wieck's Opposition.--His Allusions to Clara in the "Neue Zeitschrift."--Schumann at Vienna.--His Compositions at first Unpopular, though played by Clara Wieck and Liszt.--Schumann's Labors as a Critic.--He Marries Clara in 1840.--His Song Period inspired by his Wife.--Tour to Russia, and Brilliant Reception given to the Artist Pair.--The "Neue Zeitschrift" and its Mission.--The Davidsbund.--Peculiar Style of Schumann's Writing.--He moves to Dresden.--Active Production in Orchestral Composition.--Artistic Tour in Holland.--He is seized with Brain Disease.--Characteristics as a Man, as an Artist, and as a Philosopher.--Mme. Schumann as her Husband's Interpreter.--Chopin a Colaborer with Schumann.--Schumann on Chopin again.--Chopin's Nativity.--Exclusively a Piano-forte Composer.--His *Genre* as Pianist and Composer.--Aversion to Concert-giving.--Parisian Associations.--New Style of Technique demanded by his Works.--Unique Treatment of the Instrument.--Characteristics of Chopin's Compositions.

I.

Robert Schumann shares with Weber the honor of giving the earliest impulse to what may be called the romantic school of music, which has culminated in the operatic creations of Richard Wagner. Greatly to the gain of the world, his early aspirations as a mere player were crushed by the too intense zeal through which he attempted to perfect his manipulation, the mechanical contrivance he used having had the effect of paralyzing the muscular power of one of his hands. But this department of art work was nobly borne by his gifted wife, *nee* Clara Wieck, and Schumann concentrated his musical ambition in the higher field of composition, leaving behind him works not only remarkable for beauty of form, but for poetic richness of thought and imagination. Schumann composed songs, cantatas, operas, and symphonies, but it is in his works for the piano-forte that his idiosyncrasy was most strikingly embodied, and in which he has bequeathed the most precious inheritance to the world of art. All his powers were swept impetuously into one current, the poetic side of art, and alike as critic and composer he stands in a relation to the music of the pianoforte which places him on a pinnacle only less lofty than that of Beethoven.

Robert Schumann was born in the small Saxon town of Zwickau in the year 1810, and was designed by his father, a publisher and author of considerable reputation, for the profession of the law. The elder Schumann, though a man of talent and culture, had a deep distaste for his son's clearly displayed tendencies to music, and though he permitted him to study something of the science in the usual school-boy way (for music has always been a part of the educational course in Germany), he discouraged in every way Robert's passion. The boy had quickly become a clever player, and even at the age of eight had begun to put his ideas on paper. We are told by his biographers that he was accustomed to extemporize at school, and had such a knack in portraying the characteristics of his school-fellows in music as to make his purpose instantly recognizable. His father died when Schumann was only seventeen, and his mother, who was also bent on her son becoming a jurist, became his guardian. It was a severe battle between taste and duty, but love for his widowed mother conquered, and young Robert Schumann entered the University of Leipzig as a law student. It was with a feeling almost of despair that he wrote at this time, "I have decided upon law as my profession, and will work at it industriously, however cold and dry the beginning may be." Previously, however, he had spent a year in the household of Frederick Wieck, the distinguished teacher of music. So much he had exacted before succumbing to maternal pleading. At this time he first made the acquaintance of a charming and precocious child, Clara Wieck, who played such an important part in his future life.

Robert Schumann's law studies were inexpressibly tedious to him, and so he told his sympathetic professor, the learned Thibaut, author of the treatise "On the Purity of Music," in a characteristic manner. He went to the piano and played Weber's "Invitation to the Waltz," commenting on the different passages: "Now she speaks--that's the love prattle; now he speaks--that's the man's earnest voice; now both the lovers speak together "; concluding with the remark, "Isn't all that better far than anything that jurisprudence can utter?" The young student became quite popular in society as a pianist, heard Ernst and Paganini for the first time, and composed several works, among them the Toccata in D major. The genius for music would come to the fore in spite of jurisprudence. A vacation trip to Italy which the young man made gave fresh fuel to the flame, and he began to write the most passionate pleas to his mother that she should con sent to his adoption of a musical career. The distressed woman wrote to Wieck to know what he thought, and the answer was favorable to Robert's aspirations. Robert was intoxicated with his mother's concession, and he poured out his enthusiasm to Wieck: "Take me as I am, and, above all, bear with me. No blame shall depress me, no praise make me idle. Pails upon pails of very cold theory can not hurt me, and I will work at it without the least murmur."

Taking lodgings at the house of Wieck, Schumann devoted himself to pianoforte playing with intense ardor; but his zeal outran prudence. To hasten his proficiency and acquire an independent action for each finger, he contrived a mechanical apparatus which held the third finger of the right hand immovable, while the others went through their evolutions. The result was such a lameness of the hand that it was incurable, and young Schumann's career as a virtuoso was for ever checked. His deep sorrow, however, did not unman him long, for he turned his attention to the study of composition and counterpoint under Kupsch, and, afterward, Heinrich Dorn. He remained for three years under Wieck's roof, and the companionship of the child Clara, whose marvelous musical powers were the talk of Leipzig, was a sweet consolation to him in his troubles and his toil, though ten years his junior. The love, which became a part of his life, had already begun to flutter into unconscious being in his feeling for a shy and reserved little girl.

Schumann tells us that the year 1834 was the most important one of his life, for it witnessed the birth of the "N'eue Zeitschrift fur Musik," a journal which was to embody his notions of ideal music, and to be the organ of a clique of enthusiasts in lifting the art out of Philistinism and commonplace. The war-cry was "Reform in art," and never-ending battle against the little and conventional ideas which were believed then to be the curse of German music. Among the earlier contributors were Wieck, Schumke, Knorr, Banck, and Schumann himself, who wrote under the pseudonyms Florestan and Eusebius. Between his new journal and composing, Schumann was kept busy, but he found time to persuade himself that he was in love with Fraulein Ernestine von Fricken, a beautiful but somewhat frivolous damsel, who became engaged to the young composer and editor. Two years cooled off this passion, and a separation was mutually agreed on. Perhaps Schumann recognized something, in the lovely child who was swiftly blooming into maidenhood, which made his own inner soul protest against any other attachment.

II.

It would have been very strange indeed if two such natures as Clara Wieck and Robert Schumann had not gravitated toward each other during the almost constant intercourse between them which took place between 1835 and 1838. Clara, born in 1820, had been her father's pupil from her tenderest childhood, but the development of her musical gifts was not forced in such a way as to interfere with her health and the exuberance of her spirits. The exacting teacher was also a tender father and a man of ripe judgment, and he knew the bitter price which mere mental precocity so frequently has to pay for its existence.

But the young girl's gifts were so extraordinary, and withal her character so full of childish simplicity and gayety, that it was difficult to think of her as of the average child phenomenon. At the age of nine she could play Mozart's concertos, and Hummel's A minor Concerto for the orchestra, one of the most difficult of compositions. A year later she began to compose, and improvised without difficulty, for her lessons in counterpoint and harmony had kept pace with her studies of pianoforte technique. Paganini visited Leipzig at this period, and was so astonished at the little Clara's precocious genius that he insisted on her presence at all his concerts, and addressed her with the deepest respect as a fellow-artist. She first appeared in public concert at the age of eleven, in Leipzig, Weimar, and other places, playing Pixis, Moscheles, Mendelssohn, Beethoven, and Chopin. The latter of these composers was then almost unknown in Germany, and Clara Wieck, young as she was, contributed largely to making him popular. A year later she visited Paris in company with her father, and heard Chopin, Liszt, and Kalkbrenner, who on their part were delighted with the little artist, who, beneath the delicacy and timidity of the child, indicated extraordinary powers. Society received her with the most flattering approbation, and when her father allowed her to appear in concert her playing excited the greatest delight and surprise. Her improvisation specially displayed a vigor of imagination, a fine artistic taste, and a well-defined knowledge which justly called out the most enthusiastic recognition.

When Clara Wieck returned home, she gave herself up to work with fresh ardor, studying composition under Heinrich Dorn, singing under the celebrated Mieksch, and even violin-playing, so great was her ambition for musical accomplishments. From 1836 to 1838 she made an extended musical tour through Germany, and was welcomed as a musico-poetic ideal by the enthusiasts who gathered around her. The poet Grillparzer spoke of her as "the innocent child who first unlocked the casket in which Beethoven buried his mighty heart," and it must be confessed that Clara Wieck, even as a young girl, did more than any other pianist to develop a love of and appreciation for the music of the Titan of composers.

Long before Schumann distinctly contemplated the image of Clara as the beloved one, the half of his soul, he had divined her genius, and expressed his opinion of her in no stinted terms of praise. When she was as yet only thirteen, he had written of her in his journal: "As I know people who, having but just heard Clara, yet rejoice in their anticipation of their next occasion of hearing her, I ask, What sustains this continual interest in her? Is it the 'wonder child' herself, at whose stretches of tenths people shake their heads while they are amazed at them, or the most difficult difficulties which she sportively flings toward the public like flower garlands? Is it the special pride of the city with which a people regards its own natives? Is it that she presents to us the most interesting productions of recent art in as short a time as possible? Is it that the masses understand that art should not depend on the caprices of a few enthusiasts, who would direct us back to a century over whose corpse the wheels of time are hastening? I know not; I only feel that here we are subdued by genius, which men still hold in respect. In short, we here divine the presence of a power of which much is spoken, while few indeed possess it.... Early she drew the veil of Isis aside. Serenely the child looks up; older eyes, perhaps, would have been blinded by that radiant light.... To Clara we dare no longer apply the measuring scale of age, but only that of fulfillment.... Clara Wieck is the first German artist.... Pearls do not float on the surface; they must be sought for in the deep, often with danger. But Clara is an intrepid diver."

The child whose genius he admired ripened into a lovely young woman, and Schumann became conscious that there had been growing in his heart for years a deep, ardent love. He had fancied himself in love more than once, but now he felt that he could make no mistake as to the genuineness of his feelings. In 1836 he confessed his feelings to the object of his affections, and discovered that he not only loved but was loved, for two such gifted and sympathetic natures could hardly be thrown together for years without the growth of a mutual tenderness. The marriage project was not favored by Papa Wieck, much as he liked the young composer who had so long been his pupil and a member of his family circle. The father of Clara looked forward to a brilliant artistic career for his daughter, perhaps hoped to marry her to some serene highness, and Schumann's prospects were as yet very uncertain. So he took Clara on a long artistic journey through Germany, with a view of quenching this passion by absence and those public adulations which he knew Clara's genius would command. But nothing shook the devotion of her heart, and she insisted on playing the compositions of the young composer at her concerts, as well as those of Beethoven, Liszt, and Chopin, the latter two of whom were just beginning to be known and admired.

Hoping to overcome Papa Wieck's opposition by success, Schumann took his new journal to Vienna, and published it in that city, carrying on simultaneously with his editorial duties active labors in composition. The attempt to better his fortunes in Vienna, however, did not prove very successful, and after six months he returned again to Leipzig. Schumann's generous sympathy with other great musicians was signally shown in his very first Vienna experiences, for he immediately made a pious pilgrimage to the Waehring cemetery to offer his pious gift of flowers on the graves of Beethoven and Schubert. On Beethoven's grave he found a steel pen, which he preserved as a sacred treasure, and used afterward in writing his own finest musical fancies. He remembered, too, that the brother of Schubert, Ferdinand, was still living in a suburb of Vienna. "He knew me," Schumann says, "from my admiration for his brother, as I had publicly expressed it, and showed me many things. At last he let me look at the treasures of Franz Schubert's compositions, which he still possesses. The wealth that lay heaped up made me shudder with joy, what to take first, where to cease. Among other things, he also showed me the scores of several symphonies, of which many had never been heard, while others had been tried, but put back, on the score of their being too difficult and bombastic." One of these symphonies, that in C major, the largest and grandest in conception, Schumann chose and sent to Leipzig, where it was soon afterward produced under Mendelssohn's direction at one of the Ge-wandhaus concerts, and produced an immediate and profound sensation. For the first time the world witnessed, in a more expanded sphere, the powers of a composer the very beauties of whose songs had hitherto been fatal to his general success. During this period of Schumann's life the most important works he composed were the "Etudes Symphoniques," the famous "Carnival" dedicated to Liszt, the "Scenes of Childhood," the "Fantasia" dedicated to Liszt, the "Novellettes," and "Kreisleriana." As he writes to Heinrich Dorn: "Much music is the result of the contest I am passing through for Clara's sake." Schumann's compositions had been introduced to the public by the gifted interpretation of Clara Wieck, with whom it was a labor of love, and also by Franz Liszt, then rising almost on the top wave of his dazzling fame as a virtuoso. Liszt was a profound admirer of the less fortunate Schumann, and did everything possible to make him a favorite with the public, but for a long time in vain. Liszt writes of this as follows: "Since my first knowledge of his compositions I had played many of them in private circles at Milan and Vienna, without having succeeded in winning the approbation of my hearers. These works were, fortunately for them, too far above the then trivial level of taste to find a home in the superficial atmosphere of popular applause. The public did not fancy them, and few players understood them. Even in Leipzig, where I played the 'Carnival' at my second Gewandhaus concert, I did not obtain my customary applause. Musicians, even those who claimed to be connoisseurs also, carried too thick a mask over their ears to be able to comprehend that charming 'Carnival,' harmoniously framed as it is, and ornamented with such rich variety of artistic fancy. I did not doubt, however, but that this work would eventually win its place in general appreciation beside Beethoven's thirty-three variations on a theme by Diabelli (which work it surpasses, according to my opinion, in melody, richness, and inventiveness)." Both as a composer and writer on music, Schumann embodied his deep detestation of the Philistinism and commonplace which stupefied the current opinions of the time, and he represented in Germany the same battle of the romantic in art against what was known as the classical which had been carried on so fiercely in France by Berlioz, Liszt, and Chopin.

III.

The year 1840 was one of the most important in Schumann's life. In February he was created Doctor of Philosophy in the University of Jena, and, still more precious boon to the man's heart, Wieck's objections to the marriage with Clara had been so far melted away that he consented, though with reluctance, to their union. The marriage took place quietly at a little church in Schonfeld, near Leipzig. This year was one of the most fruitful of Schumann's life. His happiness burst forth in lyric forms. He wrote the amazing number of one hundred and thirty-eight songs, among which the more famous are the set entitled "Myrtles," the cycles of song from Heine, dedicated to Pauline Viardot, Chamisso's "Woman's Love and Life," and Heine's "Poet Love." Schumann as a song-writer must be called indeed the musical reflex of Heine, for his immortal works have the same passionate play of pathos and melancholy, the sharp-cut epigrammatic form, the grand swell of imagination, impatient of the limits set by artistic taste, which characterize the poet themes. Schumann says that nearly all the works composed at this time were written under

Clara's inspiration solely. Blest with the continual companionship of a woman of genius, as amiable as she was gifted, who placed herself as a gentle mediator between Schumann's intellectual life and the outer world, he composed many of his finest vocal and instrumental compositions during the years immediately succeeding his marriage; among them the cantata "Paradise and the Peri," and the "Faust" music. His own connection with public life was restricted to his position as teacher of piano-forte playing, composition, and score playing at the Leipzig Conservatory, while the gifted wife was the interpreter of his beautiful piano-forte works as an executant. A more perfect fitness and companionship in union could not have existed, and one is reminded of the married life of the poet pair, the Brownings. After four years of happy and quiet life, in which mental activity was inspired by the most delightful of domestic surroundings, an artistic tour to St. Petersburg was undertaken by Robert and Clara Schumann. Our composer did not go without reluctance. "Forgive me," he writes to a friend, "if I forbear telling you of my unwillingness to leave my quiet home." He seems to have had a melancholy premonition that his days of untroubled happiness were over. A genial reception awaited them at the Russian capital. They were frequently invited to the Winter Palace by the emperor and empress, and the artistic circles of the city were very enthusiastic over Mme. Schumann's piano-forte playing. Since the days of John Field, Clementi's great pupil, no one had raised such a furore among the music-loving Russians. Schumann's music, which it was his wife's dearest privilege to interpret, found a much warmer welcome than among his own countrymen at that date. In the Sclavonic nature there is a deep current of romance and mysticism, which met with instinctive sympathy the dreamy and fantastic thoughts which ran riot in Schumann's works.

On returning from the St. Petersburg tour, Schumann gave up the "Neue Zeitschrift," the journal which he had made such a powerful organ of musical revolution, and transferred it to Oswald Lorenz. Schumann's literary work is so deeply intertwined with his artistic life and mission that it is difficult, perhaps impossible, to separate the two. He had achieved a great work--he had planted in the German mind the thought that there was such a thing as progress and growth; that stagnation was death; and that genius was for ever shaping for itself new forms and developments. He had taught that no art is an end to itself, and that, unless it embodies the deep-seated longings and aspirations of men ever striving toward a loftier ideal, it becomes barren and fruitless--the mere survival of a truth whose need had ceased. He was the apostle of the musico-poetical art in Germany, and, both as author and composer, strove with might and main to educate his countrymen up to a clear understanding of the ultimate outcome of the work begun by Beethoven, Schubert, and Weber.

Schumann as a critic was eminently catholic and comprehensive. Deeply appreciative of the old lights of music, he received with enthusiasm all the fresh additions contributed by musical genius to the progress of his age. Eschewing the cold, objective, technical form of criticism, his method of approaching the work of others was eminently subjective, casting on them the illumination which one man of genius gives to another. The cast of his articles was somewhat dramatic and conversational, and the characters represented as contributing their opinions to the symposium of discussion were modeled on actual personages. He himself was personified under the dual form of Florestan and Eusebius, the "two souls in his breast"--the former, the fiery iconoclast, impulsive in his judgments and reckless in attacking prejudices; the latter, the mild, genial, receptive dreamer. Master Raro, who stood for Wieck, also typified the calm, speculative side of Schumann's nature. Chiara represented Clara Wieck, and personified the feminine side of art. So the various personages were all modeled after associates of Schumann, and, aside from the freshness and fascination which this method gave his style, it enabled him to approach his subjects from many sides. The name of the imaginary society was the Davids-bund, probably from King David and his celebrated harp, or perhaps in virtue of David's victories over the Philistines of his day.

As an illustration of Schumann's style and method of treating musical subjects, we can not do better than give his article on Chopin's "Don Juan Fantasia": "Eusebius entered not long ago. You know his pale face and the ironical smile with which he awakens expectation. I sat with Florestan at the piano-forte. Florestan is, as you know, one of those rare musical minds that foresee, as it were, coming novel or extraordinary things. But he encountered a surprise today. With the words 'Off with your hats, gentlemen! a genius,' Eusebius laid down a piece of music. We were not allowed to see the title-page. I turned over the music vacantly; the veiled enjoyment of music which one does not hear has something magical in it. And besides this, it seems that every composer has something different in the note forms. Beethoven looks differently from Mozart on paper; the difference resembles that between Jean Paul's and Goethe's prose. But here it seemed as if eyes, strange, were glancing up to me--flower eyes, basilisk eyes, peacock's eyes, maiden's eyes; in many places it looked yet brighter. I thought I saw Mozart's 'La ci darem la mano' wound through a hundred chords. **Leporello** seemed to wink at me, and **Don Juan** hurried past in his white mantle. 'Now play it,' said Florestan. Eusebius consented, and we, in the recess of a window, listened. Eusebius played as though he were inspired, and led forward countless forms filled with the liveliest, warmest life; it seemed that the inspiration of the moment gave to his fingers a power beyond the ordinary measure of their cunning. It is true that Florestan's whole applause was expressed in nothing but a happy smile, and the remark that the variations might have been written by Beethoven or Franz Schubert, had either of these been a piano virtuoso; but how surprised he was when, turning to the title-page, he read 'La ci darem la mano, varie pour le piano-forte, par Frederic Chopin, Ouvre 2,' and with what astonishment we both cried out, 'An Opus 2!' How our faces glowed as we wondered, exclaiming, 'That is something reasonable once more! Chopin? I never heard of the name--who can he be? In any case, a genius. Is not that **Zerlina's** smile, And **Leporello**, etc' I could not describe the scene. Heated with wine, Chopin, and our own enthusiasm, we went to Master Raro, who with a smile, and displaying but little curiosity for Chopin, said, 'Bring me the Chopin! I know you and your enthusiasm.' We promised to bring it the next day. Eusebius soon bade us good-night. I remained a short time with Master Raro. Florestan, who had been for some time without a habitation, hurried to my house through the moonlit streets. 'Chopin's variations,' he began, as if in a dream, 'are constantly running through my head; the whole is so dramatic and Chopin-like; the introduction is so concentrated. Do you remember **Leporello's** springs in thirds? That seems to me somewhat unfitted to the theme; but the theme--why did he write that in A flat? The variations, the finale, the adagio, these are indeed something; genius burns through every measure. Naturally, dear Julius, **Don Juan, Zerlina, Leporello, Massetto**, are the *dramatis persona; Zerlina's* answer in the theme has a sufficiently enamored character; the first variation expresses, a kind of coquettish coveteousness: the Spanish Grandee flirts amiably with the peasant girl in it. This leads of itself to the second, which is at once confidential, disputative, and comic, as though two lovers were chasing each other and laughing more than usual about it. How all this is changed in the third! It is filled with fairy music and moonshine; **Masetto** keeps at a distance, swearing audibly, but without any effect on **Don Juan**. And now the fourth--what do you think of it? Eusebius played it altogether correctly. How boldly, how wantonly, it springs forward to meet the man! though the adagio (it seems quite natural to me that Chopin repeats the first part) is in B flat minor, as it should be, for in its commencement it presents a beautiful moral warning to **Don Juan**. It is at once so mischievous and beautiful that **Leporello** listens behind the hedge, laughing and jesting that oboes and clarionettes enchantingly allure, and that the B flat major in full bloom correctly designates the first kiss of love. But all this is nothing compared to the last (have you any more wine, Julius?). That is the whole of Mozart's finale, popping champagne corks, ringing glasses, **Leporello's** voice between, the grasping, torturing demons, the fleeing **Don Juan**--and then the end, that beautifully soothes and closes all.' Florestan concluded by saying that he had never experienced feelings similar to those awakened by the finale. When the evening sunlight of a beautiful day creeps up toward the highest peaks, and when the last beam vanishes, there comes a moment when the white Alpine giants close their eyes. We feel that we have witnessed a heavenly apparition. 'And now awake to new dreams, Julius, and sleep.' 'Dear Flores-tan,' I answered, 'these confidential feelings, are perhaps praiseworthy, although somewhat subjective; but as deeply as yourself I bend before Chopin's spontaneous genius, his lofty aim, his mastership; and after that we fell asleep.'" This article was the first journalistic record of Chopin's genius.

IV.

When Schumann gave up his journal in 1845 he moved to Dresden, and he began to suffer severely from the dreadful disorder to which he fell a victim twelve years later. This disease--an abnormal formation of bone in the brain--afflicted him with excruciating pains in the head, sleeplessness, fear of death, and strange auricular delusions. A sojourn at Parma, where he had complete repose and a course of sea-bathing, partially restored his health, and he gave himself up to musical composition again. During the next three years, up to 1849, Schumann wrote some of his finest works, among which may be mentioned his opera "Genoviva," his Second symphony, the cantata "The Rose's Pilgrimage," more beautiful songs, much piano-forte and concerted music, and the musical illustrations of Byron's "Manfred," which latter is one of his greatest orchestral works.

During the years 1850 to 1854 Schumann composed his "Rhenish Symphony," the overtures to the "Bride of Messina" and "Hermann and Dorothea," and many vocal and piano-forte works. He accepted the post of musical director at Dusseldorf in 1850, removed to that city with his wife and children, and, on arriving, the artistic pair were received with a civic banquet. The position was in many respects agreeable, but the responsibilities were too great for Schumann's declining health, and probably hastened his death. In 1853 Robert and Clara Schumann made a grand artistic tour through Holland, which resembled a triumphal procession, so great was the musical enthusiasm called out. When they returned Schumann's malady returned with double force, and on February 27, 1854, he attempted to end his misery by jumping into the Rhine. Madness had seized him with a clutch which was never to be released, except at short intervals. Every possible care was lavished on him by his heartbroken and devoted wife, and the assiduous attention of the friends who reverenced the genius now for ever quenched. The last two years of his life were spent in the private insane asylum at Endenich, near Bonn, where he died July 20, 1856. Schumann possessed a wealth of musical imagination which, if possibly equaled in a few instances, is nowhere surpassed in the records of his art. For him music possessed all the attributes inherent in the other arts--absolute color and flexibility of form. That he attempted to express these phases of art expression, with an almost boundless trust in their applicability to tone and sound, not unfrequently makes them obscure to the last degree, but it also gave much of his composition a richness, depth, and subtilty of suggestive power which place them in a unique niche, and will always preserve them as objects of the greatest interest to the musical student. There is no doubt that his increasing mental malady is evident in the chaotic character of some of his later orchestral compositions, but, in those works composed during his best period, splendor of imagination goes hand in hand with genuine art treatment. This is specially noticeable in the songs and the piano-forte works. Schumann was essentially lyrical and subjective, though his intellectual breadth and culture (almost unrivaled among his musical compeers) always kept him from narrowness as a composer. He led the van in the formation of that pictorial and descriptive style of music which has asserted itself in German music, but his essentially lyric personality in his attitude to the outer world presented the external thoroughly saturated and modified by his own moods and feelings.

In his piano-forte works we find his most complete and satisfactory development as the artist composer. Here the world, with its myriad impressions, its facts, its purposes, its tendencies, met the man and commingled in a series of exquisite creations, which are true tone pictures. In this domain Beethoven alone was worthy to be compared with him, though the animus and scheme of the Beethoven piano-forte works grew out of a totally different method.

In personal appearance Schumann bore the marks of the man of genius. As he reached middle age we are told of him that his figure was of middle height, inclined to stoutness, that his bearing was dignified, his movements slow. His features, though irregular, produced an agreeable impression; his forehead was broad and high, the nose heavy, the eyes excessively bright, though generally veiled and downcast, the mouth delicately cut, the hair thick and brown, his cheeks full and ruddy. His head was squarely formed, of an intensely powerful character, and the whole expression of his face sweet and genial. Even when young he was distinguished by a kind of absent-mindedness that prevented him from taking much part in conversation. Once, it is said, he entered a lady's drawing-room to call, played a few chords on the piano, and smilingly left without speaking a word. But, among intimate friends, he could be extraordinarily fluent and eloquent in discussing an interesting topic. He was conscious of his own shyness, and once wrote to a friend: "I shall be very glad to see you here. In me, however, you must not expect to find much. I scarcely ever speak except in the evening, and most in playing the piano." His wife was the crowning blessing of his life. She was not only his consoler, but his other intellectual life, for she, with her great powers as a virtuoso, interpreted his music to the world, both before and after his death. It has rarely been the lot of an artist to see his most intimate feelings and aspirations embodied to the world by the genius of the mother of his children. Well did Ferdinand Hiller write of this artist couple: "What love beautified his life! A woman stood beside him, crowned with the starry circlet of genius, to whom he seemed at once the father to his daughter, the master to the scholar, the bridegroom to the bride, the saint to the disciple."

Clara Schumann still lives, though becoming fast an old woman in years, if still young in heart, and still able to win the admiration of the musical world by her splendid playing. Berlioz, who heard her in her youth, pronounced her the greatest virtuoso in Germany, in one of his letters to Heine; and while she was little more than a child she had gained the heartiest admiration in England, France, and Germany. Henry Chorley heard her at Leipzig in 1839, and speaks of "the organ-playing on the piano of Mme. Schumann (better known in England under the name of Clara Wieck), who commands her instrument with the enthusiasm of a sibyl and the grasp of a man." Since Schumann's death, Mme. Schumann has been known as the exponent of her husband's works, which she has performed in Germany and England with an insight, a power of conception, and a beauty of treatment which have contributed much to the recognition of his remarkable genius.

V.

The name of Frederic Francis Chopin is so closely linked in the minds of musical students with that of Schumann in that art renaissance which took place almost simultaneously in France and Germany, when so many daring and original minds broke loose from the petrifactions of custom and tradition, that we shall not venture to separate them here. Chopin was too timid and gentle to be a bold aggressor, like Berlioz, Liszt, and Schumann, but his whole nature responded to the movement, and his charming and most original compositions, which glow with the fire of a genius perhaps narrow in its limits, have never been surpassed for their individuality and poetic beauty. The present brief sketch of Chopin does not propose to consider his life biographically, full of pathos and romance as that life may be.[2]

Schumann, in his "N'eue Zeitschrift," sums up the characteristics of the Polish composer admirably; "Genius creates kingdoms, the smaller states of which are again divided by a higher hand among talents, that these may organize details which the former, in its thousand-fold activity, would be unable to perfect. As Hummel, for example, followed the call of Mozart, clothing the thoughts of that master in a flowing, sparkling robe, so Chopin followed Beethoven. Or, to speak more simply,

2   See article Chopin, in "Great German Composers."

as Hummel imitated the style of Mozart in detail, rendering it enjoyable to the virtuoso on one particular instrument, so Chopin led the spirit of Beethoven into the concert-room.

"Chopin did not make his appearance accompanied by an orchestral army, as great genius is accustomed to do; he only possessed a small cohort, but every soul belongs to him to the last hero.

"He is the pupil of the first masters--Beethoven, Schubert, Field. The first formed his mind in boldness, the second his heart in tenderness, the third his hand to its flexibility. Thus he stood well provided with deep knowledge in his art, armed with courage in the full consciousness of his power, when in the year 1830 the great voice of the people arose in the West. Hundreds of youths had waited for the moment; but Chopin was the first on the summit of the wall, behind which lay a cowardly renaissance, a dwarfish Philistinism, asleep. Blows were dealt right and left, and the Philistines awoke angrily, crying out, 'Look at the impudent one!' while others behind the besieger cried, 'The one of noble courage.'

"Besides this, and the favorable influence of period and condition, fate rendered Chopin still more individual and interesting in endowing him with an original pronounced nationality; Polish, too, and because this nationality wanders in mourning robes in the thoughtful artist, it deeply attracts us. It was well for him that neutral Germany did not receive him too warmly at first, and that his genius led him straight to one of the great capitals of the world, where he could freely poetize and grow angry. If the powerful autocrat of the North knew what a dangerous enemy threatens him in Chopin's works in the simple melodies of his mazurkas, he would forbid music. Chopin's works are cannons buried in flowers.... He is the boldest, proudest poet soul of to-day."

But Schumann could have said something more than this, and added that Chopin was a musician of exceptional attainments, a virtuoso of the very highest order, a writer for the piano pure and simple preeminent beyond example, and a master of a unique and perfect style.

Chopin was born of mixed French and Polish parentage, February 8, 1810, at Zelazowa-Wola, near Warsaw. He was educated at the Warsaw Conservatory, and his eminent genius for the piano shone at this time most unmistakably. He found in the piano-forte an exclusive organ for the expression of his thoughts. In the presence of this confidential companion he forgot his shyness and poured forth his whole soul. A passionate lover of his native country, and burning with those aspirations for freedom which have made Poland since its first partition a volcano ever ready to break forth, the folk-themes of Poland are at the root of all of Chopin's compositions, and in the waltzes and mazurkas bearing his name we find a passionate glow and richness of color which make them musical poems of the highest order.

Chopin's art position, both as a pianist and composer, was a unique one. He was accustomed to say that the breath of the concert-room stifled him, whereas Liszt, his intimate friend and fellow-artist, delighted in it as a war-horse delights in the tumult of battle. Chopin always shrank from the display of his powers as a mere executant. To exhibit his talents to the public was an offense to him, and he only cared for his remarkable technical skill as a means of placing his fanciful original poems in tone rightly before the public. It was with the greatest difficulty that his intimate friends, Liszt, Meyerbeer, Nourrit, Delacroix, Heine, Mme. George Sand, Countess D'Agoult, and others, could persuade him to appear before large mixed audiences. His genius only shone unconstrained as a player in the society of a few chosen intimate friends, with whom he felt a perfect sympathy, artistic, social, and intellectual. Exquisite, fastidious, and refined, Chopin was loss an aristocrat from political causes, or even by virtue of social caste, than from the fact that his art nature, which was delicate, feminine, and sensitive, shrank from all companions except those molded of the finest clay. We find this sense of exclusiveness and isolation in all of the Chopin music, as in some quaint, fantastic, ideal world, whose master would draw us up to his sphere, but never descend to ours.

In the treatment of the technical means of the piano-forte, he entirely wanders from the old methods. Moscheles, a great pianist in an age of great players, gave it up in despair, and confessed that he could not play Chopin's music. The latter teaches the fingers to serve his own artistic uses, without regard to the notions of the schools. It is said that M. Kalkbrenner advised Chopin to attend his classes at the Paris Conservatoire, that the latter might learn the proper fingering. Chopin answered his officious adviser by placing one of his own "Etudes" before him, and asking him to play it. The failure of the pompous professor was ludicrous, for the old-established technique utterly failed to do it justice. Chopin's end as a player was to faithfully interpret the poetry of his own composition. His genius as a composer taught him to make innovations in piano-forte effects. He was thus not only a great inventor as a composer, but as regards the technique of the piano-forte. He not only told new things well worth hearing which the world would not forget, but devised new ways of saying them, and it mattered but little to him whether his more forcible and passionate dialectic offended what Schumann calls musical Philistinism or no. Chopin formed a school of his own which was purely the outcome of his genius, though as Schumann, in the extract previously quoted, justly says: "He was molded by the deep poetic spirit of Beethoven, with whom form only had value as it expressed truthfully and beautifully symmetry of conception."

The forms of Chopin's compositions grew out of the keyboard of the piano, and their *genre* is so peculiar that it is nearly impracticable to transpose them for any other instrument. Some of the noted contemporary violinists have attempted to transpose a few of the Nocturnes and Etudes, but without success. Both Schumann and Liszt succeeded in adapting Paganini's most complex and difficult violin works for the piano-forte, but the compositions of Chopin are so essentially born to and of the one instrument that they can not be well suited to any other. The cast of the melody, the matchless beauty and swing of the rhythm, his ingenious treatment of harmony, and the chromatic changes and climaxes through which the motives are developed, make up a new chapter in the history of the piano-forte.

Liszt, in his life of Chopin, says of him: "His character was indeed not easily understood. A thousand subtle shades, mingling, crossing, contradicting, and disguising each other, rendered it almost undecipherable at first view; kind, courteous, affable, and almost of joyous manners, he would not suffer the secret convulsions which agitated him to be ever suspected. His works, concertos, waltzes, sonatas, ballades, polonaises, mazurkas, nocturnes, scherzi, all reflect a similar enigma in a most poetical and romantic form."

Chopin's moral nature was not cast in an heroic mold, and he lacked the robust intellectual marrow which is essential to the highest forms of genius in art as well as in literature and affairs, though it is not safe to believe that he was, as painted by George Sand and Liszt, a feeble youth, continually living at death's door in an atmosphere of moonshine and sentimentality. But there can be no question that the whole bent of Chopin's temperament and genius was melancholy, romantic, and poetic, and that frequently he gives us mere musical moods and reveries, instead of well-defined and well-developed ideas. His music perhaps loses nothing, for, if it misses something of the clear, inspiring, vigorous quality of other great composers, it has a subtle, dreamy, suggestive beauty all its own.

The personal life of Chopin was singularly interesting. His long and intimate connection with George Sand; the circumstances under which it was formed; the blissful idyl of the lovers in the isle of Majorca; the awakening from the dream, and the separation--these and other striking circumstances growing out of a close association with what was best in Parisian art and life, invest the career of the man, aside from his art, with more than common charm to the mind of the reader. Having touched on these phases of Chopin's life at some length in a previous volume of this series, we must reluctantly pass them by.

In closing this imperfect review of the Polish composer, it is enough to say that the present generation has more than sustained the judgment of his own as to the unique and wonderful beauty of his compositions. Hardly any concert programme is considered complete without one or more numbers selected from his works; and though there are but few pianists, even in a day when Chopin as a stylist has been a study, who can do his subtle and wonderful fancies justice, there is no composer for the piano-forte who so fascinates the musical mind.

THALBERG AND GOTTSCHALK.

I.

One of the most remarkable of the great piano-forte virtuosos was unquestionably Sigismond Thalberg, an artist who made a profound sensation in two hemispheres, and filled a large space in the musical world for more than forty-five years. Originally a disciple of the Viennese school of piano-forte playing, a pupil of Mosche-les, and a rigid believer in making the instrument which was the medium of his talent sufficient unto itself, wholly indifferent to the daring and boundless ambition which made his great rival, Franz Liszt, pile Pelion on Ossa in his grasp after new effects, Thalberg developed virtuoso-ism to its extreme degree by a mechanical dexterity which was perhaps unrivaled. But the fingers can not express more than rests in the heart and brain to give to their skill, and Thalberg, with all his immense talent, seems to have lacked the divine spark of genius. It goes without saying, to those who are familiar with the current cant of criticism, that the word genius is often applied in a very loose and misleading manner. But, in all estimates of art and artists, where there are two clearly defined factors, imagination or formative power and technical dexterity, it would seem that there should not be any error in deciding on the propriety of such a word as a measure of the quality of an artist's gifts. The lack of the creative impulse could not be mistaken in Thalberg's work, whether as player or composer. But the ability to execute all that came within the scope of his sympathies or intelligence was so prodigious that the world was easily dazzled into forgetting his deficiencies in the loftier regions of art. Trifles are often very significant. What, for example, could more vividly portray an artist's tendencies than the description of Thalberg by Moscheles, who knew him more thoroughly than any other contemporary, and felt a keener sympathy with his *genre* as an artist than with the more striking originality of Chopin and Liszt. Moscheles writes:

"I find his introduction of harp effects on the piano quite original. His theme, which lies in the middle part, is brought out clearly in relief with an accompaniment of complicated arpeggios which reminds me of a harp. The audience is amazed. He himself sits immovably calm; his whole bearing as he sits at the piano is soldierlike; his lips are tightly compressed and his coat buttoned closely. He told me he acquired this attitude of self-control by smoking a Turkish pipe while practicing his piano-forte exercises: the length of the tube was so calculated as to keep him erect and motionless." This exact discipline and mechanism were not merely matters of technical culture; they were the logical outcome of the man and surely a part of himself. But within his limits, fixed as these were, Thalberg was so great that he must be conceded to be one of the most striking and brilliant figures of an age fecund in fine artists.

Thalberg was born at Geneva, January 7, 1812, and was the natural son of Prince

Dietrichstein, an Austrian nobleman, temporarily resident in that city. His talent for music, inherited from both sides, for his mother was an artist and his father an amateur of no inconsiderable skill, became obvious at a very tender age, following the law which so generally holds in music that superior gifts display themselves at an early period. These indications of nature were not ignored, for the boy was placed under instruction before he had completed his sixth year. It is a little singular that his first teacher was not a pianist, though a very superior musician. Mittag was one of the first bassoonists of his times, and, in addition to his technical skill, a thoroughly accomplished man in the science of his profession. Thalberg was accustomed to attribute the wonderfully rich and mellow tone which characterized his playing to the influence and training of Mittag. From this instructor the future great pianist passed to the charge of the distinguished Hummel, who was not only one of the greatest virtuosos of the age, but ranked by his admirers as only a little less than Beethoven himself in his genius for pianoforte compositions, though succeeding generations have discredited his former fame by estimating him merely a "dull classic." Contemporaneously with his pupilage under Hummel, he studied the theory of music with Simon Sechter, an eminent contrapuntist. Even at this early age, for Thalberg must have been less than ten years old, he impressed all by the great precision of his fingering and the instinctive ease with which he mastered the most difficult mechanism of the art of playing. At the age of fourteen young Thalberg went to London in the household of his father, who had been appointed imperial ambassador to England, and the youth was then placed under the instruction of the great pianist Moscheles. The latter speaks of Thalberg as the most distinguished of his pupils, and as being, even at that age, already an artist of distinction and mark. It was a source of much pleasure to Moscheles that his brilliant scholar, who played much at private soirees, was not only recognized by the ***dilletante*** public generally, but by such veteran artists as Clementi and Cramer. Moscheles, in his diary, speaks of the wonderful brilliancy of a grand fancy dress ball given by Thalberg's princely father at Covent Garden Theatre. Pit, stalls, and proscenium were formed into one grand room, in which the crowd promenaded. The costumes were of every conceivable variety, and many of the most gorgeous description. The spectators, in full dress, sat in the boxes; on the stage was a court box, occupied by the royal family; and bands played in rooms adjoining for small parties of dancers.

"You will have some idea," wrote Mme. Moscheles, in a letter, "of the crowd at this ball, when I tell you that we left the ballroom at two o'clock and did not get to the prince's carriage till four." One of the interesting features of this ball was that the boy Thalberg played in one of the smaller rooms before the most distinguished people present, including the royal family, all crowding in to hear the youthful virtuoso, whose tacit recognition by his father had already opened to him the most brilliant drawing-rooms in London.

Thalberg did not immediately begin to perform in public, but, on returning to Vienna in 1827, played continually at private soirees, where he had the advantage of being heard and criticised by the foremost amateurs and musicians of the Austrian capital. It had some time since become obvious to the initiated that another great player was about to be launched on his career. The following year the young artist tried his hand at composition, for he published variations on themes from Weber's "Euryanthe," which were well received. Thalberg in after-years spoke of all his youthful productions with disdain, but his early works displayed not a little of the brilliant style of treatment which subsequently gave his fantasias a special place among compositions for the piano-forte.

It was not till 1830 that young Thalberg fairly began his career as a traveling player. The cities of Germany received him with the most *eclatant* admiration, and his feats of skill as a performer were trumpeted by the newspapers and musical journals as something unprecedented in the art of pianism. From Germany Thalberg proceeded to France and England, and his audiences were no less pronounced in their recognition. Liszt had already been before him in Paris, and Chopin arrived about the same time. Kalkbrenner, Ferdinand Hiller, and Field were playing, but the splendid, calm beauty of Thalberg's style instantly captivated the public, and elicited the most extravagant and delighted applause not only from the public, but from enlightened connoisseurs.

To follow the course of Thalberg's pianoforte achievements in his musical travels through Europe would be merely to repeat a record of uninterrupted successes. He disarmed envy and criticism everywhere, and even those disposed to withhold a frank and generous acknowledgment of his greatness did not dare to question powers of execution which seemed without a technical flaw. During his travels Thalberg composed a concerto for piano and orchestra, to play at his concerts. But this species of composition was so obviously unsuited to his abilities that he quickly forsook it, and thenceforward devoted his efforts exclusively to the instrument of which he was such an eminent master. A more extensive ambition had been rebuked in more ways than one. He composed two operas, "Fiorinda" and "Christine," and of course easily yielded to the entreaties of his admirers to have them produced. But it was clearly evident that his musical idiosyncrasy, though magnificent of its kind, was limited in range, and after the failure of his operas and attempts at orchestral writing Thalberg calmly accepted the situation.

In the year 1834 Thalberg was appointed pianist of the Imperial Chamber to the court of Austria, and accompanied the Emperor Ferdinand to Toplitz, where a convocation of the European sovereigns took place. His performances were warmly received by the assembled monarchs, and he was overwhelmed with presents and congratulations. Thalberg's way throughout the whole of his life was strewn with roses, and, though his career did not present the same romantic incidents which make the life of Franz Liszt so picturesque, it was attended by the same lavish favors of fortune. From one patron he received the gift of a fine estate, from another a magnificent city mansion in Vienna, and testimonials, like snuff-boxes set with diamonds, jeweled court-swords, superbly set portraits of his royal and imperial patrons, and costly jewelry, poured in on him continually. Imperial orders from Austria and Russia were bestowed on him, and hardly any mark of favor was denied him by that good fortune which had been auspicious to him from his very birth. In 1845, while still in the service of the Austrian emperor, though he did not intermit his musical tours through the principal European cities, Thalberg married the charming widow, whom he had known and admired before her marriage, the daughter of the great singer Lablache, Mme. Bouchot, whose first husband had been the distinguished French painter of that name. The marriage was a happy one, though scandal, which loves to busy itself about the affairs of musical celebrities, did not fail to associate Thalberg's name with several of the most beautiful women of his time. Mile. Thalberg, a daughter of this marriage, made her *debut* with considerable success in London, in 1874.

Thalberg's first visit to America was in 1853, and he came again in 1857, to more than repeat the enthusiastic reception with which he was greeted by music-loving Americans. Musical culture at that time had not attained the refinement and knowledge which now make an audience in one of our greater cities as fastidious and intelligent as can be found anywhere in the world. But Thalberg's wonderful playing, though lacking in the fire, glow, and impetuosity which would naturally most arouse the less cultivated musical sense, created a *furore*, which has never been matched since, among those who specially prided themselves on being good judges. He extended both tours to Cuba, Mexico, and South America, and it is said took away with him larger gains than he had ever made during the same period in Europe.

During the latter years of Thalberg's life he spent much of his time in elegant ease at his fine country estate near Naples, only giving concerts at some few of the largest European capitals, like London and Paris. He became an enthusiastic wine-grower, and wine from his estate gained a medal at the Exposition Universelle of 1867. Many of his best piano-forte compositions date from the period when he had given up the active pursuit of virtuosoism. His works comprise a concerto, three sonatas, many nocturnes, rondos, and etudes, about thirty fantasias, two operas, and an instruction series, which latter has been adopted by many of the best teachers, and has been the means of forming a number of able pupils. This fine artist died at his Neapolitan estate, April 27, 1871.

II.

Thalberg had but little sympathy with the dreamy romanticism which found such splendid exponents, while he was yet in his early youth, in Schumann, Chopin, and Liszt. Imagination in its higher functions he seemed to lack. A certain opulence and picturesqueness of fancy united in his artistic being with an intelligence both lucid and penetrating, and a sense of form and symmetry almost Greek in its fastidiousness. The sweet, vague, passionate aspiration^, the sensibility that quivers with every breath of movement from the external world, he could not understand. Placidity, grace, and repose he had in perfection. Yet he was very highly appreciated by those who had little in common with his artistic nature. As, for example, Robert Schumann writes of Thalberg and his playing, on the occasion of a charity concert, given in Leipzig in 1841: "In his passing flight the master's pinions rested here awhile, and, as from the angel's pinions in one of Rucker's poems, rubies and other precious stones fell from them and into indigent hands, as the master ordained it. It is difficult to say anything new of one who has been so praise beshow-ered as he has. But every earnest virtuoso is glad to hear one thing said at any time--that he has progressed in his art since he last delighted us. This best of all praise we are conscientiously able to bestow on Thalberg; for, during the last two years that we have not heard him, he has made astonishing additions to his acquirements, and, if possible, moves with greater boldness, grace, and freedom than ever. His playing seemed to have the same effect on every one, and the delight that he probably feels in it himself was shared by all. True virtuosity gives us something more than mere flexibility and execution: aman may mirror his own nature in it, and in Thalberg's playing it becomes clear to all that he is one of the favored ones of fortune, one ac-customed to wealth and elegance. Accompanied by happiness, bestowing pleasure, he commenced his career; under such circumstances he has so far pursued it, and so he will probably continue it. The whole of yesterday evening and every number that he played gave us a proof of this. The public did not seem to be there to judge, but only to enjoy; they were as certain of enjoyment as the master was of his art."

Thalberg in his appearance had none of the traditional wild picturesqueness of style and manner which so many distinguished artists, even Liszt himself, have thought it worth while to carry perhaps to the degree of affectation. Smoothly shaven, quiet, eminently respectable-looking, his handsome, somewhat Jewish-looking face composed in an expression of unostentatious good breeding, he was wont to seat himself at the piano with all the simplicity of one doing any common-place thing. He had the air of one who respected himself, his art, and the public. His performance was in an exquisitely artistic sense that of the gentleman, perfect, polished, and elaborately wrought. The distinguished American litterateur, Mr. George William Curtis, who heard him in New York in 1857, thus wrote of him: "He is a proper artist in this, that he comprehends the character of his instrument. He neither treats it as a violoncello nor a full orchestra. Those who in private have enjoyed the pleasure of hearing--or, to use a more accurate epithet, of seeing-- Strepitoso, that friend of mankind, play the piano, will understand what we mean when we speak of treating the piano as if it were an orchestra. Strepitoso storms and slams along the keyboard until the tortured instrument gives up its musical soul in despair and breaks its heart of melody by cracking all its strings.... Every instrument has its limitations, but Strepitoso will tolerate no such theory. He extracts music from his piano, not as if he were sifting the sands for gold, but as if he were raking oysters.... Now, Thalberg's manner is different from Strepitoso's. He plays the piano; that is the phrase which describes his performance. He plays it quietly and suavely. You could sit upon the lawn on a June night and hear with delight the sounds that trickled through the moonlight from the piano of this master. They would not melt your soul in you; they would not touch those longings that, like rays of starry light, respond to the rays of the stars; they would not storm your heart with the yearning passion of their strains, but you would confess it was a good world as you listened, and be glad you lived in it--you would be glad of your home and all that made it homelike; the moonlight as you listened would melt and change, and your smiling eyes would seem to glitter in cheerful sunlight as Thalberg ended."

Thalberg's style was, perhaps, the best possible illustration of the legitimate effects of the pianoforte carried to the highest by as perfect a technique as could possibly be attained by human skill.

That he lacked poetic fire and passion, that the sense of artistic restraint and a refined fastidiousness chilled and fettered him, is doubtlessly true. Whether the absence of the imaginative warmth and vigor which suffuse a work of art with the glow of something that can not be fully expressed, and kindle the thoughts of the hearer to take hitherto unknown flights, is fully compensated for by that repose and symmetry of style which know exactly what it wishes to express, and, being perfect master of the means of expression, puts forth an exact measure of effort and then stops as if shut down by an iron wall--this is an open question, and must be answered according to one's art theories. The exquisite modeling of a Benvenuto Cellini vase, wrought with patient elaboration into a thing of unsurpassable beauty, does not invoke as high a sense of pleasure as an heroic statue or noble painting by some great master, but of its kind the pleasure is just as complete. Apart from Thalberg's power as a player, however, there was something captivating in the quality of his talent, which, though not creative, was gifted with the power of seizing the very essence of the music to be interpreted. A striking example of this is shown in the fantasias he composed on the different operas, a form of writing which reached its perfection in him. His own contribution is simply a most delightful setting of the melodies of his subject, and the whole is steeped in the very atmosphere and feeling of the original, as if the master himself had done the work.

A good example is the fantasia on Mozart's "Don Giovanni." The little, wild, unformed melodies rustle in quick gusts along the keys as if wavering shadows, yet with all the familiar rhythm and family likeness, filling the mind of the hearer with the atmosphere and necessity of what is to follow, while gradually the full harmonies unfold themselves. The introduction of the minuet is one of the most striking portions. The scene of the minuet in the opera is a vision of rural loveliness and repose, whispering of flowers, fields, and happy flying hours. All this becomes poetized, and the music seems to imply rich reaches of odorous garden and moonlight, whispering foliage, and nightingales mad with the delight of their own singing, and a palace on the lawn sounding with riotous mirth. The player-composer weaves the glamour of such a dream, and the hearer finds himself strolling in imagination through the moonlit garden, listening to the birds, the waters, and the rustling leaves, while the stately beat of the minuet comes throbbing through it all, calling up the vision of gayly dressed cavaliers and beautiful ladies fantastically moving to the tune. Such poetic sentiment as this of the purely picturesque sort was in large measure Thalberg's possession, but he could never understand that turbulent ground-swell of passion which music can also powerfully express, and by which the soul is lifted up to the heights of ecstasy or plunged in depths of melancholy. Music as a vehicle for such meanings was mere Egyptian hieroglyphic, utterly beyond his limitation, absolute bathos and absurdity.

It is doubtful whether any player ever possessed a more wonderfully trained mechanism; the smallest details were polished and finished with the utmost care, the scales marvels of evenness, the shakes rivaling the trill of a canary bird. His arpeggios at times rolled like the waves of the sea, and at others resembled folds of transparent lace floating airily with the movements of the wearer. The octaves were wonderfully accurate, and the chords appeared to be struck by steel mallets instead of fingers. He was called the Bayard of pianists, "le Chevalier sans peur et sans reproche." His tone was noble, yet mellow and delicate, and the gradations between his forte and piano were traced most exquisitely. In a word, technical execution could go no further. It is said that he never played a piece in public till he had absolutely made it the property of his fingers. He was the first to divide the melody between the two hands, making the right hand perform a brilliant figure in the higher register, while the left hand exhibited a full and rich bass part, supplementing it with an accompaniment in chords. It was this characteristic which made his fantasias so unique and interesting, in spite of their lack of originality of motive, as compositions. Almost all writers for the piano have since adopted this device, even the great Mendelssohn using it in some of his concertos and "Songs without Words"; and in many cases it has been transformed into a mere trick of arrant musical charlatanism, designed to cover up with a sham glitter the utter absence of thought and motive. No better suggestion of the dominant characteristic of Thal-berg as a pianist can be found than a critical word of his friend Moscheles: "The proper ground for finger gymnastics is to be found in Thalberg's latest compositions; for mind [Geist], give me Schumann."

III.

During Thalberg's first visit to America he had an active and dangerous rival in the young and brilliant pianist, Louis Moreau Gottschalk, who was as fresh to New York audiences as Thalberg himself, though the latter had the advantage over his young competitor in a fame which was almost world-wide. Of American pianists Louis Gottschalk stands confessedly at the head by virtue of remarkable native gifts, which, had they been assisted by greater industry and ambition, might easily have won him a very eminent rank in Europe as well as in his own country. An easy, pleasure-loving, tropical nature, flexible, facile, and disposed to sacrifice the future to the present, was the only obstacle to the attainment to a place level with the foremost artists of his age.

Edward Gottschalk, who came to America in his young manhood and settled in New Orleans, and his wife, a French Creole lady, had five children, of whom the future pianist was the eldest, born in 1829. His feeling for music manifested itself when he was three years old by his ability to play a melody on the piano which he had heard. Instantly he was strong enough, he was placed under the instruction of a good teacher, and no pains were spared to develop his precocious talent. At the age of six he had made such progress on the piano that he was also instructed on the violin, and soon was able to play pieces of more than ordinary difficulty with taste and expression. We are told that the lad gave a benefit concert at the age of eight to assist an unfortunate violin-player, with considerable success, and was soon in great request at evening parties as a child phenomenon. The propriety of sending the little Louis to Paris had long been discussed, and it was finally accomplished in 1842.

On reaching Paris he was first put under the teaching of Charles Halle, but, as the latter master was a little careless, he was replaced by M. Camille Stamaty, who had the reputation of being the ablest professor in the city. The following year he began the study of harmony and counterpoint with M. Malidan, and the rapid progress he evinced in his studies was of a kind to justify his parents in their wish to devote him to the career of a pianist.

Young Louis Gottschalk was much petted in the aristocratic salons of Paris, to which he had admission through his aunts, the Comtesse de Lagrange and the Comtesse de Bourjally. His remarkable musical gifts, and more especially his talent for improvisation, excited curiosity and admiration, even in a city where the love of musical novelty had been sated by a continual supply of art prodigies. Young as he was, he wrote at this time not a few charming compositions, which were in after-years occasional features of his concerts. His delicate constitution succumbed under hard work, and for a while a severe attack of typhoid fever interrupted his studies. On his recovery, our young artist spent a few months in the Ardennes. On returning to Paris, he became the pupil of Hector Berlioz, who felt a deep interest in the young American, as an art prodigy from a land of savages in harmony, and devoted himself so assiduously to the study that he declined an invitation from the Spanish queen to become a guest of the court at Madrid.

An amusing incident occurred in a pedestrian trip which he made to the Vosges in 1846. He had forgotten his passport, and, on arriving at a small town, was arrested by a gendarme and taken before the maire. The latter official was reading a newspaper containing a notice of his last concert, and through this means he assured the worthy functionary of his identity, and was cordially welcomed to the hospitality of the official residence.

His friend Berlioz, who was ever on the alert to help the American pupil who promised to do him so much credit, arranged a series of concerts for him at the

Italian Opera in the winter of 1846-'47, and these proved brilliantly successful, not merely in filling the young artist's purse, but in augmenting his fast-growing reputation. Steady labor in study and concert-giving, many of his public performances being for charity, made two years pass swiftly by. A musical tour through France in 1849 was highly successful, and the young American returned to Paris, loaded down with gifts, and rich in the sense of having justly earned the congratulations which showered on him from all his friends. A second invitation now came from Spain, and Louis Gottschalk on arriving at Madrid was made a guest at the royal palace. From the king he received two orders, the diamond cross of Isabella la Catholique and that of Leon d'Holstein, and from the Duke de Montpensier he received a sword of honor. We are told that at one of the private court concerts Gottschalk played a duet with Don Carlos, the father of the recent pretender to the Spanish throne.

Among the romantic incidents narrated of this visit of Gottschalk to Madrid, one is too characteristic to be overlooked, as showing the tender, generous nature of the artist. An imaginative Spanish girl, whose fancy had been excited by the public enthusiasm about Gottschalk, but was too ill to attend his concerts, had a passionate desire to hear him play, and pined away in the fret-fulness of ungratified desire. Her family were not able to pay Gottschalk for the trouble of giving such an exclusive concert, but, to satisfy the sick girl, made the circumstances known to the artist. Gottschalk did not hesitate a moment, but ordered his piano to be conveyed to the humble abode of the patient. Here by her bedside he played for hours to the enraptured girl, and the strain of emotion was so great that her life ebbed away before he had finished the final chords. Gottschalk remained in Spain for two years, and it was not till the autumn of 1852 that he returned to Paris, to give a series of farewell concerts before returning again to America, where his father and brothers were anxiously awaiting him.

IV.

Before Gottschalk's departure from Paris, Hector Berlioz thus wrote of his *protege*, for whom we may fancy he had a strong bias of liking; and no judge is so generous in estimation as one artist of another, unless the critic has personal cause of dislike, and then no judge is so sweepingly unjust: "Gottschalk is one of the very small number who possess all the different elements of a consummate pianist, all the faculties which surround him with an irresistible prestige, and give him a sovereign power. He is an accomplished musician; he knows just how far fancy may be indulged in expression. He knows the limits beyond which any freedom taken with the rhythm produces only confusion and disorder, and upon these limits he never encroaches. There is an exquisite grace in his manner of phrasing sweet melodies and throwing off light touches from the higher keys. The boldness, brilliancy, and originality of his play at once dazzle and astonish, and the infantile *naivete* of his smiling caprices, the charming simplicity with which he renders simple things, seem to belong to another individuality, distinct from that which marks his thundering energy. Thus the success of M. Gottschalk before an audience of musical cultivation is immense."

But even this enthusiastic praise was pale in comparison with the eulogiums of some of the New York journals, after the first concert of Gottschalk at Niblo's Garden Theatre. One newspaper, which arrogated special strength and good judgment in its critical departments, intimated that after such a revelation it was useless any longer to speak of Beethoven! Whether Beethoven as a player or Beethoven as a composer was meant was left unknown. Gottschalk at his earlier concerts played many of his own compositions, made to order for the display of his virtuosoism, and their brilliant, showy style was very well calculated to arouse the enthusiasm of the general public. Perhaps the most sound and thoughtful opinion of Gottschalk expressed during the first enthusiasm created by his playing was that of a well-known musical journal published in Boston:

"Well, at the concert, which, by the way, did not half fill the Boston Music Hall, owing partly, we believe, to the one-dollar price, and partly, we *hope*, to distrust of an artist who plays wholly his own compositions, our expectation was confirmed. There was, indeed, most brilliant execution; we have heard none more brilliant, but are not yet prepared to say that Jaell's was less so. Gottschalk's touch is the most clear and crisp and beautiful that we have ever known. His play is free and bold and sure, and graceful in the extreme; his runs pure and liquid; his figures always clean and perfectly denned; his command of rapid octave passages prodigious; and so we might go through with all the technical points of masterly execution. It *was* great execution. But what is execution, without some thought and meaning in the combinations to be executed?... Skillful, graceful, brilliant, wonderful, we own his playing was. But players less wonderful have given us far deeper satisfaction. We have seen a criticism upon that concert, in which it was regretted that his music was too fine for common apprehension, 'too much addressed to the *reasoning* faculties,' etc. To us the want was, that it did *not* address the reason; that it seemed empty of ideas, of inspiration; that it spake little to the mind or heart, excited neither meditation nor emotion, but simply dazzled by the display of difficult feats gracefully and easily achieved. But of what use were all these difficulties? ('Difficult! I wish it was *impossible*,' said Dr. Johnson.) Why all that rapid tossing of handfuls of chords from the middle to the highest octaves, lifting the hand with such conscious appeal to our eyes? To what end all those rapid octave passages? since in the intervals of easy execution, in the seemingly quiet impromptu passages, the music grew so monotonous and commonplace: the same little figure repeated and repeated, after listless pauses, in a way which conveyed no meaning, no sense of musical progress, but only the appearance of fastidiously critical scale-practicing."

In the series of concerts given by Gottschalk throughout the United States, the public generally showed great enthusiasm and admiration, and the young pianist sustained himself very successfully against the memories of Jaell, Henri Herz, and Leopold de Meyer, as well as the immediate rivalry of Thalberg, who appealed more potently to a select few. The hold the American pianist had secured on his public did not lessen during the five years of concert-giving which succeeded. No player ever displayed his skill before American audiences who had in so large degree that peculiar quality of geniality in his style which so endears him to the public. This characteristic is something apart from genius or technical skill, and is peculiarly an emanation from the personality of the man.

In the spring of 1837 Gottschalk found himself in Havana, whither he had gone to make the beginning of a musical tour through the West Indies. His first concert was given at the Tacon Theatre, which Mr. Maretzek, who was giving operatic representations then in Havana, yielded to him for the occasion. The Cubans gave the pianist a tropical warmth of welcome, and Gott-schalk's letters from the old Spanish city are full of admiration for the climate, the life, and the people, with whom there was something strongly sympathetic in his own nature. The artist had not designed to protract his musical wanderings in the beautiful island of the Antilles for any considerable period, but his success was great, and the new experiences admirably suited his dreaming, sensuous, pleasure-loving temperament. Everywhere the advent of Gottschalk at a town was made the occasion of a festival, and life seemed to be one continued gala-day with him.

V.

In the early months of 1860 the young pianist, Arthur Napoleon, joined Gottschalk at Havana, and the two gave concerts throughout the West Indies, which were highly successful. The early summer had been designed for a tour through Central America and Venezuela, but a severe attack of illness prostrated Gottschalk, and he was not able to sail before August for his new field of musical conquest. Our artist did not return to New York till 1862, after an absence of five years, though his original plan had only contemplated a tour of two years. It must not be supposed that Gottschalk devoted his time continually to concert performances and composition, though he by no means neglected the requirements of musical labor. As he himself confesses, the balmy climate, the glorious landscapes, the languid ***dolce far niente***, which tended to enervate all that came under their magic spell, wrought on his susceptible temperament with peculiar effect. A quotation from an article written by Gottschalk, and published in the "Atlantic Monthly," entitled "Notes of a Pianist," will furnish the reader a graphic idea of the influence of tropical life on such an imaginative and voluptuous character, passionately fond of nature and outdoor life: "Thus, in succession, I have visited all the Antilles--Spanish, French, English, Dutch, Swedish, and Danish; the Guianas, and the coasts of Para. At times, having become the idol of some obscure ***pueblo***, whose untutored ears I had charmed with its own simple ballads, I would pitch my tent for five, six, eight months, deferring my departure from day to day, until finally I began seriously to entertain the idea of remaining there for evermore. Abandoning myself to such influences, I lived without care, as the bird sings, as the flower expands, as the brook flows, oblivious of the past, reckless of the future, and sowed both my heart and my purse with the

ardor of a husbandman who hopes to reap a hundred ears for every grain he con-
fides to the earth. But, alas! the fields where is garnered the harvest of expended
doubloons, and where vernal loves bloom anew, are yet to be discovered; and the
result of my prodigality was that, one fine morning, I found myself a bankrupt in
heart, with my purse at ebb-tide. Suddenly disgusted with the world and myself,
weary, discouraged, mistrusting men (ay, and women too), I fled to a desert on the
extinct volcano of M------, where, for several months, I lived the life of a cenobite,
with no companion but a poor lunatic whom I had met on a small island, and who
had attached himself to me. He followed me everywhere, and loved me with that
absurd and touching constancy of which dogs and madmen alone are capable. My
friend, whose insanity was of a mild and harmless character, fancied himself the
greatest genius in the world. He was, moreover, under the impression that he suffered from a gigantic, monstrous tooth. Of the two idiosyncrasies, the latter alone
made his lunacy discernible, too many individuals being affected with the other
symptom to render it an anomalous feature of the human mind. My friend was in
the habit of protesting that this enormous tooth increased periodically, and threatened to encroach upon his entire jaw. Tormented, at the same time, with the desire
of regenerating humanity, he divided his leisure between the study of dentistry, to
which he applied himself in order to impede the progress of his hypothetical tyrant,
and a voluminous correspondence which he kept up with the Pope, his brother,
and the Emperor of the French, his cousin. In the latter occupation he pleaded the
interests of humanity, styled himself 'the Prince of Thought,' and exalted me to the
dignity of his illustrious friend and benefactor. In the midst of the wreck of his intellect, one thing still survived--his love of music. He played the violin; and, strange
as it may appear, although insane, he could not understand the so-called *music of
the future*.

"My hut, perched on the verge of the crater, at the very summit of the mountain, commanded a view of all the surrounding country. The rock upon which it was
built projected over a precipice whose abysses were concealed by creeping plants,
cactus, and bamboos. The species of table-rock thus formed had been encircled
with a railing, and transformed into a terrace on a level with the sleeping-room,
by my predecessor in this hermitage. His last wish had been to be buried there;
and from my bed I could see his white tombstone gleaming in the moonlight a few

steps from my window. Every evening I rolled my piano out upon the terrace; and there, facing the most incomparably beautiful landscape, all bathed in the soft and limpid atmosphere of the tropics, I poured forth on the instrument, and for myself alone, the thoughts with which the scene inspired me. And what a scene! Picture to yourself a gigantic amphitheatre hewn out of the mountains by an army of Titans; right and left, immense virgin forests full of those subdued and distant harmonies which are, as it were, the voices of Silence; before me, a prospect of twenty leagues marvelously enhanced by the extreme transparency of the air; above, the azure of the sky: beneath, the creviced sides of the mountain sweeping down to the plain; afar, the waving savannas; beyond them, a grayish speck (the distant city); and, encompassing them all, the immensity of the ocean closing the horizon with its deep-blue line. Behind me was a rock on which a torrent of melted snow dashed its white foam, and there, diverted from its course, rushed with a mad leap and plunged headlong into the gulf that yawned beneath my window.

"Amid such scenes I composed 'Reponds-moi la Marche des Gibaros,' 'Polonia,' 'Columbia,' 'Pastorella e Cavaliere,' 'Jeunesse,' and many other unpublished works. I allowed my fingers to run over the keys, wrapped up in the contemplation of these wonders; while my poor friend, whom I heeded but little, revealed to me with a childish loquacity the lofty destiny he held in reserve for humanity. Can you conceive the contrast produced by this shattered intellect expressing at random its disjointed thoughts, as a disordered clock strikes by chance any hour, and the majestic serenity of the scene around me? I felt it instinctively. My misanthropy gave way. I became indulgent toward myself and mankind, and the wounds of my heart closed once more. My despair was soothed; and soon the sun of the tropics, which tinges all things with gold--dreams as well as fruits--restored me with new confidence and vigor to my wanderings.

"I relapsed into the manners and life of these primitive countries: if not strictly virtuous, they are at all events terribly attractive. Existence in a tropical wilderness, in the midst of a voluptuous and half-civilized race, bears no resemblance to that of a London cockney, a Parisian lounger, or an American Quaker. Times there were, indeed, when a voice was heard within me that spoke of nobler aims. It reminded me of what I once was, of what I yet might be; and commanded imperatively a return to a healthier and more active life. But I had allowed myself to be enervated by this baneful languor, this insidious *far niente*; and my moral torpor was such that the mere thought of reappearing before a polished audience struck me as super-latively absurd. 'Where was the object?' I would ask myself. Moreover, it was too late; and I went on dreaming with open eyes, careering on horseback through the savannas, listening at break of day to the prattle of the parrots in the guava-trees, at nightfall to the chirp of the *grillos* in the cane-fields, or else smoking my cigar, tak-ing my coffee, rocking myself in a hammock--in short, enjoying all the delights that are the very heart-blood of a *guajiro*, and out of the sphere of which he can see but death, or, what is worse to him, the feverish agitation of our Northern society. Go and talk of the funds, of the landed interest, of stock-jobbing, to this Sybarite lord of the wilderness, who can live all the year round on luscious bananas and delicious cocoa-nuts which he is not even at the trouble of planting; who has the best tobacco in the world to smoke; who replaces today the horse he had yesterday by a better one, chosen from the first *calallada* he meets; who requires no further protection from the cold than a pair of linen trousers, in that favored clime where the seasons roll on in one perennial summer; who, more than all this, finds at eve, under the rustling palm-trees, pensive beauties, eager to reward with their smiles the one who murmurs in their ears those three words, ever new, ever beautiful, 'Yo te quiero.'"

VI.

Mr. Gottschalk's return to America in February, 1862, was celebrated by a con-cert in Irving Hall, on the anniversary of his *debut* in New York. This was the beginning of another brilliant musical series, in pursuance of which he appeared in every prominent city of the country. While many found fault with Gottschalk for descending to pure "claptrap" and bravura playing, for using his great powers to merely superficial and unworthy ends, he seemed to retain as great a hold as ever over the masses of concert-goers. Gottschalk himself, with his epicurean, easy-going nature, laughed at the lectures read him by the critics and connoisseurs, who would have him follow out ideals for which he had no taste. It was like asking the butterfly to live the life of the bee. Great as were the gifts of the artist, it was not to be expected that these would be pursued in lines not consistent with the limitations of his temperament. Gottschalk appears to have had no desire except to amuse and delight the world, and to have been foreign to any loftier musical aspiration, if we may judge by his own recorded words. He passed through life as would a splendid wild singing-bird, making music because it was the law of his being, but never directing that talent with conscious energy to some purpose beyond itself.

In 1863 family misfortunes and severe illness of himself cooperated to make the year vacant of musical doings, but instantly he recovered he was engaged by M. Strakosch to give another series of concerts in the leading Eastern cities. Without attempting to linger over his career for the next two years, let us pass to his second expedition to the tropics in 1865. Four years were spent in South America, each country that he visited vieing with the other in doing him honor. Magnificent gifts were heaped on him by his enthusiastic Spanish-American admirers, and life was one continual ovation. In Peru he gave sixty concerts, and was presented with a costly decoration of gold, diamond, and pearl. In Chili the Government voted him a grand gold medal, which the board of public schools, the board of visitors of the hospitals, and the municipal government of Valparaiso supplemented by gold medals, in recognition of Gottschalk's munificence in the benefit concerts he gave for various public and humane institutions. The American pianist, through the whole of his career, had shown the traditional benevolence of his class in offering his services to the advancement of worthy objects. A similar reception awaited Gottschalk in Montevideo, where the artist became doubly the object of admiration by the substantial additions he made to the popular educational fund. While in this city he organized and conducted a great musical festival in which three hundred musicians engaged, exclusive of the Italian Opera company then at Montevideo.

The spring of 1869 brought Gottschalk to the last scene of his musical triumphs, for the span of his career was about to close over him. Rio Janeiro, the capital of Brazil, gave Gottschalk an ardent reception, which made this city properly the culmination of his toils and triumphs. Gottschalk wrote that his performances created such a *furore* that boxes commanded a premium of seventy-five dollars, and single seats fetched twenty-five. He was frequently entertained by Dom Pedro at the palace; in every way the Brazilians testified their lavish admiration of his artistic talents. In the midst of his success Gottschalk was seized with yellow fever, and brought very low. Indeed, the report came back to New York that he was dead, a report, however, which his own letters, written from the bed of convalescence, soon contradicted.

In October of 1869 Gottschalk was appointed by the emperor to take the leadership of a great festival, in which eight hundred performers in orchestra and chorus would take part. Indefatigable labor, in rehearsing his musicians and organizing the almost innumerable details of such an affair, acted on a frame which had not yet recovered its strength from a severe attack of illness. With difficulty he dragged himself through the tedious preparation, and when he stood up to conduct the first concert of the festival, on the evening of November 26, he was so weak that he could scarcely stand. The next day he was too ill to rise, and, though he forced himself to go to the opera-house in the evening, he was so weak as to be unable to conduct the music, and he had to be driven back to his hotel. The best medical skill watched over him, but his hour had come, and after three weeks of severe suffering he died, December 18, 1869. The funeral solemnities at the Cathedral of Rio were of the most imposing character, and all the indications of really heart-felt sorrow were shown among the vast crowd of spectators, for Gottschalk had quickly endeared himself to the public both as man and artist. At the time of Gott-schalk's death, it was his purpose to set sail for Europe at the earliest practicable moment, to secure the publication of some of his more important works, and the production of his operas, of which he had the finished scores of not less than six.

Louis Moreau Gottschalk was an artist and composer whose gifts were never more than half developed; for his native genius as a musician was of the highest order. Shortly before he died, at the age of forty, he seemed to have ripened into more earnest views and purposes, and, had he lived to fulfill his prime, it is reasonable to hazard the conjecture that he would have richly earned a far loftier niche in the pantheon of music than can now be given him. A rich, pleasure-loving, Oriental temperament, which tended to pour itself forth in dreams instead of action; vivid emotional sensibilities, which enabled him to exhaust all the resources of pleasure where imagination stimulates sense; and a thorough optimism in his theories, which saw everything at its best, tended to blunt the keen ambition which would otherwise inevitably have stirred the possessor of such artistic gifts. Gottschalk fell far short of his possibilities, though he was the greatest piano executant ever produced by our own country. He might have dazzled the world even as he dazzled his own partial countrymen.

His style as a pianist was sparkling, dashing, showy, but, in the judgment of the most judicious, he did not appear to good advantage in comparison with Thalberg, in whom a perfect technique was dominated by a conscious intellectualism, and a high ideal, passionless but severely beautiful.

Gottschalk's idiosyncrasy as a composer ran in parallel lines with that of the player. Most of the works of this musician are brilliant, charming, tender, melodious, full of captivating excellence, but bright with the flash of fancy, rather than strong with the power of imagination. We do not find in his piano-forte pieces any of that subtile soul-searching force which penetrates to the deepest roots of thought and feeling. Sundry musical cynics were wont to crush Gottschalk's individuality into the coffin of a single epigram. "A musical bonbon to tickle the palates of sentimental women." But this falls as far short of justice as the enthusiasm of many of his admirers overreaches it. The easy and genial temperament of the man, his ability to seize the things of life on their bright side, and a naive indolence which indisposed the artist to grapple with the severest obligations of an art life, prevented Gottschalk from attaining the greatness possible to him, but they contributed to make him singularly lovable, and to justify the passionate attachment which he inspired in most of those who knew him well. But, with all of Gottschalk's limitations, he must be considered the most noticeable and able of pianists and composers for the piano yet produced by the United States.

FRANZ LISZT.

The Spoiled Favorite of Fortune.--His Inherited Genius.--Birth and Early Training.--First Appearance in Concert.--Adam Liszt and his Son in Paris.--Sensation made by the Boy's Playing.--His Morbid Religious Sufferings.--Franz Liszt thrown on his own Resources.--The Artistic Circle in Paris.--Liszt in the Banks of Romanticism.--His Friends and Associates.--Mme. D'Agoult and her Connection with Franz Liszt.--He retires to Geneva.--Is recalled to Paris by the Thalberg **Furore**.--Rivalry between the Artists, and their Factions.--He commences his Career as Traveling Virtuoso.--The Blaze of Enthusiasm throughout Europe.--Schumann on Liszt as Man and Artist.--He ranks the Hungarian Virtuoso as the Superior of Thalberg.--Liszt's Generosity to his own Countrymen.--The Honors paid to him in Pesth.--Incidents of his Musical Wanderings.--He loses the Proceeds of Three Hundred Concerts.--Contributes to the Completion of the Cologne Cathedral.--His Connection with the Beethoven Statue at Bonn, and the Celebration of the Unveiling.--Chorley on Liszt.--Berlioz and Liszt.--Character of the Enthusiasm called out by Liszt as an Artist.--Remarkable Personality as a Man.--Berlioz characterizes the Great Virtuoso in a Letter.--Liszt erases his Life as a Virtuoso, and becomes Chapel-Master and Court Conductor at Weimar.--Avowed Belief in the New School of Music, and Production of Works of this School.--Wagner's Testimony to Liszt's Assistance.--Liszt's Resignation of his Weimar Post after Ten Years.--His Subsequent Life.--He takes Holy Orders.--Liszt as a Virtuoso and Composer.--Entitled to be placed among tire most Remarkable Men of his Age.

I.

There are but few names in music more interesting than that of Franz Liszt, the spoiled favorite of Europe for more than half a century, and without question the greatest piano-forte virtuoso that ever lived. His life has passed through the sunniest regions of fortune and success, and from his cradle upward the gods have showered on him their richest gifts. His career as an artist and musician has been most remarkable, his personal life full of romance, and his connection with some of the most vital changes in music which have occurred during the century interesting and significant. From his first appearance in public, at the age of twelve, his genius was acknowledged with enthusiasm throughout the whole republic of art, from Beethoven down to the obscurest *dilletante*, and it may be asserted that the history of music knows no instance of success approaching that achieved by the performances of this great player in every capital of Europe, from Madrid to St. Petersburg. When he wearied of the fame of the virtuoso, and became a composer, not only for the piano-forte, but for the orchestra, his invincible energy soon overcame all difficulties in his path, and he has lived to see himself accepted as one of the greatest of living musical thinkers and writers.

The life of Liszt is so crowded with important incidents that it is difficult to condense into the brief limits of a sketch any fairly adequate statement of his career. He was born October 22, 1811, in the village of Raiding, in Hungary, and it is said that his father Adam Liszt, who was in the service of the Prince Esterhazy, was firmly convinced that the child would become distinguished on account of the appearance of a remarkable comet during the year. Adam Liszt himself was a fine pianist, gifted indeed with a talent which might have made him eminent had he pursued it. All his ambition and hope, however, centered in his son, in whom musical genius quickly declared itself; and the father found teaching this gifted child not only a labor of love, but a task smoothed by the extraordinary aptness of the pupil. He was accustomed to say to the young Franz: "My son, you are destined to realize the glorious ideal that has shone in vain before my youth. In you that is to reach its fulfillment which I have myself but faintly conceived. In you shall my genius grow up and bear fruit; I shall renew my youth in you even after I am laid in the grave." Such prophetic words recall the vision of the Genoese woman, who foresaw the future greatness of the little Nicolo Paganini, a genius who resembled in many ways the phenomenal musical force embodied in Franz Liszt. When the lad was very young, perhaps not more than six, he read the "Kene" of Chateaubriand, and it made such an indelible impression on his mind that he in after years spoke of it as having been one of the most potent influences of his life, since it stimulated the natural melancholy of his character when his nature was most flexible and impressible.

At the age of nine he made his first appearance in public at Odenburg, playing Bies's concerto in three flats, and improvising a fantasia so full of melodic ideas, striking rhythms, and well-arranged harmony as to strike the audience with surprise and admiration. Among the hearers was Prince Esterhazy, who was so pleased with the precocious talent shown that he put a purse of fifty ducats in the young musician's hand. Soon after this Adam Liszt went to Pres-burg to live, and several noblemen, among whom were Prince Esterhazy, and the Counts Amadee and Szapary, all of them enthusiastic patrons of music, determined to bear the burden of the boy's musical education. To this end they agreed to allow him six hundred florins a year for six years. Young Liszt was placed at Vienna under the tutelage of the celebrated pianist and teacher Czerny, and soon made such progress that he was able to play such works as those even of Beethoven and Hummel at first sight. When Liszt did this for one of Hummel's most difficult concertos, at the rooms of the music publisher one day, it created a great sensation in Vienna, and he quickly became one of the lions of the drawing-rooms of the capital. Czerny himself was so much delighted with the genius of his charge that he refused to accept the three hundred florins stipulated for his lessons, saying he was but too well repaid by the success of the pupil.

Though toiling with incessant industry in musical study and practice, for the boy was working at composition with Salieri and Randhartinger, as well as the piano-forte with Czerny, he found time to indulge in those strange, mystical, and fantastic dreams which have molded his whole life, oscillating between pietistic delirium, wherein he saw celestial visions and felt the call to a holy life, and the most voluptuous images and aspirations for earthly pleasures. Franz Liszt at this early age had a sensibility so delicate, and an imagination so quickly kindled, that he himself tells us no one can guess the extremes of ecstasy and despair through which he alternately passed. These spiritual experiences were perhaps fed by the mysticism of Jacob Boehme, whose works came into his possession, and furnished a most delusive and dangerous guide for the young enthusiast's fancy. But, dream and suffer as he might, nothing was allowed to quench the ardor of his musical studies.

Eighteen months were passed in diligent labor under the guidance of the masters, who found teaching almost unnecessary, as the wonderful lad needed but a hint to work out for himself the most difficult problems, and he toiled so incessantly that he often became conscious of the change of day into night only by the failure of the light and the coming of the candles. Finally, by advice of Salieri, after eighteen months of labor, he determined to appear in concert in Vienna. On this occasion the audience was composed of the most distinguished people of Vienna, drawn thither to hear the young musical wonder of whom every one talked. Among the hearers was Beethoven, who after the concert gave the proud boy the most cordial praise, and prophesied a great career for him.

The elder Liszt was already in Paris, and it was determined that Franz should go to that city, to avail himself of the instructions of Cherubini, at the Conservatoire, who as a teacher of counterpoint had no equal in Europe. The Prince Metternich sent letters of the warmest recommendation, but they were of no avail, for Cherubini, who was singularly whimsical and obstinate in his notions, refused to accept the new candidate, on account of the rule of the Conservatoire excluding pupils of foreign birth, a plea which the famous director did not hesitate to break when he chose. Franz, however, continued his studies under Reicha and Paer, and, while the gates of the Conservatoire were closed, all the salons of Paris opened to receive him. Everywhere he was feted, courted, caressed. This fair-haired, blue-eyed lad, with the seal of genius burning on his face, had made the social world mad over him. The young adventurer was sailing in a treacherous channel, full of dangerous reefs. Would he, in the homage paid to him, an unmatured youth, by scholars, artists, wealth, beauty, and rank, forgot in mere self-love and vanity his high obligations to his art and the sincere devotion which alone could wrest from art its richest guerdon? This problem seems to have troubled his father, for he determined to take his young Franz away from the palace of Circe. The boy had already made an attempt at composition in the shape of an operetta, in one act, "Don Sanche," which was very well received at the Academie Royale. Adolph Nourrit, the great singer, had led the young composer on the stage, where he was received with thunders of applause by the audience, and was embraced with transport by Rudolph Kreutzer, the director of the orchestra.

Adam Liszt and his son went to England, and spent about six months in giving concerts in London and other cities. Franz was less than fourteen years old, but the pale, fragile, slender boy had, in the deep melancholy which stamped the noble outline of his face, an appearance of maturity that belied his years. English audiences everywhere received him with admiration, but he seemed to have lost all zest for the intoxicating wine of public favor. A profound gloom stole over him, and we even hear of hints at an attempt to commit suicide. Adam Liszt attributed it to the sad English climate, which Hein-rich Heine cursed with such unlimited bitterness, and took his boy back again to sunnier France. But the dejection darkened and deepened, threatening even to pass into epilepsy. It assumed the form of religious enthusiasm, alternating with fits of remorse as of one who had committed the unpardonable sin, and sometimes expressed itself in a species of frenzy for the monastic life. These strange experiences alarmed the father, and, in obedience to medical advice, he took the ailing, half-hysterical lad to Boulogne-sur-Mer, for sea-bathing.

II.

While by the seaside Franz Liszt lost the father who had loved him with the devotion of father and mother combined. This fresh stroke of affliction deepened his dejection, and finally resulted in a fit of severe illness. When he was convalescent new views of life seemed to inspire him. He was now entirely thrown on his own resources for support, for Adam Liszt had left his affairs so deeply involved that there was but little left for his son and widow. A powerful nature, turned awry by unhealthy broodings, is often rescued from its own mental perversities by the sense of some new responsibility suddenly imposed on it. Boy as Liszt was, the Titan in him had already shown itself in the agonies and struggles which he had undergone, and, now that the necessity of hard work suddenly came, the atmosphere of turmoil and gloom began to clear under the imminent practical burden of life. He set resolutely to work composing and giving concerts. The religious mania under which he had rested for a while turned his thoughts to sacred music, and most of his compositions were masses. But the very effort of responsible toil set, as it were, a background against which he could appoint the true place and dimensions of his art work. There was another disturbance, however, which now stirred up his excitable mind. He fell madly in love with a lady of high rank, and surrendered his young heart entirely to this new passion. The unfortunate issue of this attachment, for the lady was much older than himself, and laughed with a gentle mockery at the infatuation of her young adorer, made Liszt intensely unhappy and misanthropical, but it did not prevent him from steady labor. Indeed, work became all the more welcome, as it served to distract his mind from its amorous pains, and his fantastic musings, instead of feeding on themselves, expressed themselves in his art. Certainly no healthier sign of one beginning to clothe himself in his right mind again can easily be imagined.

Liszt was now twenty years of age, and had regularly settled in Paris. He became acquainted intimately with the leaders of French literature, and was an habitue of the brilliant circles which gathered these great minds night after night. Lamartine and Chateaubriand were yielding place to a young and fiery school of writers and thinkers, but cordially clasped hands with the successors whom they themselves had made possible. Mme. George Sand, Balzac, Dumas, Victor Hugo, and others were just then beginning to stir in the mental revolution which they made famous. Liszt felt a deep interest in the literary and scientific interests of the day, and he threw himself into the new movement with great enthusiasm, for its strong wave moved art as well as letters with convulsive throes. The musician found in this fresh impulse something congenial to his own fiery, restless, aspiring nature. He entered eagerly into all the intellectual movements of the day. He became a St. Simonian and such a hot-headed politician that, had he not been an artist, and as such considered a harmless fanatic, he would perhaps have incurred some penalties. Liszt has left us, in his "Life of Chopin," and his letters, some very vivid portraitures of the people and the events, the fascinating literary and artistic reunions, and the personal experiences which made this part of his life so interesting; but, tempting as it is, we can not linger. There can be no question that this section of his career profoundly colored his whole life, and that the influence of Victor Hugo, Balzac, and Mme. George Sand is very perceptible in his compositions not merely in their superficial tone and character, but in the very theory on which they are built. Liszt thenceforward cut loose from all classic restraints, and dared to fling rules and canons to the winds, except so far as his artistic taste approved them. The brilliant and daring coterie, defying conventionality and the dull decorum of social law, in which our artist lived, wrought also another change in his character. Liszt had hitherto been almost austere in his self-denial, in restraint of passion and license, in a religious purity of life, as if he dwelt in the cold shadow of the monastery, not knowing what moment he should disappear within its gates. There was now to be a radical change.

One of the brilliant members of the coterie in which he lived a life of such keen mental activity was Countess D'Agoult, who afterward became famous in the literary world as "Daniel Stern." Beautiful, witty, accomplished, imaginative, thoroughly in sympathy with her friend George Sand in her views of love and matrimony, and not less daring in testifying to her opinion by actions, the name of Mme. D'Agoult had already been widely bruited abroad in connection with more than one romantic escapade. In the powerful personality of young Franz Liszt, instinct with an artistic genius which aspired like an eagle, vital with a resolute, reckless will, and full of a magnetic energy that overflowed in everything--looks, movements, talk, playing--the somewhat fickle nature of Mme. D'Agoult was drawn to the artist like steel to a magnet. Liszt, on the other hand, easily yielded to the refined and delicious sensuousness of one of the most accomplished women of her time, who to every womanly fascination added the rarest mental gifts and high social place.

The mutual passion soon culminated in a tie which lasted for many years, and was perhaps as faithfully observed by both parties as could be expected of such an irregular connection. Three children were the offspring of this attachment, a son who died, and two daughters, one of whom became the wife of M. Ollivier, the last imperial prime minister of France, and the other successively Mme. Von Bulow and Mme. Wagner, under which latter title she is still known. The ***chroniques scandaleuses*** of Paris and other great cities of Europe are full of racy scandals purporting to connect the name of Liszt with well-known charming and beautiful women, but, aside from the uncertainty which goes with such rumors, this is not a feature of Liszt's life on which it is our purpose to dilate. The errors of such a man, exposed by his temperament and surroundings to the fiercest breath of temptation, should be rather veiled than opened to the garish day. Of the connection with Mme. D'Agoult something has been briefly told, because it had an important influence on his art career. Though the Church had never sanctioned the tie, there is every reason to believe that the lady's power over Liszt was consistently used to restrain his naturally eccentric bias, and to keep his thoughts fixed on the loftiest art ideals.

III.

Soon after Liszt's connection with Mme. D'Agoult began, he retired with his devoted companion to Geneva, Switzerland, a city always celebrated in the annals of European literature and art. In the quiet and charming atmosphere of this city our artist spent two years, busy for the most part in composing. He had already attained a superb rank as a pianist, and of those virtuosos who had then exhibited their talents in Paris no one was considered at all worthy to be compared with Liszt except Chopin. Aside from the great mental grasp, the opulent imagination, the fire and passion, the dazzling technical skill of the player, there was a vivid personality in Liszt as a man which captivated audiences. This element dominated his slightest action. He strode over the concert stage with the haughty step of a despot who ruled with a sway not to be contested. Tearing his gloves from his fingers and hurling them on the piano, he would seat himself with a proud gesture, run his fingers through his waving blonde locks, and then attack the piano with the vehemence of a conqueror taking his army into action. Much of this manner was probably the outcome of natural temperament, something the result of affectation; but it helped to add to the glamour with which Liszt always held his audiences captive. When he left Paris for a studious retirement at Geneva, the throne became vacant. By and by there came a contestant for the seat, a player no less remarkable in many respects than Liszt himself, Sigismond Thalberg, whose performances aroused Paris, alert for a new sensation, into an enthusiasm which quickly mounted to boiling heat. Humors of the danger threatened to his hitherto acknowledged ascendancy reached

Liszt in his Swiss retreat. The artist's ambition was stirred to the quick; he could not sleep at night with the thought of this victorious rival who was snatching his laurels, and he hastened back to Paris to meet Thalberg on his own ground. The latter, however, had already left Paris, and Liszt only felt the ground-swell of the storm he had raised. There was a hot division of opinion among the Parisians, as there had been in the days of Gluck and Piccini. Society was divided into Lisztians and Thalbergians, and to indulge in this strife was the favorite amusement of the fashionable world. Liszt proceeded to reestablish his place by a series of remarkable concerts, in which he introduced to the public some of the works wrought out during his retirement, among them transcriptions from the songs of Schubert and the symphonies of Beethoven, in which the most free and passionate poetic spirit was expressed through the medium of technical difficulties in the scoring before unknown to the art of the piano-forte. There can be no doubt that the influence of Thalberg's rivalry on Liszt's mind was a strong force, and suggested new combinations. Without having heard Thalberg, our artist had already divined the secret of his effects, and borrowed from them enough to give a new impulse to an inventive faculty which was fertile in expedients and quick to assimilate all things of value to the uses of its own insatiable ambition.

Franz Liszt's career as a traveling virtuoso commenced in 1837, and lasted for twelve years. Hitherto he had resisted the impulsion to such a course, all his desires rushing toward composition, but the extraordinary rewards promised cooperated with the spur of rivalry to overcome all scruples. The first year of these art travels was made memorable by the great inundation of the Danube, which caused so much suffering at Pesth. Thousands of people were rendered homeless, and the scene was one that appealed piteously to the humanitarian mind. The heart of Franz Liszt burned with sympathy, and he devoted the proceeds of his concerts for nearly two months to the alleviation of the woes of his countrymen. A princely sum was contributed by the artist, which went far to assist the sufferers. The number of occasions on which Liszt gave his services to charity was legion. It is credibly stated that the amount of benefactions contributed by his benefit concerts, added to the immense sums which he directly disbursed, would have made him several times a millionaire.

The blaze of enthusiasm which Liszt kindled made his track luminous throughout the musical centers of Europe. Caesar-like, his very arrival was a victory, for it aroused an indescribable ferment of agitation, which rose at his concerts to wild excesses. Ladies of the highest rank tore their gloves to strips in the ardor of their applause, flung their jewels on the stage instead of bouquets, shrieked in ecstasy and sometimes fainted, and made a wild rush for the stage at the close of the music to see Liszt, and obtain some of the broken strings of the piano, which the artist had ruined in the heat of his play, as precious relics of the occasion. The stories told of the Liszt craze among the ladies of Germany and Russia are highly amusing, and have a value as registering the degree of the effect he produced on impressible minds. Even sober and judicious critics who knew well whereof they spoke yielded to the contagion. Schumann writes of him, *apropos* of his Dresden and Leipzig concerts in 1840: "The whole audience greeted his appearance with an enthusiastic storm of applause, and then he began to play. I had heard him before, but an artist is a different thing in the presence of the public compared with what he appears in the presence of a few. The fine open space, the glitter of light, the elegantly dressed audience--all this elevates the frame of mind in the giver and receiver. And now the demon's power began to awake; he first played with the public as if to try it, then gave it something more profound, until every single member was enveloped in his art; and then the whole mass began to rise and fall precisely as he willed it. I never found any artist except Paga-nini to possess in so high a degree this power of sub-jecting, elevating, and leading the public. It is an instantaneous variety of wildness, tenderness, boldness, and airy grace; the instrument glows under the hand of its master.... It is most easy to speak of his outward appearance. People have often tried to picture this by comparing Liszt's head to Schiller's or Napoleon's; and the comparison so far holds good, in that extraordinary men possess certain traits in common, such as an expression of energy and strength of will in the eyes and mouth. He has some resemblance to the portraits of Napoleon as a young general, pale, thin, with a remarkable profile, the whole significance of his appearance culminating in his head. While listening to Liszt's playing, I have often almost imagined myself as listening to one I heard long before. But this art is scarcely to be described. It is not this or that style of piano-forte playing; it is rather the outward expression of a daring character, to whom Fate has given as instruments of victory and command, not the dangerous weapon of war, but the peaceful ones of art. No matter how many and great artists we possess or have seen pass before us of recent years, though some of them equal him in single points, all must yield to him in energy and boldness. People have been very fond of placing Thalberg in the lists beside him, and then drawing comparisons. But it is only necessary to look at both heads to come to a conclusion. I remember the remark of a Viennese designer who said, not inaptly, that his countryman's head resembled that of a handsome countess with a man's nose, while of Liszt he observed that he might sit to every painter for a Grecian god. There is a similar difference in their art. Chopin stands nearer to Liszt as a player, for at least he loses nothing beside him in fairy-like grace and tenderness; next to him Paganini, and, among women, Mme. Malibran; from these Liszt himself says he has learned the most.... Liszt's most genial performance was yet to come, Weber's 'Concert-stuck,' which he played at the second performance. Virtuoso and public seemed to be in the freshest mood possible on that evening, and the enthusiasm during and after his playing almost exceeded anything hitherto known here. Although Liszt grasped the piece from the begin-ing with such force and grandeur that an attack on the battle-field seemed to be in question, yet he carried this on with continually increasing power, until the passage where the player seems to stand at the summit of the orchestra, leading it forward in triumph. Here, indeed, he resembled that great commander to whom he has been compared, and the tempestuous applause that greeted him was not unlike an adoring 'Vive l'Empereur.'"

Flattering to his pride, however, as were the universal honors bestowed on the artist, none were so grateful as those from his own countrymen. The philanthropy of his conduct had made a deep impression on the Hungarians. Two cities, Pesth and Odenburg, created him an honorary citizen; a patent of nobility was solicited for him by the *comitat* of Odenburg; and the "sword of honor," according to Hungarian custom, was presented to him with due solemnities. A brief account from an Hungarian journal of the time is of interest.

"The national feeling of the Magyars is well known; and proud are they of that star of the first magnitude which arose out of their nation. Over the countries of Europe the fame of the Hungarian Liszt came to them before they had as yet an opportunity of admiring him. The Danube was swollen by rains, Pesth was inundated, thousands were mourning the loss of friends and relations or of all their property. During his absence in Milan Liszt learned that many of his countrymen were suffering from absolute want. His resolution was taken. The smiling heaven of Italy, the *dolce far niente* of Southern life, could not detain him. The following morning he had quitted Milan and was on his way to Vienna. He performed for the benefit of those who had suffered by the inundation at Pesth. His art was the horn of plenty from which streamed forth blessings for the afflicted. Eighteen months afterward he came to Pesth, not as the artist in search of pecuniary advantage, but as a Magyar. He played for the Hungarian national theatre, for the musical society, for the poor of Pesth and of Odenburg, always before crowded houses, and the proceeds, fully one hundred thousand francs, were appropriated for these purposes. Who can wonder that admiration and pride should arise to enthusiasm in the breasts of his grateful countrymen? He was complimented by serenades, garlands were thrown to him; in short, the whole population of Pesth neglected nothing to manifest their respect, gratitude, and affection. But these honors, which might have been paid to any other artist of high distinction, did not satisfy them. They resolved to bind him for ever to the Hungarian nation from which he sprang. The token of manly honor in Hungary is a sword, for every Magyar has the right to wear a sword, and avails himself of that right. It was determined that their celebrated countryman should be presented with the Hungarian sword of honor. The noblemen appeared at the theatre, in the rich costume they usually wear before the emperor, and presented Liszt, midst thunders of applause from the whole assembled people, with a costly sword of honor." It was also proposed to erect a bronze statue of him in Pesth, but Liszt persuaded his countrymen to give the money to a struggling young artist instead.

IV.

In the autumn of 1840 Liszt went from Paris, at which city he had been playing for some time, to the north of Germany, where he at first found the people colder than he had been wont to experience. But this soon disappeared before the magic of his playing, and even the Hamburgers, notorious for a callous, bovine temperament, gave wild demonstrations of pleasure at his concerts. He specially pleased the worthy citizens by his willingness to play off-hand, without notes, any work which they called for, a feat justly regarded as a stupendous exercise of memory.

From Hamburg he went to London, where he gave nine concerts in a fortnight, and stormed the affections and admiration of the English public as he had already conquered the heart of Continental Europe. While in London a calamity befell him. A rascally agent in whom he implicitly trusted disappeared with the proceeds of three hundred concerts, an enormous sum, amounting to nearly fifty thousand pounds sterling. Liszt bore this reverse with cheerful spirits and scorned the condolences with which his friends sought to comfort him, saying he could easily make the money again, that his wealth was not in money, but in the power of making money.

The artist's musical wanderings were nearly without ceasing. His restless journeying carried him from Italy to Denmark, and from the British Islands to Russia, and everywhere the art and social world bowed at his feet in recognition of a genius which in its way could only be designated by the term "colossal." It seems cumbersome and monotonous to repeat the details of successive triumphs; but some of them are attended by features of peculiar interest. He offered, in the summer of 1841, to give the proceeds of a concert to the completion of the Cathedral of Cologne (who that loves music does not remember Liszt's setting of Heine's song "Im Rhein," where he translates the glory of the Cathedral into music?). Liszt was then staying at the island of Nonneworth, near Bonn, and a musical society, the Liedertafel, resolved to escort him up to Cologne with due pomp, and so made a grand excursion with a great company of invited guests on a steamboat hired for the purpose. A fine band of music greeted Liszt on landing, and an extensive banquet was then served, at which Liszt made an eloquent speech, full of wit and feeling. The artist acceded to the desire of the great congregation of people who had gathered to hear him play; and his piano was brought into the ruined old chapel of the ancient nunnery, about which so many romantic Rhenish legends cluster. Liszt gave a display of his wonderful powers to the delighted multitude, and the long-deserted hall of Nonneworth chapel, which for many years had only heard the melancholy call of the owl, resounded with the most magnificent music. Finally the procession with Liszt at the head marched to the steamboat, and the vessel glided over the bosom of the Rhine amid the dazzling glare of fireworks and to the music of singing and instruments. All Cologne was assembled to meet them, and Liszt was carried on the shoulders of his frantic admirers to his hotel.

In common with all other great musicians, Liszt has throughout life been a reverential admirer of the genius of Beethoven, an isolated force in music without peer or parallel. In his later years Liszt bitterly reproached himself because, in the vanity and impetuosity of his youth, he had dared to take liberties with the text of the Beethoven sonatas. Many interesting facts in Liszt's life connect themselves, directly or indirectly, with Beethoven. Among these is worthy of mention our artist's part in the Beethoven festival at Bonn in 1845, organized to celebrate the erection of a colossal bronze statue. The enterprise had been languishing for a long time, when Liszt promptly declared he would make up the deficiency single-handed, and this he did with great celerity. In an incredibly short time the money was raised, and the commission put in the hands of the sculptor Hilbnel, of Dresden, one of the foremost artists of Germany.

The programme for the celebration was drawn up by Liszt and Dr. Spohr, who were to be the joint conductors of the festival music. A thousand difficulties intervened to embarrass the organization of the affair, the jealousies of prominent singers, who revolted against the self-effacement they would needs undergo, a certain truly German parsimony in raising the money for the expenses, and the envious littleness of certain great composers and musicians, who feared that Liszt would reap too much glory from the prominence of the part he had taken in the affair, But Liszt's energy had surmounted all these obstacles, when finally, only a month before the festival, which was to take place in August, it was discovered that there was no suitable Pesthalle in Bonn. The committee said, "What if the affair should not pay expenses? would they not be personally saddled with the debt?" Liszt promptly answered that, if the proceeds were not sufficient, he himself would pay the cost of the building. The architect of the Cologne Cathedral was placed at the head of the work, a waste plot of ground selected, the trees grubbed up, timber fished up from one of the great Rhine rafts, and the Festhalle rose with the swiftness of Aladdin's palace. The erection of the statue of Beethoven at his birthplace, and the musical celebration thereof in August, 1845, one of the most interesting events of its kind that ever occurred, must be, for the most part, attributed to the energy and munificence of Franz Liszt. Great personages were present from all parts of Europe, among them King William of Prussia and Queen Victoria of England. Henry Chorley, who has given a pretty full description of the festival, says that Liszt's performance of Beethoven's concerto in E flat was the crowning glory of the festival, in spite of the richness and beauty of the rest of the programme. "I must lastly commemorate, as the most magnificent piece of piano-forte playing I ever heard, Dr. Liszt's delivery of the concerto in E flat.... Whereas its deliverer restrained himself within all the limits that the most sober classicist could have prescribed, he still rose to a loftiness, in part ascribable to the enthusiasm of time and place, in part referable to a nature chivalresque, proud, and poetic in no common degree, which I have heard no other instrumentalist attain.... The triumph in the mind of the executant sustained the triumph in the idea of the compositions without strain, without spasm, but with a breadth and depth and height such as made the genius of the executant approach the genius of the inventor.... There are players, there are poets; and as a poet Liszt was possibly never so sublimely or genuinely inspired as in that performance, which remains a bright and precious thing in the midst of all the curiously parti-colored recollections of the Beethoven festival at Bonn."

In 1846, among Liszt's other musical experiences, he played in concerts with Berlioz throughout Austria and Southern Germany. The impetuous Osechs and Magyars showed their hot Tartar blood in the passion of enthusiasm they displayed. Berlioz relates that, at his first concert at Pesth, he performed his celebrated version of the "Rakoczy March," and there was such a furious explosion of excitement that it wellnigh put an end to the concert. At the end of the performance Berlioz was wiping the perspiration from his face in the little room off the stage, when the door burst open, and a shabbily dressed man, his face glowing with a strange fire, rushed in, throwing himself at Berlioz's feet, his eyes brimming with tears. He kissed the composer over and over again, and sobbed out brokenly: "Ah, sir! Me Hungarian... poor devil... not speak French... ***un, poco l'taliano***.... Pardon... my ecstasy... Ah! understand your cannon... Yes! yes! the great battle... Germans, dogs!" Then, striking great blows with his fists on his chest, "In my heart I carry you... A Frenchman, revolutionist... know how to write music for revolutions." At a supper given after the performance, Berlioz tells us Liszt made an inimitable speech, and got so gloriously be-champagned that it was with great difficulty that he could be restrained from pistolling a Bohemian nobleman, at two o'clock in the morning, who insisted that he could carry off more bottles under his belt than Liszt. But the latter played at a concert next day at noon "assuredly as he had never played before," says Berlioz.

Before passing from that period of Liszt's career which was distinctly that of the virtuoso, it is proper to refer to the unique character of the enthusiasm which everywhere followed his track like the turmoil of a stormy sea. Europe had been familiar with other great players, many of them consummate artists, like Hummel, Henri Herz, Czerny, Kalkbrenner, Field, Moscheles, and Thalberg, the most brilliant name of them all. But the feeling which these performers aroused was pale and passionless in comparison with that evoked by Franz Liszt. This was not merely the outcome of Liszt as a player and musician, but of Liszt as a man. The man always impressed people as immeasurably bigger than what he did, great as that was. His nature had a lavishness that knew no bounds. He lived for every distinguished man and beautiful woman, and with every joyous thing. He had wit and sympathy to spare for gentle and simple, and his kindliness was lavished with royal profusion on the scum as well as the salt of the earth. This atmosphere of personal grandeur radiated from him, and invested his doings, musical and otherwise, with something peculiarly fine and fascinating. And then as a player Liszt rose above his mates as something of a different genius, a different race, a different world, to every one else who has ever handled a piano. He is not to be considered among the great composers, also pianists, who have merely treated their instrument as an interpreting medium, but as a poet, who executively employed the piano as his means of utterance and material for creation. In mere mechanical skill, after every one else has ended, Liszt had still something to add, carrying every man's discovery further. If he was surpassed by Thalberg in richness of sound, he surpassed Thalberg by a variety of tone of which the redoubtable Viennese player had no dream. He had his delicate, light, freakish moods in which he might stand for another Chopin in qualities of fancy, sentiment, and faery brilliancy. In sweep of hand and rapidity of finger, in fire and fineness of execution, in that interweaving of exquisite momentary fancies where the work admits, in a memory so vast as to seem almost superhuman; in that lightning quickness of view, enabling him to penetrate instantaneously the meaning of a new composition, and to light it up properly with its own inner spirit (some touch of his own brilliancy added); briefly, in a mastery, complete, spontaneous, enjoying and giving enjoyment, over every style and school of music, all those who have heard Liszt assert that he is unapproached among players and the traditions of players.

In a letter from Berlioz to Liszt, the writer gives us a vivid idea of the great virtuoso's playing and its effects. Berlioz is complaining of the difficulties which hamper the giving of orchestral concerts. After rehearsing his mishaps, he says: "After all, of what use is such information to you? You can say with confidence, changing the mot of Louis XIV, '***L'orchestre, c'est moi; le chour, c'est moi; le chef c'est encore moi***.' My piano-forte sings, dreams, explodes, resounds; it defies the flight of the most skillful forms; it has, like the orchestra, its brazen harmonies; like it, and without the least preparation, it can give to the evening breeze its cloud of fairy chords and vague melodies. I need neither theatre, nor box scene, nor much staging. I have not to tire myself out at long rehearsals. I want neither a hundred, fifty, nor twenty players. I do not even need any music. A grand hall, a grand pianoforte, and I am master of a grand audience. I show myself and am applauded; my memory awakens, dazzling fantasies grow beneath my fingers. Enthusiastic acclamations answer them. I sing Schubert's "Ave Maria," or Beethoven's "Adelaida" on the piano, and all hearts tend toward me, all breasts hold their breath.... Then come luminous bombs, the banquet of this grand firework, and the cries of the public, and the flowers and the crowns that rain around the priest of harmony, shuddering on his tripod; and the young beauties, who, all in tears, in their divine confusion kiss the hem of his cloak; and the sincere homage drawn from serious minds and the feverish applause torn from many; the lofty brows that bow down, and the narrow hearts, marveling to find themselves expanding '.... It is a dream, one of those golden dreams one has when one is called Liszt or Paganini."

That such a man as this, brilliant in wit, extravagant in habit and opinion, courted for his personal fascination by every one greatest in rank and choicest in intellect from his prodigious youth to his ripe manhood, should suddenly cease from display at the moment when his popularity was at its highest, when no rival was in being, is a remarkable trait in Dr. Franz Liszt's remarkable life. But this he did in 1849, by settling in Weimar as conductor of the court theatre, his age then being thirty-eight years.

V.

Liszt closed his career as a virtuoso, and accepted a permanent engagement at Weimar, with the distinct purpose of becoming identified with the new school of music which was beginning to express itself so remarkably through Richard Wagner. His new position enabled him to bring works before the world which would otherwise have had but little chance of seeing the light of day, and he rapidly produced at brief intervals eleven works, either for the first time, or else revived from what had seemed a dead failure. Among these works were "Lohengrin," "Rienzi," and "Tannhauser" by Wagner, "Benvenuto Cellini" by Berlioz, and Schumann's "Genoveva," and music to Byron's "Manfred." Liszt's new departure and the extraordinary band of artists he drew around him attracted the attention of the world of music, and Weimar became a great musical center, even as in the days of Goethe it had been a visiting shrine for the literary pilgrims of Europe. Thus a nucleus of bold and enthusiastic musicians was formed whose mission it was to preach the gospel of the new musical faith.

Richard Wagner says that, after the revolution of 1849, when he was compelled to fly for his life, he was thoroughly disheartened as an artist, and that all thought of musical creativeness was dead within him. From this stagnation he was rescued by a friend, and that friend was Franz Liszt. Let us tell the story in Wagner's own words:

"I met Liszt for the first time during my earliest stay in Paris, at a period when I had renounced the hope, nay, even a wish of a Paris reputation, and, indeed, was in a state of internal revolt against the artistic life which I found there. At our meeting he struck me as the most perfect contrast to my own being and situation. In this world into which it had been my desire to fly from my narrow circumstances, Liszt had grown up from his earliest age so as to be the object of general love and admiration at a time when I was repulsed by general coldness and want of sympathy. In consequence, I looked upon him with suspicion. I had no opportunity of disclosing my being and working to him, and therefore the reception I met with on his part was of a superficial kind, as was indeed natural in a man to whom every day the most divergent impressions claimed access. But I was not in a mood to look with unprejudiced eyes for the natural cause of this behavior, which, though friendly and obliging in itself, could not but wound me in the then state of my mind. I never repeated my first call on Liszt, and, without knowing or even wishing to know him, I was prone to look on him as strange and adverse to my nature. My repeated expression of this feeling was afterward told to him, just at the time when my "Rienzi" at Dresden was attracting general attention. He was surprised to find himself misunderstood with such violence by a man whom he had scarcely known, and whose acquaintance now seemed not without value to him. I am still moved when I think of the repeated and eager attempts he made to change my opinion of him, even before he knew any of my works. He acted not from any artistic sympathy, but led by the purely human wish of discontinuing a casual disharmony between himself and another being; perhaps he also felt an infinitely tender misgiving of having really hurt me unconsciously. He who knows the selfishness and terrible insensibility of our social life, and especially of the relations of modern artists to each other, can not be struck with wonder, nay, delight, with the treatment I received from this remarkable man.... At Weimar I saw him for the last time, when I was resting for a few days in Thuringia, uncertain whether the threatening persecution would compel me to continue my flight from Germany. The very day when my personal danger became a certainty, I saw Liszt conducting a rehearsal of my 'Tannhouser,' and was astonished at recognizing my second self in his achievement. What I had felt in inventing this music, he felt in performing it; what I had wanted to express in writing it down, he expressed in making it sound. Strange to say, through the love of this rarest friend, I gained, at the very moment of becoming homeless, a real home for my art which I had hitherto longed for and sought for in the wrong place.... At the end of my last stay in Paris, when, ill, miserable, and despairing, I sat brooding over my fate, my eye fell on the score of my 'Lohengrin,' which I had totally forgotten. Suddenly I felt something like compassion that this music should never sound from off the death-pale paper. Two words I wrote to Liszt; the answer was that preparation was being made for the performance on the grandest scale which the limited means of Weimar permitted. Everything that man or circumstances could do was done to make the work understood.... Errors and misconceptions impeded the desired success. What was to be done to supply what was wanted, so as to further the true understanding on all sides and, with it, the ultimate success of the work? Liszt saw it at once, and did it. He gave to the public his own impression of the work in a manner the convincing eloquence and overpowering efficacy of which remain unequaled. Success was his reward, and with this success he now approaches me, saying, 'Behold, we have come so far! Now create us a new work, that we may go still farther.'"

Liszt remained at Weimar for ten years, when he resigned his place on account of certain narrow jealousies and opposition offered to his plans. Since 1859 he has lived at Weimar, Pesth, and Rome, always the center of a circle of pupils and admirers, and, though no longer occupying an active place in the world, full of unselfish devotion to the true interests of music and musicians. In 1868 he took minor orders in the Roman priesthood. Since his early youth Liszt had been the subject of strong paroxysms of religious feeling, which more than once had nearly carried him into monastic life, and thus his brilliant career would have been lost to the world and to art. After he had gained every reward that can be lavished on genius, and tasted to the very dregs the wine of human happiness, so far as that can come of a splendid prosperity and the adoration of the musical world for nearly half a century, a sudden revulsion seems to have recalled again to the surface that profound religious passion which the glory and pleasure of his busy life had never entirely suppressed. It was by no means astonishing to those who knew Liszt's life best that he should have taken holy orders.

Abbe Liszt lives a portion of each year with the Prince-Cardinal Hohenlohe, in the well-known Villa d'Este, near Rome, a chateau with whose history much romance is interwoven. He is said to be very zealous in his religious devotions, and to spend much time in reading and composing. He rarely touches the piano, unless inspired by the presence of visitors whom he thoroughly likes, and even in such cases less for his own pleasure than for the gratification of his friends. Even his intimate friends would hardly venture to ask Liszt to play. His summer months are divided between Pesth and Weimar, where his advent always makes a glad commotion among the artistic circles of these respective cities. Of the various pupils who have been formed by Liszt, Hans von Bulow, who married his daughter Cosima, is the most distinguished, and shares with Rubenstein the honor of being the first of European pianists, now that Liszt has for so long a time withdrawn himself from the field of competition.

VI.

Liszt has been a very industrious and prolific writer, his works numbering thirty-one compositions for the orchestra; seven for the piano-forte and orchestra; two for piano and violin; nine for the organ; thirteen masses, psalms, and other sacred music; two oratorios; fifteen cantatas and chorals; sixty-three songs; and one hundred and seventy-nine works for the piano-forte proper. The bulk of these compositions, the most important of them at least, were produced in the first forty years of his life, and testify to enormous energy and capacity for work, as they came into being during his active period as a virtuoso. In addition to his musical works, Liszt has shown distinguished talent in letters, and his articles and pamphlets, notably the monographs on Robert Franz, Chopin, and the Music of the Gypsies, indicate that, had he not chosen to devote himself to music, he might have made himself an enviable name in literature.

Perhaps no better characterization of Liszt could be made than to call him the musical Victor Hugo of his age. In both these great men we find the same restless and burning imagination, a quickness of sensibility easily aroused to vehemence, a continual reaching forward toward the new and untried and impatience of the old, the same great versatility, the same unequaled command of all the resources of their respective crafts, and, until within the last twenty years, the same ceaseless fecundity. Of Liszt as a player it is not necessary to speak further. Suffice it that he is acknowledged to have been, while pursuing the path of the virtuoso, not only great, but the greatest in the records of art, with the possible exception of Paganini. To the possession of a technique which united all the best qualities of other players, carrying each a step further, he added a powerful and passionate imagination which illuminated the work before him. Wagner wrote of him: "He who has had frequent opportunities, particularly in a friendly circle, of hearing Liszt play, for instance, Beethoven, must have understood that this was not mere reproduction, but production. The actual point of division between these two things is not so easily determined as most people believe, but so much I have ascertained without a doubt, that, in order to reproduce Beethoven, one must produce with him." It was this quality which made Liszt such a vital interpreter of other composers, as well as such a brilliant performer of his own works. As a composer for the piano Franz Liszt has been accused of sacrificing substantial charm of motive for the creation of the most gigantic technical difficulties, designed for the display of his own skill. This charge is best answered by a study of his transcriptions of songs and symphonies, which, difficult in an extreme degree, are yet rich in no less excess with musical thought and fullness of musical color. He transcribed the "Etudes" of Pa-ganini, it is true, as a sort of "tour deforce", and no one has dared to attempt them in the concert room but himself; but for the most part Liszt's piano-forte writings are full of substance in their being as well as splendid elaboration in their form. This holds good no less of the purely original compositions, like the concertos and "Rhapsodies Hongroises," than of the transcriptions and paraphrases of the *Lied*, the opera, and symphony.

As a composer for the orchestra Liszt has spent the ripest period of his life, and attained a deservedly high rank. His symphonies belong to what has been called, for want of a better name, "programme music," or music which needs the key of the story or legend to explain and justify the composition. This classification may yet be very misleading. Liszt does not, like Berlioz, refer every feature of the music to a distinct event, emotion, or dramatic situation, but concerns himself chiefly with the pictorial and symbolic bearings of his subject. For example, the "Mazeppa" symphony, based on Victor Hugo's poem, gets its significance, not in view of its description of Mazeppa's peril and rescue, but because this famous ride becomes the symbol of man: "*Lie vivant sur la croupe fatale, Genie, ardent Coursier*." The spiritual life of this thought burns with subtle suggestions throughout the whole symphony.

Liszt has not been merely a devoted adherent of the "Music of the Future" as expressed in operatic form, but he has embodied his belief in the close alliance of poetry and music in his symphonies and transcriptions of songs. Anything more pictorial, vivid, descriptive, and passionate can not easily be fancied. It is proper also to say in passing that the composer shows a command over the resources of the orchestra similar to his mastery of the piano, though at times a tendency to violent and strident effects offends the ear. Franz Liszt, take him for all in all, must be regarded as one of the most remarkable men of the last half century, a personality so stalwart, picturesque, and massive as to be not only a landmark in music, but an imposing figure to those not specially characterized by their musical sympathies. His influence on his art has been deep and widespread; his connection with some of the most important movements of the last two generations well marked; and his individuality a fact of commanding force in the art circles of nearly every country of Europe, where art bears any vital connection with social and public life.

The Codes Of Hammurabi And Moses
W. W. Davies

QTY

The discovery of the Hammurabi Code is one of the greatest achievements of archaeology, and is of paramount interest, not only to the student of the Bible, but also to all those interested in ancient history...

Religion   ISBN: *1-59462-338-4*   Pages:132
MSRP $12.95

The Theory of Moral Sentiments
Adam Smith

QTY

This work from 1749. contains original theories of conscience amd moral judgment and it is the foundation for systemof morals.

Philosophy ISBN: *1-59462-777-0*   Pages:536
MSRP $19.95

Jessica's First Prayer
Hesba Stretton

QTY

In a screened and secluded corner of one of the many railway-bridges which span the streets of London there could be seen a few years ago, from five o'clock every morning until half past eight, a tidily set-out coffee-stall, consisting of a trestle and board, upon which stood two large tin cans, with a small fire of charcoal burning under each so as to keep the coffee boiling during the early hours of the morning when the work-people were thronging into the city on their way to their daily toil...

Childrens   ISBN: *1-59462-373-2*   Pages:84
MSRP $9.95

My Life and Work
Henry Ford

QTY

Henry Ford revolutionized the world with his implementation of mass production for the Model T automobile. Gain valuable business insight into his life and work with his own auto-biography... "We have only started on our development of our country we have not as yet, with all our talk of wonderful progress, done more than scratch the surface. The progress has been wonderful enough but..."

Biographies/   ISBN: *1-59462-198-5*   Pages:300
MSRP $21.95

The Art of Cross-Examination
Francis Wellman

QTY

I presume it is the experience of every author, after his first book is published upon an important subject, to be almost overwhelmed with a wealth of ideas and illustrations which could readily have been included in his book, and which to his own mind, at least, seem to make a second edition inevitable. Such certainly was the case with me; and when the first edition had reached its sixth impression in five months, I rejoiced to learn that it seemed to my publishers that the book had met with a sufficiently favorable reception to justify a second and considerably enlarged edition. ..

Pages:412

Reference   **ISBN:** *1-59462-647-2*   *MSRP $19.95*

On the Duty of Civil Disobedience
Henry David Thoreau

QTY

Thoreau wrote his famous essay, On the Duty of Civil Disobedience, as a protest against an unjust but popular war and the immoral but popular institution of slave-owning. He did more than write—he declined to pay his taxes, and was hauled off to gaol in consequence. Who can say how much this refusal of his hastened the end of the war and of slavery ?

Law   **ISBN:** *1-59462-747-9*   **Pages:48**

MSRP $7.45

Dream Psychology Psychoanalysis for Beginners
Sigmund Freud

QTY

Sigmund Freud, born Sigismund Schlomo Freud (May 6, 1856 - September 23, 1939), was a Jewish-Austrian neurologist and psychiatrist who co-founded the psychoanalytic school of psychology. Freud is best known for his theories of the unconscious mind, especially involving the mechanism of repression; his redefinition of sexual desire as mobile and directed towards a wide variety of objects; and his therapeutic techniques, especially his understanding of transference in the therapeutic relationship and the presumed value of dreams as sources of insight into unconscious desires.

Pages:196

Psychology   **ISBN:** *1-59462-905-6*   *MSRP $15.45*

The Miracle of Right Thought
Orison Swett Marden

QTY

Believe with all of your heart that you will do what you were made to do. When the mind has once formed the habit of holding cheerful, happy, prosperous pictures, it will not be easy to form the opposite habit. It does not matter how improbable or how far away this realization may see, or how dark the prospects may be, if we visualize them as best we can, as vividly as possible, hold tenaciously to them and vigorously struggle to attain them, they will gradually become actualized, realized in the life. But a desire, a longing without endeavor, a yearning abandoned or held indifferently will vanish without realization.

Pages:360

Self Help   **ISBN:** *1-59462-644-8*   *MSRP $25.45*

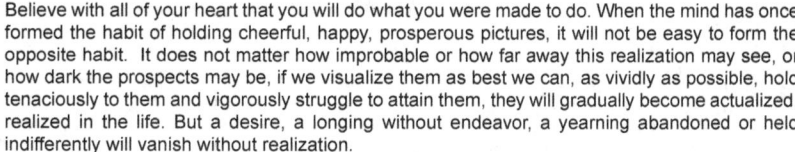

www.bookjungle.com *email: sales@bookjungle.com fax: 630-214-0564 mail: Book Jungle PO Box 2226 Champaign, IL 61825*

QTY

The Rosicrucian Cosmo-Conception Mystic Christianity by *Max Heindel*　ISBN: *1-59462-188-8*　**$38.95**
The Rosicrucian Cosmo-conception is not dogmatic, neither does it appeal to any other authority than the reason of the student. It is: not controversial, but is: sent forth in the, hope that it may help to clear...　New Age/Religion Pages 646

Abandonment To Divine Providence by *Jean-Pierre de Caussade*　ISBN: *1-59462-228-0*　**$25.95**
"The Rev. Jean Pierre de Caussade was one of the most remarkable spiritual writers of the Society of Jesus in France in the 18th Century. His death took place at Toulouse in 1751. His works have gone through many editions and have been republished...　Inspirational/Religion Pages 400

Mental Chemistry by *Charles Haanel*　ISBN: *1-59462-192-6*　**$23.95**
Mental Chemistry allows the change of material conditions by combining and appropriately utilizing the power of the mind. Much like applied chemistry creates something new and unique out of careful combinations of chemicals the mastery of mental chemistry...　New Age Pages 354

The Letters of Robert Browning and Elizabeth Barret Barrett 1845-1846 vol II　ISBN: *1-59462-193-4*　**$35.95**
by *Robert Browning and Elizabeth Barrett*　Biographies Pages 596

Gleanings In Genesis (volume I) by *Arthur W. Pink*　ISBN: *1-59462-130-6*　**$27.45**
Appropriately has Genesis been termed "the seed plot of the Bible" for in it we have, in germ form, almost all of the great doctrines which are afterwards fully developed in the books of Scripture which follow...　Religion/Inspirational Pages 420

The Master Key by *L. W. de Laurence*　ISBN: *1-59462-001-6*　**$30.95**
In no branch of human knowledge has there been a more lively increase of the spirit of research during the past few years than in the study of Psychology, Concentration and Mental Discipline. The requests for authentic lessons in Thought Control, Mental Discipline and...　New Age/Business Pages 422

The Lesser Key Of Solomon Goetia by *L. W. de Laurence*　ISBN: *1-59462-092-X*　**$9.95**
This translation of the first book of the "Lernegton" which is now for the first time made accessible to students of Talismanic Magic was done, after careful collation and edition, from numerous Ancient Manuscripts in Hebrew, Latin, and French...　New Age/Occult Pages 92

Rubaiyat Of Omar Khayyam by *Edward Fitzgerald*　ISBN:*1-59462-332-5*　**$13.95**
Edward Fitzgerald, whom the world has already learned, in spite of his own efforts to remain within the shadow of anonymity, to look upon as one of the rarest poets of the century, was born at Bredfield, in Suffolk, on the 31st of March, 1809. He was the third son of John Purcell...　Music Pages 172

Ancient Law by *Henry Maine*　ISBN: *1-59462-128-4*　**$29.95**
The chief object of the following pages is to indicate some of the earliest ideas of mankind, as they are reflected in Ancient Law, and to point out the relation of those ideas to modern thought.　Religion/History Pages 452

Far-Away Stories by *William J. Locke*　ISBN: *1-59462-129-2*　**$19.45**
"Good wine needs no bush, but a collection of mixed vintages does. And this book is just such a collection. Some of the stories I do not want to remain buried for ever in the museum files of dead magazine-numbers an author's not unpardonable vanity..."　Fiction Pages 272

Life of David Crockett by *David Crockett*　ISBN: *1-59462-250-7*　**$27.45**
"Colonel David Crockett was one of the most remarkable men of the times in which he lived. Born in humble life, but gifted with a strong will, an indomitable courage, and unremitting perseverance...　Biographies/New Age Pages 424

Lip-Reading by *Edward Nitchie*　ISBN: *1-59462-206-X*　**$25.95**
Edward B. Nitchie, founder of the New York School for the Hard of Hearing, now the Nitchie School of Lip-Reading, Inc, wrote "LIP-READING Principles and Practice". The development and perfecting of this meritorious work on lip-reading was an undertaking...　How-to Pages 400

A Handbook of Suggestive Therapeutics, Applied Hypnotism, Psychic Science　ISBN: *1-59462-214-0*　**$24.95**
by *Henry Munro*　Health/New Age/Health/Self-help Pages 376

A Doll's House: and Two Other Plays by *Henrik Ibsen*　ISBN: *1-59462-112-8*　**$19.95**
Henrik Ibsen created this classic when in revolutionary 1848 Rome. Introducing some striking concepts in playwriting for the realist genre, this play has been studied the world over.　Fiction/Classics/Plays 308

The Light of Asia by *sir Edwin Arnold*　ISBN: *1-59462-204-3*　**$13.95**
In this poetic masterpiece, Edwin Arnold describes the life and teachings of Buddha. The man who was to become known as Buddha to the world was born as Prince Gautama of India but he rejected the worldly riches and abandoned the reigns of power when...　Religion/History/Biographies Pages 170

The Complete Works of Guy de Maupassant by *Guy de Maupassant*　ISBN: *1-59462-157-8*　**$16.95**
"For days and days, nights and nights, I had dreamed of that first kiss which was to consecrate our engagement, and I knew not on what spot I should put my lips..."　Fiction/Classics Pages 240

The Art of Cross-Examination by *Francis L. Wellman*　ISBN: *1-59462-309-0*　**$26.95**
Written by a renowned trial lawyer, Wellman imparts his experience and uses case studies to explain how to use psychology to extract desired information through questioning.　How-to/Science/Reference Pages 408

Answered or Unanswered? by *Louisa Vaughan*　ISBN: *1-59462-248-5*　**$10.95**
Miracles of Faith in China　Religion Pages 112

The Edinburgh Lectures on Mental Science (1909) by *Thomas*　ISBN: *1-59462-008-3*　**$11.95**
This book contains the substance of a course of lectures recently given by the writer in the Queen Street Hall, Edinburgh. Its purpose is to indicate the Natural Principles governing the relation between Mental Action and Material Conditions...　New Age/Psychology Pages 148

Ayesha by *H. Rider Haggard*　ISBN: *1-59462-301-5*　**$24.95**
Verily and indeed it is the unexpected that happens! Probably if there was one person upon the earth from whom the Editor of this, and of a certain previous history, did not expect to hear again...　Classics Pages 380

Ayala's Angel by *Anthony Trollope*　ISBN: *1-59462-352-X*　**$29.95**
The two girls were both pretty, but Lucy who was twenty-one who supposed to be simple and comparatively unattractive, whereas Ayala was credited, as her Bombwhat romantic name might show, with poetic charm and a taste for romance. Ayala when her father died was nineteen...　Fiction Pages 484

The American Commonwealth by *James Bryce*　ISBN: *1-59462-286-8*　**$34.45**
An interpretation of American democratic political theory. It examines political mechanics and society from the perspective of Scotsman James Bryce　Politics Pages 572

Stories of the Pilgrims by *Margaret P. Pumphrey*　ISBN: *1-59462-116-0*　**$17.95**
This book explores pilgrims religious oppression in England as well as their escape to Holland and eventual crossing to America on the Mayflower, and their early days in New England...　History Pages 268

QTY

The Fasting Cure *by Sinclair Upton* ISBN: *1-59462-222-1* **$13.95**
In the Cosmopolitan Magazine for May, 1910, and in the Contemporary Review (London) for April, 1910, I published an article dealing with my experiences in fasting. I have written a great many magazine articles, but never one which attracted so much attention... New Age/Self Help/Health Pages 164

Hebrew Astrology *by Sepharial* ISBN: *1-59462-308-2* **$13.45**
In these days of advanced thinking it is a matter of common observation that we have left many of the old landmarks behind and that we are now pressing forward to greater heights and to a wider horizon than that which represented the mind-content of our progenitors... Astrology Pages 144

Thought Vibration or The Law of Attraction in the Thought World ISBN: *1-59462-127-6* **$12.95**
by William Walker Atkinson *Psychology/Religion Pages 144*

Optimism *by Helen Keller* ISBN: *1-59462-108-X* **$15.95**
Helen Keller was blind, deaf, and mute since 19 months old, yet famously learned how to overcome these handicaps, communicate with the world, and spread her lectures promoting optimism. An inspiring read for everyone... Biographies/Inspirational Pages 84

Sara Crewe *by Frances Burnett* ISBN: *1-59462-360-0* **$9.45**
In the first place, Miss Minchin lived in London. Her home was a large, dull, tall one, in a large, dull square, where all the houses were alike, and all the sparrows were alike, and where all the door-knockers made the same heavy sound... Childrens/Classic Pages 88

The Autobiography of Benjamin Franklin *by Benjamin Franklin* ISBN: *1-59462-135-7* **$24.95**
The Autobiography of Benjamin Franklin has probably been more extensively read than any other American historical work, and no other book of its kind has had such ups and downs of fortune. Franklin lived for many years in England, where he was agent... Biographies/History Pages 332

Name	
Email	
Telephone	
Address	
City, State ZIP	

☐ **Credit Card**   ☐ **Check / Money Order**

Credit Card Number	
Expiration Date	
Signature	

Please Mail to: Book Jungle
PO Box 2226
Champaign, IL 61825
or Fax to: 630-214-0564

ORDERING INFORMATION

web: *www.bookjungle.com*
email: *sales@bookjungle.com*
fax: *630-214-0564*
mail: *Book Jungle PO Box 2226 Champaign, IL 61825*
or PayPal *to sales@bookjungle.com*

Please contact us for bulk discounts

DIRECT-ORDER TERMS

**20% Discount if You Order
Two or More Books**
Free Domestic Shipping!
Accepted: Master Card, Visa,
Discover, American Express